A PROMISE FOR FAITH

BRIAR CREEK LOVE BOOK ONE

STACY T. SIMMONS

ISBN: 978-1-951839-47-5

Celebrate Lit Publishing

304 S. Jones Blvd #754

Las Vegas, NV, 89107

http://www.celebratelitpublishing.com/

"Now faith is confidence in what we hope for and assurance about what we do not see." Hebrews 11:1 NIV

"Faith is the strength by which a shattered world shall emerge into the light."
Helen Keller

CHAPTER ONE

A geyser that could pass for Old Faithful's miniature cousin spewed from Faith Fuller's SUV's hood. Nine hours into the drive to Briar Creek, North Carolina, Faith's patience had grown parchment paper thin. Clutching the wheel, she pulled from the road and onto a stream's pebbled shoreline. Faith alighted from the car and zipped up her jacket against the chill of the waning late afternoon sunlight. Flinging open the trunk, she pushed past Tetris piles of moving boxes and found her chef's grade ovenproof mitts. Pushing them onto her hands, she shot a prayer for safety into the purpling sky and cranked wide the blue hood. Water sizzled and belched from the belly of the motor. An acrid chemical stench caused her eyes to water. Where to start? Faith's knowledge of car mechanisms was severely limited. She moved to the side of the engine and inspected a large black hose. No water. Faith surveyed the tangle of tubes nearby, but nothing seemed wrong with her car other than a hissing spray of water. *Is it the radiator?* It was drier than her mom's Sunday dinner biscuits. Marching to the rear of her SUV, she threw the mitts into the box and crossed her arms across her chest, eyeing the road for a sign of life.

A car's motor droned on the other side of the hill. Faith's eyes focused on the road, and she lifted a hand to wave. The gray sedan sped past. Her stalwart smile faded in the taillight's afterglow. Faith pressed her glowing phone screen to make a call. Her shoulders sank. Zero bars. In imitation of her old hometown's treasured statue, she held her phone aloft, like the Statue of Liberty and pivoted to try to get one single bar. Walking a few feet from her car, she tried again. *The tall evergreens are blocking my reception. Will I have to walk into town?*

"Need help?"

Instinctively, her muscles corded together, and Faith swallowed the last drop of moisture in her mouth and turned, her keys laced between each finger.

Him. Faith scrutinized his face, investigating any changes over the years. A wrinkle above one eye was new. Still had that beach-blonde-brown hair that didn't like a comb and amazing green eyes. And he was ripped, with strong arms.

Her past had become her present as the keys plummeted to the ground.

"I'll get 'em." Caleb bent down to scoop them up and placed them in her hand. "How are you? It's been, what, eight years?"

Eight years, five days, too many hours since we broke up. Faith batted the wispy end of a curl brushing her cheek. "I'm good. Busy." Faith's tympani-drum heart punched against her chest.

"What brings you here?"

"Visiting my best friend Taylor and her hubby." Awakened embers of hurt fired through her body. "You live around here?"

"Briar Creek, not too far from Taylor and Jarod. I was coming back from the grocery store supercenter when I noticed the geyser." He headed to the car, "Let's have a look."

"Okay."

She followed at a distance. Caleb's spicy cologne teased her nose and tightened her stomach. Arriving at the still-noisy car, steaming water ran from underneath in a river. She noticed a frown pulling on his lips.

"Looks like a water pump or broken hose."

"Is there a gas station ahead?"

"In town, twenty miles away."

Caleb pulled out his cell phone. *Traitor, he has two bars.*

"Hello. We need a tow," Caleb closed the hood. His voice carried in the still air. "Belle's, um, my friend's car is beside the road, near the town marker sign, on Highway 194. You're nearby? See you soon."

Belle. He used to call me that when we were dating. She remembered their frequent visits to bookstores around New York City. They'd show each other the oddest books they could find. Faith always won, and that was how she earned the nickname "Belle," after one of her favorite movie characters.

Caleb came closer. "He's ten minutes away." He pointed to her car. "This might take a while to fix. How long are you here?"

"A week."

"Tay, Jarod and I are going kayaking tomorrow, you should come and see what I've been up to."

Her veins iced. *Boats.* She and boats didn't mix. "By rafting?"

"I'll show you."

He thumbed through photos on his phone and held it closer to Faith. She saw a wooden building with a bubbling river beyond. The visual did nothing to warm her chilled body.

"I own Hawk's Creek Outfitters. We take clients rafting and kayaking."

"Nice."

"What's going on with you? Still a test-kitchen chef in New York City?"

What do I say? I'm jobless, I was fired. Spin. Embellish. Weave a web. "I'm looking at other possibilities."

"Here?"

"No. I'm taking a pit stop here to visit."

Faith watched his bright smile fade under the curtains of his lips. Heat washed her face.

Over the din of the crickets, Caleb responded. "You loved New York and your job."

"I've changed."

"Seems so."

Faith hugged herself as searing shame lit the exposed soft spots in her heart.

A grinding rumble sounded, and a tow truck eased toward them.

An overall-clad man leaped from the truck cab and assessed the scene. "Evening, I'll get it ready to go to the mechanics in a jiffy." He pulled on his nanny goat beard. "Wanna ride with me, young lady?"

Caleb stood in between Faith and the driver. "I'll give her a ride, Chuck."

"Can I borrow your phone? I need to contact Taylor."

He handed her the phone and climbed into his car. "Sure."

She tapped a message onto the keyboard. The phone began to thrum. Slanting her gaze toward the screen, Taylor's face appeared.

Faith, whose phone is this?

I'm borrowing someone's.

I'll explain later. He's waving to me to get in the car.

Okay, I can't wait to hear all the story. See you soon.

Riding down the road in the sleek SUV, she watched every shimmy of her old Bessie, attached by flimsy chains to the back of the tow truck. She prayed the old girl would not fall apart and leave her stranded. Nervously, Faith picked at a hangnail.

"Hawk's Creek is over there."

Outlined in the greying night stood a party hat peaked roof and dull siding.

With the whirr of a button, her window slid down as spring

A PROMISE FOR FAITH

mountain air moved around her, along with a gurgle of moving water. She eased back into the seat and held in a sigh.

"Shouldn't be too bad tomorrow. With the rains, we'll only get a few rapids."

Shutting out the water's call with a flick of the button, Faith's hands dampened, and her heart galloped. *He never knew what happened, and he never will.* Pushing past her whirlpool of emotions, Faith placed a grin on her face as Caleb told her something funny. She'd deal with what tomorrow would bring later. On her own terms.

CHAPTER TWO

*P*anic swam in a steady current as the mechanic shop manager added more numbers to the estimate. The cost was more than she had currently in her checking account. Faith would have to tap into her savings account, the one she'd promised to never touch unless something dire had arisen. With no more paychecks on the foreseeable horizon, what was she going to do?

"Faith." Her best friend since childhood, Taylor Evans, and her husband Jarod rushed into the garage. Taylor gathered Faith in a hug. "I've missed you."

"Hey, Tay. Hey, Jarod." Faith's emotions calmed under her friend's soothing voice and warm hug. "Me too. Good to see you both."

Jarod pointed to the garage, "What did they say about your car?"

"It's the water pump," interjected the man behind the counter around his thick wad of over-exposed gum. "I knew right away. Gonna take a few days or so to fix."

Caleb blew out a long breath, and Jarod whistled as Faith's shoulders sank.

"Let's get the boxes out of your car, so we can load them in Jarod's truck." Caleb headed toward the garage bay door, "Show me what you want to take."

He held the door open for their friends. Faith tightened the coat around her as the temperature had fallen in the minutes they'd been in the shop. All four of them worked to move the high-end chef's supply boxes to the back of Jarod's truck.

"See you three tomorrow at Hawk's Creek," said Caleb when they'd finished.

"See you then. Thanks for the help."

"Welcome." Caleb waved and walked to his SUV, hopped in, and drove away.

Faith's shoulders eased and her heart rate slowed with his departure.

"So," Tay swiveled toward Faith. "It was a rotten way to meet Caleb again, but how are you doing?"

"Shocked, but glad he helped me."

"You know that he owns a rafting and kayaking company, right? It sounds like he's convinced you to go." Taylor took her hand and gave it a squeeze. "I remember what happened."

Her skin crawled as if a thousand ants marched over her.

"You don't have to do this, Faith."

"I've got to try. I haven't been on a boat since then."

They climbed into the truck and she answered their questions about her road trip. By the time the truck bounced into Jarod and Tay's driveway, a blanket of exhaustion lay on Faith.

"Honey, can you get Faith's suitcase?" Taylor asked Jarod. "I'm going to take our tired friend in the house and show her where she'll sleep."

"Sure."

The walkway curved to the front porch of the home, and Faith noted the pots spilling with bright blue and yellow flowers on either side of the door. Walking over the threshold she noticed a lamp lit the tan sofas her friend had decorated with splashes of color from the square pillows resting on the cushions.

"Your new place, it's gorgeous."

"Thank you. We're happy with how it turned out. Let's show you to your room."

Taylor and her dog Sugar led the way upstairs. As she entered the room, Faith's feet sunk into the plush sea green rug next to the bed. Sugar leapt onto the pristine white bedding.

Pointing a finger at the dog, Taylor commanded, "Get down, Sugar."

Sugar's yellow arrow tail tucked beneath her, and two big brown eyes stared at Faith.

"Aww, she's fine." Running a hand over the silky coat, Faith grinned. "This is her home, and I'm a visitor. She's got first rights."

"You know, Faith, it's not sounding too good for Old Bessie. We can help you if you need it."

"It's gonna be fine. Thanks."

Jarod came into the room and put the suitcase across the arms of an overstuffed green and tan chair. Faith smiled in thanks.

"I'm glad Caleb happened by at the right time." Jarod put an arm around his wife's shoulders. "He's a good guy."

"He is." Faith yawned. "Sorry, twelve hours in a car. I'm beat."

"We'll talk more tomorrow." Taylor touched her arm and smiled.

"Night." The couple exited the room with Sugar padding behind them.

Sitting down on the bed, she ran her fingers through her hair as her head dipped. Prayers moved across her lips, for finances, for the future, and for tomorrow.

"Like I said last night, you don't have to do this," Tay said to Faith the next morning when it was time to leave for the rafting trip.

"Tay, I can't be a chicken."

"You're not. Don't force it. Bring a book, relax. You drove all day yesterday from New York to North Carolina and had car trouble. Talk about a lot of stress. That's exhausting."

"I don't know."

Jarod said, "We need to go."

Taylor glanced at Faith.

Faith nodded at her friend and tucked the mystery novel she'd left on the side table in her bag. "I'm ready. I'll raft."

"Let's go then, Faithful." Taylor used the childhood nickname for her best friend, Faith Fuller.

Settled into the back seat of the truck, Jarod soon had them out in the country. Twenty-five minutes later, Jarod made a sharp turn into a parking lot. Faith's stomach took a similar turn into an immediate flip-flop.

Still woozy, she alighted from the car to the sound of rushing water in the background. Faith spotted a bright, pencil-yellow flit of a boat beyond them in the water. Why had she said she'd come? She planted her feet in the shifting pea gravel parking lot.

"Walk with me?" she asked Taylor.

"Sure."

"I don't think I can go through with it."

"Don't. You've got nothing to prove."

"I do. To myself."

"You're as pale as my legs." Tay put a hand on her shoulder and a smile peeked at the corners of her mouth. "Read. I'll tell Caleb something."

Faith's gaze shifted beyond the shore. Her eyes landed on a rowboat near the edge. An older man and young girl sat inside. She froze, captive to the image as the scene in front of Faith blurred and hidden memories unfurled in her mind. A dinghy. Her favorite Back Street Boys t-shirt. Her handsome Grandpa Fuller. The bobber's ping when it hit the grey-green water. A bright pink fishing pole.

"Faith, come over here," Taylor called, pulling Faith from the edge of her dark reverie.

With a pinch around her heart, she shoved away the memory, all except a pair of bright blue eyes and a matching golf shirt. What happened next stayed safely buried.

CHAPTER THREE

*M*oisture stung her eyes. *I can't go.*

"Faith?" Taylor ran a hand over Faith's hair in a mothering way.

Pinpricks of pain eased as the repetitive motion and soft lapping water rounded the jagged edges of her nerve.

"I thought I could go, but I can't. My parents' boat is huge, and I still can't step foot on it. That raft down there, it's scary to me, too. I don't know what I was thinking."

"You're brave to even try. I understand. What're you going to say?"

Caleb and Jarod walked to where Faith and Taylor stood.

"Everyone ready?" asked Caleb as he handed everyone a water bottle.

"I'm more tired than I thought. I'll sit and read. You three go on." Her hand shook as she fished the book from her bag then eased back into the chair.

"You're sure?"

"Positive."

"I'll stay with you."

"No, go have fun for me, too."

Caleb moved closer to Faith. "You okay? You seem upset."

"I'm fine. Tired."

"You're sure."

She nodded.

Caleb arrowed a glance toward her as if he needed to double check Faith. "See you later."

Plastering a smile on her face, she said, "Bye."

Taylor grinned. "I'll tell you about it."

As Tay moved away, she couldn't stop herself from saying, "Please be careful."

"We're in good hands. It's going to be okay. Really. Enjoy your book. We'll see you later."

"Sure." Faith watched while they loaded into the kayaks. Her friends skimmed their paddles into the placid water and playfully splashed each other. At the sound of their laughter, a twinge of regret passed through Faith.

As Caleb pushed the raft away from the bank with an oar, Faith uttered a silent prayer of safety for her friends. A sense of calm swept over her. She shifted her gaze to the scenery around the deck. The green grass bent its head in the slight breeze, and the soothing water rippled steps away from where she sat. Pulling out a protein bar, she nibbled absentmindedly while reading. Her head popped up when a noise sounded. A rafting group clambered into a bobbing boat. Faith put the partially finished bar in her bag and returned to her novel.

Faith was halfway through the book by the time a loud noise drew her gaze. Sometime later Taylor, Jarod, and Caleb piled out of a shuttle in the parking lot below, safe and sound.

She watched as they climbed upstairs to the deck.

"How'd it go?" she asked.

"Fantastic! The rapids were amazing." Taylor wrung out her damp hair and grinned.

"Glad you had fun." Faith placed a bookmark into the crease of the novel, stood, stretched, and walked across the deck.

Caleb strode up the bank behind them, water dripping down his face in small rivers.

"You okay?" he asked.

"Fine. Thanks." She put the book into her bag, busy doing anything to not see him. When she did look around her gaze met Caleb's. Again, she averted her glance toward her almost empty water bottle.

"Caleb, are you ready for the youth volleyball game this afternoon?" Taylor asked.

"Wouldn't miss it."

"Your team against Jarod's, this'll be good. Faith, you're coming, aren't you?"

Faith crossed her arms. *It feels like they're pushing us together.* "Why?"

"It's going to be fun."

Caleb pulled his shirt away from his body, and it immediately clung back in place. "I don't know about you two, but I need to get home and put on dry clothes. And get my cheerleader."

Faith recalled exactly who his cheerleader was as her stomach tied in knots. She didn't want to see Caleb with someone else.

"Let's go." Taylor walked ahead with Jarod.

Caleb waited behind. "You going to the game?"

"To keep Taylor company."

"Is that the only reason?"

"Cheering Jarod on."

"Not my team?"

"Exactly." Without waiting for a response, Faith put her bag over her shoulder and caught up with her friends.

She noticed on the car ride a coffee shop near Hawk's Creek she hadn't seen before and mentioned it to her friends. "It matches the exterior of Caleb's business."

Jarod half-turned in the seat. "It's Hawk's Creek Coffee.

Caleb opened it a few months ago." He shifted his glance back to the narrow country road.

"I'm impressed." The words tumbled from her mouth before she could stuff them back in. Taylor did a double take. The corner of Faith's lip turned up as she raised a shoulder.

"They've got the best mochas, don't they, honey?" Taylor poked Jarod in the shoulder.

"Hmm. Yeah."

"And the most delicious cinnamon rolls."

"They do. I'm starting to feel dry already." Jarod grinned. "U-turn." He nosed the car into the coffee shop parking lot.

"What a surprise." Taylor bounced from the car.

Jarod groaned. "Hardly."

Curious, Faith exited the car. She noticed Caleb's SUV pull into the space next to Jarod's truck.

Caleb alighted from his car and motioned with a muscled arm. "It's on me, come on."

"Won't your cheerleader mind?"

"They'll wait."

Remaining silent, Faith followed. The sound of laughter filled the room as she entered. A spicy aroma held center court over the nutty scent of fresh ground coffee. The burnt sunset, orange-red color on the walls warmed the room as the sunlight beamed through the numerous windows. *Beautiful. It looks like a place I'd like to own.* Her eyes landed on the carved wooden display cases. Faith's appetite awakened. "Tay, are these your Aunt Joy's recipes? You gave them to Caleb?"

"I did."

A dark-haired man working behind the counter gave a cookie to her.

She took a bite, letting her eyes close until she finished savoring the crunched walnuts and cinnamon chips bursting inside her mouth. "They're the best. Everyone at Rocky Shoals

Church Camp waited for your Aunt Joy's care packages, which you always shared."

Taylor's laughter bubbled. Snorting, she reddened. "I remember sitting on those tree stumps by the mailroom. Those were good times but really hard on the backend!"

They darted looks at each other and giggled as sparks of the memory swirled and danced around them.

Caleb coughed and spoke. "Ryan's ready to take our coffee orders."

Once placed, they found a table near the windows, overlooking the beautiful blue-green river that gamboled beyond the coffee shop. Faith glanced at Caleb and smiled. "I like this place; it's cozy."

"Yeah?" Caleb clasped his fingers together on the table. "What would you add?"

"A deck or patio, extending the seating."

"You're business-minded. Why haven't you opened a bakery?"

She put her half-raised coffee cup on the table and shrugged. "New York was too expensive."

Caleb leaned forward. "Is that why you left?"

"No." *Nosy.* Faith snatched a glance at his dimpled smile. She swallowed a sigh. *He's off limits.* Picking up her mug, Faith hid a frown behind the amber-colored shield.

As the creak of the door drew Faith's attention, she noticed an attractive older woman enter. Her dark, coarse hair, laced with gray, was woven into an intricate bun atop her head. This, coupled with her petite size and beautiful café au lait skin, gave the impression of a wood nymph or pixie queen. She wore a freshly pressed pink top and a smile as dazzling as the spring day.

Caleb stood and walked over to the woman. "Hello, Lizzie."

"Afternoon. Lucas has been crowing about the oatmeal cookies. My husband has a sweet tooth to rival mine."

"Ryan," Caleb said to the man behind the coffee bar.

The dark-haired man whipped his head around. "Yes?"

"Please fix a box for Mr. Lucas and Miss Lizzie."

"Will do."

Caleb returned to the table.

"Good to see Lizzie doing better." Jarod flicked at his straw wrapper on the table. "Her health's been bad recently."

"Ryan's doing the baking and most of the managing so Lizzie can stay home. Our business is brisk, and with summer coming, I'll need a manager. Not sure if Lizzie can keep up the pace."

Faith noticed how Lizzie flitted from table to table as Ryan assembled her order. A smile for a young child busy chomping on a cookie, whose scattered crumbs painted the table and floor around their chair. Another for a middle-aged group of ladies sipping tea and pointing to their book covers on the table. While small, the space filled with happiness thanks to this woman. "I hope she can, people seem to adore her."

Caleb introduced Faith to Lizzie, and after chatting for a few minutes, it felt like she'd known her for years.

Jarod flicked a glance to his phone. "We need to go. The church kids are meeting us at the park in a couple of hours." The group said their goodbyes to Miss Lizzie and headed for the door.

Out into the sunlight, Faith squinted and glanced at the coffee shop. She pictured a low deck beyond the building, with tables and brightly colored plants. A twinge pinched her heart as it left a seed of an idea planted yet not watered. To own her own bakery... but how?

CHAPTER FOUR

*C*aleb slammed the trunk as he heard his son Jackson's voice through the open car door.

"Out."

"Hold on a sec, Jack."

"Okay."

He shouldered the navy blue child's chair with a cartoon character tiger on its bag. "Ready for the game?" Caleb unbuckled the seatbelt and swooped his son out of the car and into the air. Jack's blond hair haloed around his head.

"Me. Flywing."

"Uh huh."

"Higher."

He spotted a group of Jarod's church kids waiting for them. "I see your friends." Jack wiggled to get out of his hands.

"Down." Caleb put him on the soft grass and grinned as Jack's two-and-a-half-year-old legs ran as fast as he could toward the teens. Several girls' sonic screeches short-circuited his thirty-year old ears. His son's name crested above the wave of giggles. Caleb unfolded the chair near the canopy of a tree by the volleyball area and watched as Jack tossed the ball with two of the girls. He felt a clap on his back and turned.

"Jack's a charmer," Jarod said.

"Like me."

Jarod set two adult chairs next to Jack's smaller one. "Your wife was always more social than you."

Caleb noticed Taylor and Faith approaching. "Not now." He bobbed his head in the ladies' direction. Jarod glanced their way and nodded. Caleb checked to see what was going on with Jack. Jack's laughter was his answer.

"Thanks." Taylor put a hand on her husband's shoulder. "I take it Faith and I are going to have company?" She pointed to the little chair.

Jack walked over to them, holding on to the hand of a girl from the youth group. "He wanted to see his dad."

"Thanks, Gabi."

Caleb picked him up.

The girl smiled and walked back toward her friends.

"You've got a child. So, I take it you're married?" Faith's hands were clasped together.

"I . . . was. It's a long story. I don't talk about it in front of you-know who."

"Down, pwease."

Caleb put lowered his son to the ground, and held his hand.

"Oh." Faith nodded. "I didn't see a car seat the other night."

"I needed the extra space for groceries. Jack stayed with his favorite sitter."

Jack pointed to Faith. "Lady."

"This is Faith; she's a friend."

"Hi, Fay."

Faith giggled and high-fived Jack. "Nice to meet you; I like your cool light-up shoes."

Suddenly, Jack broke away from his dad, and ran several feet beyond the group. "Fast!"

"You are very fast." Faith clapped.

Smiling, Jack rejoined them.

"Come here, running boy." Taylor held out her arms and Jack wiggled into them. "You two need to get your teams ready."

Jack said, "Taywor."

"Yes?"

"Pwetty." Jack played with one of Taylor's curls, but Caleb started to brush his hand away.

"He always does this." Taylor sat down and held Jack on her lap, while Faith sat on the chair on the end.

"Be back in a while. Bye, tiger."

Jack held up a still chubby hand and waved. Warmth spread through Caleb. *I'd like to hear what Faith says, but the game won't wait.*

Jarod's victorious team whooped and celebrated with the popsicles he'd pulled from the cooler moments earlier. Caleb's team enjoyed them, too, even though some sulked on the outskirts of the group.

"Me?" Jack held out his hand to his dad. Taylor held his other one.

"Sure."

Jack grabbed the blue and red popsicle and began to consume it. Caleb wiped the red trail going down his chin with a finger.

Faith gestured to him. "His dad's wearing some, too."

Caleb saw where she'd pointed red and blue streaked his arm. *Smooth.* "The hazards of parenting." Taylor pulled a tissue from her bag that he used to wipe it away.

Before long, Jack gave Caleb the rest of the treat and decorated his arm again with his sticky hand.

"I've got some hand sanitizer." Faith pulled a small bottle from her purse and Taylor proffered a wad of tissues.

He grabbed them and they adhered like permanent glue to his fingers. Caleb tore the tissues off, leaving fragments on his finger pads.

"I've got it." Faith took the bottle and dabbed it onto the tissue. "Can this go near Jack's face?"

"No, he's going straight into the shower at home." Caleb swallowed a groan at the sticky strands of red and blue in Jack's blond hair, like a post-modern homage to the flag. "We'd better go. Okay with the group?"

"Sure." Jarod folded Jack's chair. "Parents are pulling in now."

Caleb shouldered the chair and found a less-sticky spot on Jack's arm to hold. "Jack and I are going fishing tomorrow. Want to go, Faith?" He felt the ends of his ears burn. *Where'd that come from?*

"Uh, sure. What time?"

"I'll pick you up around 3:30, he takes a long nap after church on Sunday."

"Okay. See you then."

Jack waved his goodbye.

As he buckled Jack, he heard, "Lady goes?"

"Taylor?"

Jack's head shook. "No."

"Faith? Yeah, she is."

Jack leaned his face to Caleb's. He could smell the scent of cherry popsicle and warm, grassy sunshine on his son. "Nice."

He raised his head, hit it on the roof and winced. Pain coupled with surprise. *He likes her.* Caleb closed the door and walked to his door, glancing back at the group. He noticed Faith, head tilted back, laughing with their friends. *Three people fishing. Nothing else.* Caleb rubbed his thumb over his ring finger, the ridge was still noticeable from when he took it off a year ago. Caleb's deep sigh filled the car's interior as he reversed and headed home with his boy. The short drive home invigorated Jack. He shimmied in his car seat until Caleb unbuckled him.

Jack popped from his chair and grabbed Caleb's hand in a sugary clasp. "I'm hungy."

"All right. Grilled chicken leftovers."

Big brown eyes met his, and Jack shook his head. "Ceeal."

"Leftovers. Then, shower."

"No, bath."

"Dinner. Shower. Bedtime story. Bed."

Jack's bottom lip stuck out as he settled into his chair in the family room.

Caleb turned on the television, and found Jack's favorite show. His son's lip soon returned to normal.

He headed to the kitchen to prepare their food. His cell phone blared, and Caleb swiped to answer.

"Caleb. It's Lucas. We're in the ER."

"What's going on?" Instantly, blood pounded in his ears.

"Lizzie's got another bout of pneumonia."

"I'm sorry. What can I do?"

"Pray. Doctor's saying she's got to rest at home for a month. This one is a doozy. The worst I've seen. It came on suddenly. Sorry to leave you short a person."

"No apologies. Hug your wife for me. I'll be praying."

"Sure."

Dinner was quickly enjoyed.

"Bath time, sport."

Minutes later, once he had a clean boy that smelled like banana and strawberries, Caleb helped him pull on his shirt.

"I do it," Jack said.

He stepped back and viewed the cobra dance his son performed as he got his body settled into his pajamas.

Once his son was soundly asleep, the silence of the house

allowed his thoughts to wander. Caleb silently prayed for his friend, Miss Lizzy. *Who do I know that can assist at the coffee shop? Someone I can trust?*

CHAPTER FIVE

"*W*hy didn't you tell me? I had no idea Caleb had a child. I stopped looking at any of his social media a long time ago." Faith tossed the last of the leftover popsicles into Jarod's cooler. "He's really cute. Jack resembles Caleb in everything but his coloring."

"I didn't want to hurt you." Taylor began to fold the chairs and glanced away. "His mom had blonde hair."

"Was she nice?"

"Mmm hmm."

"Are they. . . divorced?"

"No."

Faith knew she needed to stop, yet something inside of her begged for an answer. "Separated?"

Taylor's shoulders fell. "She died. Two years ago."

"That's horrible." After every scenario she'd played in her head, this was not one of them. Losing the mother of your child had to be beyond imaginable. "I need to say something to him."

"Don't." Taylor snapped the last chair closed. "If he wants you to know, he'll tell you."

They walked to the car in silence. A thousand questions circled Faith, yet she remained mute.

∼

Taylor and Jarod's Shih-tzu, Sugar, sat perched on the bed's edge, tongue lolling and eyes trailing her every move. "Don't you have a ball to chase this afternoon?"

Sugar stared.

"You're making me nervous."

Faith rummaged through her suitcase to find her favorite jeans and a shirt that wasn't wrinkled. The doorbell rang downstairs, and Sugar jumped from the bed yowling. "Shh, Sugar." She pulled on the jeans with ripped knees and threw on a green plaid shirt and her pale grey Converse. One quick glance in the mirror to swipe on a light lipstick and finger-comb her hair and she headed downstairs. Excitement unfolded with each step. It had been a long time since she'd been fishing, especially with as cute a fishing buddy as Cal— Jack. Near the bottom step she spotted Jarod and Caleb talking at the door while Jack ran around with Sugar.

Caleb glanced at her, and she smiled. "Hi, you two."

"Hey, ready?" He put a hand on Jack's shoulder and opened the front door.

Warmth tingled in her. "Yes." Faith swept the wave of curls from blocking her sight and grabbed her bag off the foyer bench.

Jarod stood at the door with Sugar. "Have fun! Catch dinner for me."

Caleb guffawed. "Better go to the store, we catch and release."

"Does that mean I have to release?" Faith grimaced.

"I might help." Caleb grinned as he hoisted Jack into his seat. "Maybe."

24

"I'll remember that." Faith sat in the passenger seat and felt someone run their fingers through her hair. She turned to see the culprit.

Jack giggled and kicked his feet in his chair.

"Time to buckle you in." Caleb snapped the buckles into place. "Your hair should be safe now."

"I thought it was cute." Faith fluttered her fingers on his legs as he wiggle-wormed away from them. "Are you excited, Jack?

"Yesh."

"Me too."

Caleb slid into the driver's seat and closed the door. He turned on some music after starting his car. "Jack's favorite."

She soon overheard Jack's musical noises from the backseat, and to her surprise, Caleb sang along. "Nice voice. I've never heard you sing."

"Sing with us. The words are easy. Banana. Anna. Ramma."

Faith waved a hand in the air. "I'm more of a 'make a joyful noise' kind of person. Trust me, it's better for your ears if I listen." Songs and giggles filled the remainder of the short car ride.

Plop. Plink. Plunk. All three of them put their lines into the clear emerald waters. "Thanks for bringing an extra pole." Faith bobbled her pole as the line floated near Caleb's.

"I had another one at home. My dad likes to come with us sometimes."

"I bet that's fun."

"Jack loves it when his granddaddy makes a big deal over his catch." Caleb winked at Faith. "Even when it's a minnow."

"He's probably better than me." Faith cut a glance to Jack.

Jack's Spiderman pole dragged nearer to the water, and he began to get close to the lapping river. Faith's hand collided with Caleb's as they both went in to grab the pole. She quickly moved hers away.

"Yeah. I think he's hooked something big. Let me help you,

tiger." Caleb looked at Faith over his shoulder. "Could you take this?" Caleb handed Faith his pole.

Faith eyed movement in the rippling water, delight trickling inside. With each turn of the reel, Jack's prize grew closer. Jack jumped up and down on the grassy bank.

"Fish. I got it."

"You did." The two lines began to tangle, she shoved her pole farther from her body. A splash drew her attention back to the action. Jack's line held a small trout, no longer than a pencil. "That's a good-looking fish, Jack."

"Fanks." He stuck his tongue between his teeth as he helped his dad take the hook out of the fish's mouth.

"Careful, we don't want to hurt the fish. Let's put him into the water." Dad and son released the flapping fish back into the water, where it disappeared under the cover of some moss-flecked rocks at the bottom of the stream. Faith glanced at the two as they shared a hug, and tingling threads of happiness weaved through her.

"See dat? He goes."

"He did. Almost as fast as you ran yesterday," said Faith.

Jack took off down the bank of the river. Caleb followed and steered him in the right direction.

"Why don't we catch its friend?"

"Hungy."

"Okay." Caleb opened his backpack and got out a container of wet wipes. "Wash first." Jack handed the dirty wipe to his dad. "Now we can have grapes. Want some, too?"

Faith waved the two rods still in her hands.

"Sorry, forgot." He ran and grabbed them from her and wrapped the lines along the pole. "Wipe?"

"Yes, Dad."

"Ha ha." Caleb offered the wipe to her anyway.

One look at her hands and she used it. Faith reached for her bag to dispose of it right as Caleb took it from her and stuffed it into the trash bag.

"I didn't want your purse to get wet," Caleb said before he popped a green grape globe into his mouth.

"Considerate of you."

"I can be." Caleb pulled out three water bottles from his bag. "Want one?"

His kindness surprised her. "Sure."

He handed it over to her and opened a smaller bottle for Jack.

"Do you two come here often?"

"Not very. Sundays are my only day off, and we usually do something around the house after church, keep it low-key."

"That has to grow old. All that work."

"Owning a business has its drawbacks. When you have your own someday, you'll know."

"Maybe."

"Are you thinking about living in Florida near family permanently?"

"No."

"Stop me if I'm being rude, but why did you leave New York?"

She pressed a foot down on the green grass and lifted it up. As the uneven fringe sprang back, it eased her sensitive nerves. *The grass is like me, knocked down but bouncing back up.* "Fired."

"That stinks, sorry."

"Appreciate it." Faith felt a release, the tight bands around her chest loosening. "I'll find something soon."

Caleb's green eyes met hers. "Don't think I'm weird for asking. Lizzie is out ill for at least a month. Would you consider working for me? It's not New York, but it's a temporary job in a nice small-town area."

Faith ran a hand through her hair and glanced skyward. "I'm sorry Lizzie is sick. I hope she'll be better soon."

"Me too."

"When would I start?"

"Tomorrow. I've asked around and had no takers."

This is an answer to prayers, Old Bessie's costing a lot to fix. Play it cool, Faith. "Um. I don't have experience in a coffee shop. Remember, I was a test kitchen chef?"

"How could I forget? All those things you cooked when we dated caused me to have to let my Wall Street suits out at the tailors." He patted his stomach. "I stay away from that stuff now."

As her eyes trailed where his hand touched, her face warmed. *Yes, you do.* The water bottle tumbled from her fingers and she bent to pick it up. She brushed the dirty side off and grimaced.

"How long again? A month?"

"No more than. It's strictly temporary." Caleb offered Faith the bag of grapes. She shook her head. When he gave her the figures for what she'd make, Faith raised an eyebrow.

"I 'll check to see if Tay and Jarod don't mind me staying. I can come this week. We'll see about the rest of the month."

Caleb's mouth turned up. "I'll let Ryan know. You really are saving me."

"You owe me."

"I do."

"Me too." Jack held his grape in the air like a salute. Faith and Caleb looked at each other and laughed.

Once everything was packed into his car, they drove toward town. Faith heard soft snuffles behind her and turned to see the source. Jack had his thumb in his mouth; his head was lolled to the side of the seat. "Is he okay?" She noticed Caleb's eyes veer to the rearview mirror.

"He's fine, that's why we. . . I mean . . . I bought the extra head cushions for his seat." Caleb's smile faded in the waning sun.

Words stuck inside Faith's mouth. She took a sip from the water bottle. Cool water bruised her tightened esophagus. Instinctively, Faith grabbed her throat. Caleb's chin jutted forward.

"You know what happened." Caleb's pain penetrated her heart.

"I do and I'm sorry."

"Feel pity, don't you?"

He braced an arm on his door and the other Faith noticed was white knuckled on the wheel. "Everyone does. Go on. Pour out your sympathy. I'm numb to it."

Her gaze fell to the floorboards, salt stung her eyes. "I'm not giving it." *Like a robot. He didn't let me in when we dated, and he's not now.* She flung the door open in the driveway and went to force it closed. *Jack.* Faith peered into the window where he still slept. *Oh, the blessed oblivion of a child.*

"Be at the coffee shop at seven."

Faith gently closed the door despite herself and he left. She made her way up the sidewalk and rapped on the door. When Tay opened it, Faith spilled the tense conversation in one breath.

"He's so angry. I don't know if I can work for him."

"What?" Taylor pulled on her arm.

"Caleb guessed that I knew."

Taylor blew a curl from her face. "He's simmering in hurt. We've tried to talk to him. It's getting better than it was. The other thing you said about work?"

"Lizzie's ill and won't be working for a month. He asked me to step in."

"I hope she's better soon, that sweet lady's been ill a lot recently. Maybe you should text Caleb."

"Not tonight, he's heard enough from me for today. He's changed, Tay. I'm not sure I know Caleb."

"Behind that somewhat crusty exterior lies a big heart."

"Then it's buried deep down under a layer of hot, molten anger. I'm exhausted. Night."

"It's eight."

"The drama tired me. There's a romantic mystery I'm going to fall asleep reading."

"Sweet dreams."

Faith texted three words to Caleb. *I'll be there.* Not waiting for a response, she washed the grime from the fishing trip away in the shower. As she did, Faith remembered Jack's excitement in catching the fish. She smiled. One Gaines liked her: Jack. The other: far from it. Tomorrow would be interesting.

CHAPTER SIX

*A*rriving at the coffee shop twenty minutes early, Faith climbed from Tay's truck and waved.

"Thanks."

Taylor raised a hand from out of the driver's side window. "Welcome. Pick you up at five. Be nice."

"See you, and I might."

Taylor's bright blue truck zoomed from the small lot.

Faith moved toward the door. Her shirt caught on a thorn from a rose bush in the plantings adjacent to the sidewalk. Removing it, she ripped a small hole in the cloth. *Fantastic.* She shifted her body to hide the ripped portion as Ryan smiled in her direction. Faith noticed his bright grey eyes shielded under a mass of black curls. "Hi Ryan."

"Hello. I'll show you around in a sec." Ryan's tall frame disappeared under the granite counter, a ripping sound filled the air, and he hefted a square brown box onto the counter. He gave her a Hawk's Creek Coffee shirt and hat. "Your uniform." Ryan's eyes darted to the rip in her shirt, and she covered it with her hand.

"I'll go change." Faith took the clothes and marched to the

ladies' room. In the soft light coming from the mason jar chandelier, the mocha-colored polo and black logo hat didn't look awful on her. Not as flattering as her other shirt but serviceable. She walked down the short hall and back into the coffee shop area.

Ryan motioned for her to come to the cash register so he could show her the system. After a few attempts, she understood the ordering system and payment methods. Next came the coffee orders, which she handled with the grace of a newborn calf. Café au lait and the burned odor of espresso soon decorated and scented her shirt.

"You'll get it, Faith. I'll handle the more involved orders for the next several days. By the time I leave for Hawaii next week, you'll be ready."

"I didn't know you were going on vacation. Who's helping?"

"I think you know them." Ryan moved to the opposite end of the counter to take the first person's order. Faith felt like blurting to Ryan to tell her, but she was swamped in warming and packaging the baked goods for the customers' orders.

For several hours it was busy. Faith couldn't believe there were so many things to keep up with on the fancy Italian coffee maker, items in the bakery case, and clean up. She glanced at the iron maiden of footwear she was wearing—her pointy-toed flats — and narrowed her eyes. Tomorrow, her barely-used tennis shoes would be worn and not these harbingers of torture. Tiny hairs raised on the back of her neck as the door creaked. Throwing a glance in the door's direction, her nose wrinkled.

"Happy to see me this afternoon?"

"Not really."

"How's it going, Ryan?"

Ryan adjusted his ball cap. "Busy."

"Two coffees?" Caleb jerked a thumb in Faith's direction. Ryan nodded.

"Lose a fight with the coffee maker?" Caleb gestured to her Rorschach test shirt.

"I'm learning."

"Come sit with me. Ryan's got it."

Faith walked to the nearest chair and sat, wincing.

"What's wrong?" Caleb leaned into the table.

"My feet. I wore the wrong shoes."

"Be back soon." Caleb darted from the seat and out the door.

"Caleb coming back?" Ryan handed Faith her coffee and put a mug decorated with an airplane on the table.

"He said he was." She sipped the dark brew, the acid notes mingled with a smoke flavor. Delicious. Two more sips and Caleb reappeared carrying an orange Hawk's Creek bag.

Caleb gave the cloth bag to Faith. "For you."

"What is it?"

"Look."

Faith dipped her fingers into the bag, felt something squishy, and glanced inside. Warmth sprinkled over her. "Tie-dye flip flops?"

"From the gift shop. Did I get the right size?"

Faith pulled them from the bag and closed one eye against the glare of the kaleidoscopic rainbow sherbet shoes. An unparalleled fashion don't. "Yes."

"I wasn't positive."

"Thanks." Faith slid a foot into the sandal, the padded sole cushioning her pained foot. She put the other on, wiggled her toes, and bagged her flats.

"Nice, huh? They look like that ice cream you'd get from Crème," said Caleb.

"Sunset. I can taste the orange and raspberry swirls. You've got a good memory."

"Not true. I can't remember my order."

"Grapefruit tango."

As she shifted, the shoes' rubber soles squeaked. "How much do I owe you?"

"No charge. Are you liking it?"

"I do, all the customers made the time go quickly. This is the first time I've sat."

"Mondays are always busy, and Fridays, too. So, are you staying for the month?"

"Yes. Ryan told me about his trip this morning. But not who was helping."

"Me."

A vein in her temple pounded. "What about your other business?"

"I've got assistant managers. That's why I have two people lead. One can't be there, the other will."

"Who's your co-leader?"

"She's. . . gone."

"Oh." Faith observed Caleb's drooping mouth and shoulders. "If you want to talk—"

Shoving from the table, he stood and grabbed his mug. "See you." Before Faith uttered a syllable, he'd departed.

CHAPTER SEVEN

*H*urt seized his midsection, the rushing water past the trees mimicked his over-amplified nerves. *When will it get better?* He jerked open the door to Hawk's Creek and straightened a stuffed animal in the kids' section of the gift shop, pausing when he heard door creak. Tiny arms encircled his legs. A swell of love wrapped his heart. "Hey, Jack. Thanks for bringing him by, Mrs. Settles."

Jack's part-time sitter smiled and blew Jack a kiss as she left. "See you two tomorrow."

"Bye." Turning his attention to a stuffed monkey from the miniature canoe display, he hugged it close to his body and swung back and forth. Big brown eyes focused in on his face. "Mine. Pweas?"

"But you already have five of them." He couldn't look at his son any longer, so he stared at the ceiling. Tug. Pull. Heave. A clammy little hand touched his leg.

"One more."

He didn't lisp. Caleb was electrified. He'd locked away the unspoken worry that his son would need speech therapy as he had as a young boy. "All right. This is the last monkey."

"Thanks." The brown monkey danced up his arm as far as Jack could reach, and the smile on his little face stretched from ear to ear.

"Help me in the office for a bit, then we'll go home." He pulled an apple and a bottle of water out from the mini-fridge and handed it to Jack.

Back to working on taxes. He exhaled and took another glance at his son who was busy playing with his new toy and the non-messy markers and paper he kept in his office for Jack. Work.

While he printed files on his copier, Jack would get up and bring them to him, smelling of crisp apple and a whiff of over-heated child. He noted he needed to make sure Jack showered, not played in the water tonight.

Squinting at the screen, the numbers merged, and his head felt two sizes bigger. He rubbed his eyes and swigged his water. Before he could attempt to start working again, someone knocked on the office door.

"Come in," Jack yelled.

Caleb put a finger to his mouth. "Whisper, please, I'm getting a headache." Jack nodded. The door swung open and the visitor stepped inside. By the look on her face, she wasn't happy.

"Hi, Fay." Jack waved.

"I'm doing my taxes. Need something?"

"Hi, Jack. I like your monkey." Faith shrugged. "It's not important."

Caleb held his head. The pounding felt like drums.

Two lines V'd between her brows. "Allergy headache?"

"Migraine." Putting the water bottle to his temple numbed only the small area. He wished it would cover his head. "Stress."

"Are you able to drive?"

"Probably. I'm not getting the flashes yet." Shutting down the computer he rose from his seat, and streamers of light flickered in his vision. "Too late."

"I'll drive, let me text Tay and let her know. Point to what you need and I'll get it." At his direction, Faith gathered his backpack and phone for him.

"Thanks." Everything looked out of focus like he was looking into Fun House mirrors at a carnival. He squinted which caused the pain to pulsate more intensely.

"Give me your keys and I'll pull up to the front door."

Within a few moments, Faith pulled to the front, and he put Jack into the seat and buckled him in. Pulling on sunglasses dampened the migraine-noise in his head, and he leaned back in the leather seat and closed his eyes. What seemed like moments later, a climbing choke of nausea traced a path in his throat as the car swung side to side on the curves of the mountain road. Through his cycloptic vision, he spied a stand of trees. He held a hand over his mouth and pointed to the side.

"Pull over?"

He gave Faith a thumbs-up signal and made it to the trees before illness steamrolled him.

"Daddy sick." Caleb heard the hitch in his son's voice.

Sweat beaded his face, yet he had to get back to the cold air in the car. Taking a few quick breaths, he forced the words, "I'm fine."

A rose scented cloth bobbed in front of him. It smelled like one of those perfume shops his mom liked. His lip curled.

"Wipe." Faith put the white, girly cloth in his hand. "You need to freshen up."

"Got anything else?"

"Not a thing."

Softness, like a dryer sheet, touched his skin as he tried not to choke on the cloying smell. Faith held out a crumpled baggie and he put the stink bomb inside and closed it. "I'll throw it away later." He crammed it into his bag.

"Okay, Daddy?"

"Sure." Eyes closed, he could feel the concerned stares from

Faith and his son. Embarrassing as the episode should be, he didn't care—pain controlled his mood. As the car stopped, he opened his eyes. He'd never been so glad to see his house before. "I'll get Jack."

Faith pointed a finger at him. "Unlock your front door. Jack and I will come in after you."

Opening the door, his dog jumped up and punched him with oversized paws in his gut. Pain arrowed to his head. He fought the swells of nausea.

"Hey—"

Caleb blurted, "His name's Ranger." He gripped the dog collar to make sure the overexcited animal wouldn't knock Faith down. "You might want to back away, he slobbers." Too late. Her hand shot out toward Ranger's gooey maw.

"He's gorgeous."

Ranger's tail whomped on the tile foyer floor, and his watermelon-colored tongue bathed her hand. The stickiness left a shiny imprint on the back of her hand, Caleb noticed.

"Sorry, he's friendly."

"I'm fine."

"Jack, show her the guest bathroom." Obediently, Jack took Faith's hand and led her down the hall.

Caleb dragged to the master bathroom and downed two extra-strength headache relievers, then went to the kitchen and sat down at the table.

"Hungy, Daddy."

Pressing a hand to his stomach, he peeled himself away from his resting place, words dripping thicker than honey. "Okay, Jack."

Faith made a shooing motion. "Go. I've got this. I'd imagine you're not hungry."

"No." Caleb held up a hand and waved before heading down the hall to the master suite where he showered and fell into bed.

38

Before his eyes closed, a joy-buzzer of panic hit. He'd left his son. Weariness claimed him as he realized he'd trusted her with even his most precious gift— Jack.

CHAPTER EIGHT

*F*aith found her way around the kitchen as she pulled on the brass knobs in search of cookware. Finding the pans that she needed, she and her miniature sous-chef Jack put together a delicious dinner of grilled cheeses and fresh tomato soup. Last minute, she chopped some fruit and put it into a big bowl for them to share at the table. Jack popped a large chunk of banana in his mouth and grinned.

"Please close your mouth, Jack." He promptly put his lips together. She couldn't believe he'd obeyed, but he paid her back for her light scolding by asking fifty questions during dinner. It reminded her of the speed dating she'd done in New York, without the yards of desiccated conversation and oily, too-eager men. By the time her ears stopped ringing, Jack declared it was shower time. She followed his quick steps down the hall and into his room, where he dug a pair of turtle-patterned pajamas from the drawer.

"I'll start the water." Faith surveyed the racecar red Spiderman shower curtain and matching bath rugs and smiled. It was definitely a little boy's dream.

Running a hand through the warm water she turned to Jack. "All ready. Need anything?"

"Me do."

Faith stepped into Jack's bedroom, and the bathroom door closed behind her. *Is he old enough to bathe himself?* She'd not been around many little children. With privacy in mind, she cracked the door slightly to listen for any alarming noises.

Rushing water streamed for what she hoped was long enough to clean a rather messy young man, and he emerged, leaving a vapor trail in his wake. She listened for footsteps down the hall. None came.

A dancing monkey kissed her face before Jack and his fiber-filled friend settled into bed. "Wead, pwease?"

"I'd love to." Unsure of where to sit, she lowered to the floor beside his bed and propped her back against the small white nightstand. Faith read the story and giggled along with Jack at the little boy who thought he could drive a car. Closing the book, she slipped a glance at the bed. An angel-kissed cheek rested on the monkey, and little snuffles marked the quiet spaces in the cool air. *This is unexpectedly nice, maybe this is what being a mom feels a bit like.* Faith softly smiled.

She peeked into the hall, checking for any signs of Caleb awakening, but the dark hall remained quiet. She flicked on the airplane nightlight and kept the door cracked open. Tiptoeing on the tile floor she found her bag, sat on the living room sofa, and wiped the makeup off her face with a cloth. Crickets chirruped outside and the moonlight peeped through the blinds. Ranger settled on the floor next to her as Faith snuggled into the cushions on the family room sofa and read a book on her phone. Hope's photo replaced the words of her book. She flicked to answer.

"Hey, sis. How's school?"

"Work and more work."

"Nice."

Hope asked, "How's your job?"

"I'll make you a coffee when you come visit sometime."

"I take it you're moving there?"

"Not sure. It's quiet, and the people are nice. Tay and Jarod are here, so I might."

"After New York, anything's less crowded."

"How's photography class? Anything new with it?"

"An exhibition on campus soon."

"Send me a photo."

"Noted. Let me know if you're moving there."

"Will do."

Faith returned to the book. A chapter later, her eyes drifted closed.

Heavy footsteps brought her back from her dreams. *Caleb.* Faith ducked farther down into the soft blue blanket. Through half-closed eyes, Faith watched a tall form loom over her, his hand brushing a piece of hair from her face, his fingers warm against her skin. She sighed.

Caleb's slight chuckle broke the quiet of the night.

"Come on, boy," whispered Caleb.

Faith returned to her dreams, only to be awoken by the whir of a blender.

Light streamed from the blinds. She darted a look around the room. *Caleb's up.* She hurried to the bathroom, finger-combed her hair, rinsed out her stale mouth, then padded to the kitchen.

"Morning, Faith. I'm making a kale and strawberry smoothie. Want one?"

There wasn't enough strawberry in anything to make her want to drink that chunky green concoction. "No, thanks. Are you feeling better?"

"I am. I haven't had a bad migraine in years—since before Jack was born."

"Glad you're okay. I'm curious, does Jack drink those, too?"

Faith gestured at the science experiment reject while trying to not sniff the grass-green scent.

"Nope. He thinks they're gross. Mrs. Settles, the sitter, makes his breakfast. I have to leave early today for a kayak lesson before the shop opens." Opening a cabinet, he shook a cereal box toward her. "There's some apple cinnamon flax cereal."

"I'm good."

"Thanks for staying. How was Jack last night?" Caleb's grin was infectious.

She returned his smile. "Welcome. He was great. I fed him dinner, he got ready for bed, and we read a book. Jack's a great little boy."

"He is. Did you wear the reading cape?"

"No. No cape."

"You'd look good in it." Caleb's mouth quirked into a grin. "Not like me though. Jack calls me Superman."

"Conceited much?"

"Honest." He poured the thick gloppy drink into a glass and took a sip.

"You missed." Biting back a snort, she motioned with a finger to the Incredible Hulk experiment on his white t-shirt.

She noticed his smirk as he pulled the shirt away from his body to investigate. "My favorite one. Gotta get it in the wash." As he raised the shirt over his head, smooth skin and sleek muscles appeared.

Veering her eyes toward the doorway, she stated, "I need to go get ready for work."

"I'll show you out." Caleb's broad, muscled back led the way to the front door.

Faith's eyes stayed glued on his flexing muscles until he turned around after opening the door. Putting on her sunglasses against the bright sunrise, she waved and walked through the door. "See you." Maneuvering around his car, she shot down the road toward a home with real food. *Flax cereal and kale smooth-*

ies? When did Caleb turn into a clean eater? He'd been dubbed "pizza man" by their friends when they'd dated. He'd changed. Over a bagel and coffee, Faith shared the details with her best friend about the night.

"You did the right thing by staying," said Tay.

"I felt sorry for him." Faith pushed aside her half-eaten breakfast.

"How was Jack?"

"We cooked dinner together, and then I read him a bedtime story. He's so sweet. Caleb's raising him well."

Taylor sipped her coffee and raised an eyebrow. Faith waved her hands in front of her. "Don't say it, Tay. I'm not changing my mind about kids. He's a precious little boy, period." She took a bite of her bagel and swallowed. "This is much better than the kale smoothie Caleb offered to make for me. Yuck."

"Ever since Avery's death, he's eating better. For Jack."

Every ounce of wind escaped Faith's lungs. "Oh." Guilt ping-ponged within. "I guess I would change, too, if I had a child. But I'm not going to date his dad. He eats all that good-for-you stuff. I bake with butter, not the substitute made from plants."

Taylor pinched off a sliver of bagel. "Dating?"

Faith's face heated. "Don't know why I mentioned . . . dating."

"Don't throttle yourself. Be his friend. He needs one. Besides, you're only here for a week." Taylor left the kitchen to get ready for work.

I didn't mean to say that. I'm overtired. Dragging herself upstairs, she readied for work. A screeching voice said, "It's your mom." Ring, ring, "It's your mom," cautioned her cell phone. After drinking the last drop of coffee, she answered.

"Hi Mom."

"Are you coming home next Wednesday?"

"No, I'm working tempor—"

Her mom interrupted. "Wonderful, you've got a job. I'll tell your dad. He'll be relieved, too."

Faith gripped the phone tighter. "Relieved? I was saying it's a month-long job."

Once again, her mom ignored the last part of her statement. "We're remodeling. Our contractor got us on the books earlier than planned. Dad, Grace, and I are moving, week after next, into a two-bedroom apartment until the work is completed. They said it would take six months."

"Half a year?"

"We're gutting the whole house."

"I can help you pack."

"The movers are doing that and storing most of it."

"Then, I'll squeeze in Grace's bedroom when I get home in a month. My things from NYC are still in storage, I won't take up much space."

"The bedroom's too small. It will barely fit Grace's furniture and a twin bed."

"No room for Hope?" Faith referred to her middle sister who was in college.

Her mom said, "Hope's taking summer courses, so she's staying put at FSU. You said you have a job, right? You understand, don't you, honey?"

Lead settled in her midsection. They didn't have room for her. *Say something.* "I do."

"Fine, I've got a case to prepare for court. Tell me about your job soon."

Before Faith could say anything else, Faith heard the click of her mother hanging up.

"Crud muffin!" Numbness threaded through her and the air became thinner than onion skin as her shriveled lungs worked to gain oxygen She prayed. Faith needed a job and home, quick. Jamming her phone into her bag, she drove to her very temporary job.

45

~

As the door slammed behind her in the coffee shop, she jumped, fueled by too much caffeine and too little sleep. Flicking off the steam wand, she eyed the source of the sound.

"You look tired." Caleb pointed his airplane mug in her direction. "And I thought my sofa was comfortable."

She bit back a tired retort. "What're you ordering?"

"Black coffee. Come sit." He flicked a smile as Faith prepared the dark coffee and Caleb sat at a nearby table.

Faith watched in fascination as he gulped the cinder-hot liquid like a water-thirsty camel. Caleb wiped his lips with an organic cotton paper napkin and winked at Faith. "Perfect. Thanks."

"I don't see how you drink that swill water." Faith arched her upper lip.

"Wrong side?"

"Come again?"

"Of the bed." He steepled his fingers.

She ignored his remark and tossed her hair over a shoulder. Bitterness danced at the knifed edges of her emotions. Strong. Dark. Swirling. "I got bad news this morning." She kicked the floor. It was the only thing she could kick.

"I've got time." Caleb crossed a leg and folded his arms on his chest.

Faith's eyes met his. "It's my problem."

"You're, um, an employee."

Faith's eyebrow arched. "Not really."

"Semantics."

The rising volcano within seeped from the cracks. "I've got no place to go," she blurted. Shame singed her face.

"Florida?"

"Not anymore."

Caleb loudly exhaled. "I'd hire you full-time."

"You're more concerned than my parents." Faith flicked a hangnail.

"Oh."

"Yeah." The bagel rose in her throat. *Should've kept quiet.*

"That had to sting."

Tightness banded her chest, and she swallowed the mountain parked in her throat. "When you're treated like that most of the time, the surprise isn't there anymore."

"I'd never be indifferent to Jack."

"No." Faith tugged on the skin around her nailbed as it reddened and refused to budge. "You're a kind man who wouldn't."

His hand inched closer to hers. "No one deserves to be neglected or ignored."

Like a thorn from the rosebush beyond the concrete walls of the building, his words struck beneath her exterior.

He cleared his throat. "Stay."

The thorn released its grip, and a tenuous ray of sunlight split the darkness. "Maybe."

"Jack would miss you if you left." Caleb rose to his feet. "So would I." The corner of his mouth slipped upward, and he turned, making his way to the door.

Like the Tinman receiving his oil, his words eased a place that had been fused shut for a long time. She glanced at the departing man, whose beastly form was turning altogether more pleasant. A petal of hope unfurled.

CHAPTER NINE

*C*aleb's black shorts were the perfect length to show off his tan-from-the-outdoors muscular legs. *Something's hot.* She eyed the coffee cup in her hands. "Want a cup before we open?"

Caleb nodded. "Sure."

Faith heard Caleb's stomach argue. "Did you miss breakfast?"

He nodded.

"You open the shop and I'll be back in a sec." *I'll remind him how well I can cook and bake. I need a job... maybe I can accept the one he offered.*

Faith went to the kitchen, whipped a quick omelet together and put a raspberry twist on the side. She carried it to the front as the steam from the plate kissed her face and rocked her heels. Prickles of anticipation at his reaction swelled through her. "Enjoy." She slid the plate onto the nearest table as a customer walked through the door.

"My favorite, raspberry twists. Are you trying to bribe your boss?" Caleb smiled and sank down into a chair.

She silently cheered as he tilted his head back and closed his eyes.

Score one for me. "Maybe. It's a recipe I created, and I'm testing it at the shop. Do you mind?"

"Good, you can bribe me anytime. If you ever need a taste tester, I'll make that sacrifice for you."

"You will, huh? I'll alert you next time I experiment on a recipe." She eyed him as he began to eat his breakfast. *Hope he likes it.*

Caleb inhaled the omelet and twist. He chugged the coffee after and took the plate toward the kitchen. "Man, this was way better than my eggs cooked with ketchup and water."

Faith spoke under her breath. "Yuck." She didn't miss the sullen glance from the waiting customer. Throwing the biggest grin on her face she could manage, Faith took his order and finished it with record speed.

Caleb held a fresh cup in his hand. "The new machine came. Show me how to use it."

He was so close; Faith could smell the strong coffee on his breath mixed with a minty scent. Odd, yet homey. "Put the beans into the top from the jar to your left. There's a scoop inside. It'll grind them." Scooping an overly generous portion, Caleb spilled most on the wooden floor.

He started toward the back. "I'll get the broom."

Faith wagged a finger. "Later. Put the mug underneath, then press this lever." Their hands collided at the handle. Heat travelled to her face. Faith bit her lip and pulled away. "You do it."

"It's gonna be yours. Still take it with cream and cinnamon?"

"Yes."

Caleb doused the cup with cream and shook the cinnamon until it sparkled and danced in the air.

Faith turned to scrub her burning nose with the back of a hand. A sneeze moved with the intensity of a runaway horse. "Achoo!" Embarrassment flooded her until she heard Caleb's matching trumpeted sneeze. Faith smirked.

"Take a sip." Caleb tilted the cup toward her as the cinnamon confetti skated across the creamy dairy lake.

Stomach knotting, she put her hands over his and took a child's tea party sip as the heat of the bittersweet cinnamon engulfed her taste buds. "Mmhmm."

"Too strong?"

Swaying her hand side to side, Faith swallowed the fireball. Caleb handed her a glass of water, and in a hurry it dribbled down her neck as the cool water doused rioting flames inside.

Caleb sniffed the contents of the mug. "Whew, it's pretty bad. I'll make another one."

Pushing past the bubbling burn, Faith protested. "I'm good." She swiped the mug from the table and put it in the sink.

Following behind her, Caleb stated, "Today, you fix the coffee. I'll ring up the customers." Caleb separated from her and went to the cash register.

"Great." Her taut shoulders eased. "We've got another customer." She was happy to have an excuse to end the conversation. "I'll show you later."

He nodded.

Sipping a cold tea, Faith ran through her social media on an afternoon break. Wavy hair connected to a tall person appeared on the phone's screen. Caleb. She turned, pasting a mock scowl on her face. "Nosey."

"Some might say curious." Caleb slid into the seat across from her. "Didn't know you were on the social sites. You could've requested to friend me."

"I haven't been on until recently. Too busy."

"I can keep you busy."

"How?" Her stomach pitched and swayed. She grabbed the counter for support. "Giving kayak lessons?"

"No."

The tension receded from her midsection. "Where?"

"Here. Run the coffee shop." He ran a hand through his hair. "I know. The pay. It isn't New York standards. You can work here until you find something."

Shadows of possibilities settled near her heart. "I might leave soon."

"Considered. Speaking of leaving, I need to get Jack from school. We'll come help you close."

"He'd be bored."

"He likes helping. I'll see how tired he is. If he's ready to help, we'll come back."

"Sure, he'd make it fun."

"He's good at that. Make sure to lock up. Bye." The door whooshed behind Caleb.

Several hours later, Faith locked the door and rubbed her complaining back. Cleaning time. She went over the checklist for closing and cleaned the front. Now the kitchen. Up to her elbows in suds, Faith heard footsteps. With shaking hands, she grabbed a rolling pin and walked toward the front of the coffee shop; the splats of dishwater hitting the floor heralding her arrival. For good measure, she hit the pin against her free palm. It made a satisfying "swack" sound. Her heart in her throat she rounded the corner and heard a deep laugh.

Caleb hid Jack behind his back and grinned. "Nice weapon."

Jack giggled. "Fay not scary. Wet."

Bubbles ran down her arms saturating her jeans. "Agreed."

"Let's help." Caleb led the way to the kitchen as Jack and Faith followed. "Jack will make sure we're doing a good job cleaning."

"Can our boss have a cookie?" Faith pointed to Jack who was seated by the baking racks with one hand precariously inching toward the cookies.

"Son, those cookies aren't for you." In two steps, Caleb stood next to Jack.

"One. For helping." Faith ignored Caleb's pointed glance.

"One." A smile creased the corners of his mouth.

Faith handed the warm cookie to Jack on a paper towel.

"Fanks." Jack spoke between bites of the crumbly cookie. "Yum." Clump. Clump. Giggle. Jack sprinted to the coffee shop. "Me fast." Red-faced, Jack returned with a small piece of cookie in his hand. "Dwopped."

"Aww, I'll get another one."

"He won't eat dinner."

Faith pulled her hand from the container. "Okay."

"Before we go, can I wrap up another one for him to take for after dinner?"

"As long as you make it two." Caleb put the towel next to the sink, and he winked. "Can't let him eat dessert by himself."

"No, you can't." Sidestepping to the container area she snuck three macadamia chunk cookies and some blueberry lemon leftover scones for breakfast the following day into a box. She taped it shut before giving it to him.

"There's more than two cookies in here."

"Something for breakfast tomorrow." Faith grabbed her bag off the hook by the back door. "So I don't have to hear your stomach growl."

"I might skip eating whatever's in the box for more of your omelet tomorrow." He shook his head and his green eyes glinted in the narrow beams of sunlight coming from the slatted blinds. "You're a better cook than me. Tonight, Jack and I are having spaghetti sauce out of a jar and some buttered bread slices and salad. Do you put water in your sauce?"

Faith pursed her lips and controlled her gaze which threatened to shoot upward. "You put water in your eggs and jar sauce?"

"Isn't that right?"

Not even close. "I could show you."

"Tonight. Come over for dinner."

Faith saw Jack tug at his dad's hand. "Food, Daddy."

"I need to get my car. It's ready."

"We'll take you."

"Got it covered, thanks. Jarod's taking me to get my car. Then I'll run to the store and meet you two at your house. Don't cook without me."

"I won't even walk into the kitchen."

"Excellent. We'll cook together."

"Me too?" questioned Caleb. He seemed to be uncomfortable as he pulled on his shirt collar.

She nodded to Caleb and left.

Groceries gathered at the adequate local grocery store, she navigated to their home, pinpricks of happiness skittering through her. *I love to cook, that's it.* She pulled into the short driveway and admired once again the home's exterior, clad in a crisp, white clapboard siding with an inviting brick porch. The only thing lacking were flowers dotting the barren beds to greet visitors. Before she had the car door opened, Jack, Caleb, and Ranger came out of the front door.

"I'll get the bags. Jack, take Faith inside."

Jack and Ranger led the way through the front door and into the kitchen. Caleb came in shortly and put the bags onto the other side of the island on the grey granite countertop.

"I really like your house; it's pretty."

"Avery did all the decorating." Caleb softly shrugged.

"She had a great eye." Where to go from here? Her elbow creases began to dampen, and the room seemed smaller.

Jack pointed to the awaiting bags.

Smart boy. "Right, dinner." She went around the other side of the island, began to pull out the groceries from the cloth bag, and exhaled.

"We'll help." Caleb pulled a small apron out of a drawer and tied it around Jack. "It's the only one we have, or I'd give one to you."

"Splatters don't bother me. Jack, come help me like you did last night."

Jack ran over to the island.

"Wait. Jack, you helped Faith cook?"

Jack's head nodded up and down as he pulled on the black apron. "Fay said I'm a chef."

Caleb held out a hand. "High five. That's awesome. I'm proud of you."

"Hold on a sec, I forgot." Faith fished around her purse and pulled out Jack's present. Lightning bugs plinked against her ribcage. "For you." She gave him the bright red spoon decorated with superhero stickers on the handle.

Big chocolate eyes followed the trail of the gift. "Fanks." He took it and waved it in the air like a conductor's wand.

"You didn't have to do that." Caleb moved the step stool next to Faith, and Jack leaped onto it to eagerly look at the ingredients for dinner.

"I knew he'd love it." Getting lost in his eyes for a second, she leaned closer to him. Thrashing bugs lit her insides as he closed the gap.

"I love it, too."

"Yeah?" Warm air tickled her cheeks.

"Definitely."

Hovering inches apart, a heart-shaped object separated their lips. Faith stepped back and tamped down outpouring ardent disappointment.

Jack gave her a tomato. "Yum."

Snuffing a sigh, Faith instructed. "We're making sauce. Point me, please, to your cutting board." Not looking toward her,

Caleb jerked a finger in the stove's direction. She pulled out a pristine white plastic rectangle. "I need your biggest pot."

"On it." Caleb pulled out a turkey roaster.

Faith sighed. "Smaller."

One noisy interlude later, he found a pot that was suitable, to Faith's delight. She had Jack stir the ingredients together before putting the sauce on the burner. Ranger stayed on crumb patrol. He cheetah-pounced when a microscopic piece fell to the wooden floor.

"Wanger. No." Jack pointed the rosy-red spoon at the dog as the sauce splattered on Faith's jeans.

She jumped back from the island.

"Sorry about that," Caleb gave her a sheepish smile and a wet paper towel.

Faith dabbed at the splotch.

Brushing past her, he said, "I'll put the sauce on the stove."

After she threw the used paper towel in the trash, Faith turned to Jack. "Now I need help with this salad." Faith swung the cellophane bag side to side and smiled down at Jack. "Is anyone strong enough to open this?"

Jack's pudgy hand waved in the air. "Me."

Caleb wiggled his fingers toward Faith. She put the bag into his outstretched palm. "I'll give it a little start."

He turned around and all Faith heard was the sharp snip of scissors.

Caleb gave the bag to his son. "Use your muscles."

When the bag gave way, Jack wiggled and smiled. Faith shot a protective hand toward his back as the step stool tremored. Jack the he-man held up one shoestring arm and declared, "I'm strong."

"You are." Caleb hugged Jack.

Faith's gaze stayed on the sweet scene until the boy crawled from his dad's hug.

"Thirsty," said his son.

"All right, I'll get your milk." Caleb swung the jug out of the refrigerator door. "Something to drink, Faith?"

"Water, please."

He poured a plastic cup of milk and made a glass of water for Faith.

She took it from him and grinned in thanks.

"Need any help?" asked Caleb.

"I've got the rest."

"Jack, let's go throw the ball with Ranger to stay out of Faith's way."

"Okay."

She stirred the sauce and then slid the bread in the oven. Caleb played fetch with his dog as his son looked on, and at the sight of his flexing biceps, she bit her lip.

Caleb held the ball midair as their eyes met. She looked in the opposite direction. A pull from deep within fought to convince her to look again. *Resist, he's got a family. Remember how he hurt you before?* She opened the back door and yelled, "Dinner's ready in a few."

Noticing a red dot of sauce on the light grey granite she wiped it with a wet blue sponge. Looking down at her reflection on the side of the large pasta pot, she saw the contented look on her face. *This has been fun. I never though cooking with kids would be so entertaining. Maybe I should re-think my whole "no kids" approach?*

After dinner, Faith sat back and put a hand on her full stomach. No spills, plenty of laughs and three empty plates meant dinner was a success.

Jack slumped in his chair, his head bobbing toward his gooey plate.

"Bath time, buddy." Caleb picked Jack up from his seat and glanced toward Faith. "I'll clean up when I'm finished putting Jack to bed. Want to stay longer?"

"I can." Gathering the dishes in her hands, she ran water over them in the sink.

"Night, Fay."

She turned toward the little boy and smiled. "Goodnight."

Caleb and Jack left the room.

While Faith turned on the dishwasher, Ranger dropped a squeaky toy at her feet. "Those brown eyes. Who can refuse them?"

"How about mine?"

Faith turned to see Caleb with a superhero cape wrapped around his shoulders.

Her mouth fell open, her shoulders quaked. "Special occasion?"

"Aagh." He quickly pulled it from his shoulders. "The reading cape." He held up a hand. "I know. I know. It's. . . awkward."

No superhero is as appealing as you. Faith's eyes widened as her stomach curled into a ball. "I wouldn't say awkward."

"Thanks for tonight. You should be wearing the cape." He put the cape over the back of the breakfast room chair. "You saved me and Jack from another dinner flop."

She felt a nip of regret from Caleb's honesty. "It can't be that bad."

"Remember my coffee?" Caleb winced and flicked the air. "It was a bad coffee drinking challenge."

"Yeah."

"But you won." Caleb swung the door open. "I've got a prize for you."

"You do?"

"Hold on a sec." He ran into another room and returned. "Here." Caleb gave her a plastic card.

As she read the words, *Hawk's Creek Outfitters*, her heart skipped several beats. "Gift card?"

"Kayak lessons. It'd be fun to teach you. If you're sticking around." He hefted a shoulder. "Are you?"

"Am I what?"

"Staying? Do you want the job?"

Kayak lessons. Her throat closed. The ghost from her childhood gripped her with grim force. She slipped the card in her bag. "I'm not sure yet, but I'll let you know soon." She nodded. "Thanks for the gift."

"Hope you'll use it. It'd be fun."

She bit the inside of her cheek, her brows pinching. "Mmhmm,"

"About the job, I know it's not a New York City size paycheck, but I'll do the best I can."

"I know you would. I really appreciate the offer. I'll let you know soon." Faith gathered her things. "It's getting late, thanks for everything. See you later." She went through the door and to her car as her pulse galloped far too fast for the short walk. How she'd get out of the lessons was anyone's guess. But fear could make an honest person the best liar in the world.

CHAPTER TEN

*J*ack dragged his spoon through his milk and played with the cereal-o's in the bowl. Caleb glanced at the half-full dish. "Not hungry?"

He shook his head and pointed to the bakery box on top of the fridge.

Distract him. He snapped his fingers. "Who do you want to invite to your birthday party?"

Jack lifted his square shoulders.

Caleb started counting people off on his fingers. "Your friends from preschool and church, your grandparents and aunt and uncles. Who else?"

"Fay."

Heat radiated from his hands and zinged up his arms. *Gotta turn the air down in here.* Caleb reached for the box, took out a scone, and began to absentmindedly eat a piece.

"Me too." Jack's spoon clanked against the cereal bowl rim." Daddy." He held out a hand for a piece.

Caleb broke off a piece and gave it to his son who hummed while he ate the blueberry-filled treat. Whatever Faith made was delicious. Caleb recalled last night's dinner and their good time together. "We'll invite Fay. . . Faith to your party."

Jack licked his lips and pointed to the box. "Fun. More."

"One more." Caleb broke off a small piece and put it on Jack's napkin. "Drink your milk. Strong men need calcium." Jack swigged his milk, and Caleb laughed when he noticed Jack's milky mouth ring. "Let's brush your teeth, then we'll roll." Jack scooted from his favorite chair and ran out of the kitchen, Ranger barking after him.

As they pulled out from the driveway, their loud singing drew curious stares from the neighbors. *Let 'em look.* He waved at the spy-next-door watering his yard and cranked up the volume in his adequate singing voice. He glanced in the rearview mirror as Jack moved his head back and forth and belted out the "wash your hands song." Several more songs followed before they pulled into a parking spot, and he and Jack went into the building. After a hug and an I love you, Jack vanished into the crowd of kids watching their class pet rabbit, Jasper, eat his hay bundle. Shutting the door to the school, his joy dampened as a piece of him remained in the classroom.

He drove the short way to the coffee shop, and his mood elevated as he thought about the day ahead and who he'd spend it with. Something twisted in his stomach. *Must be all the carbs.*

Caleb threw back his shoulders and opened the coffee shop door. His smile faded when he noticed Faith was wearing a yellow dress which highlighted all her workout routine success. He felt his ears grow warm.

"Morning, can I fix a coffee for you?" Caleb felt proud he'd strung a sentence together since his mind was occupied on the beautiful woman in front of him.

"Yes, please. No cinnamon. A squeeze of honey and milk."

Caleb's lip curled and his stomach skittered. "Honey?"

"Better for me than other things, try it."

"I'll make one for myself, too." Pride hung on Caleb like a

badge of honor as Faith sipped the coffee and made a satisfied noise. "Pass the test?"

She nodded and drank more.

Exhaling, he sipped the honey-laced coffee. "It's pretty good. I still like my coffee unsweetened, but it's not bad. Jack liked your breakfast this morning."

Faith smiled. "He's a sweet little guy."

A lump sat in his throat. "I'm fortunate. By the way, he's got a birthday party coming up on June 20th. Wanna come?"

"I'll have to see. Do you need me to bake the cake?" Her hazel eyes brightened and her long hair wrapped around her face. When he didn't answer right away, her brows furrowed. "You're not speaking, so . . . I guess you already have someone doing the cake."

"Uh, his aunt, Avery's sister, always makes a cake for his party."

"Oh, family will be there."

"My parents, my brother, and Avery's sister and her husband." Caleb edged toward Faith as he observed her face paling. "It's not only family but also people from church and his school. Tay and Jarod come, too. It gets chaotic. You could help me corral the kids."

"I don't know anything about kids." Faith crossed her arms across her chest.

"There'll be enough adults to help. Jack wanted you to come," he prodded.

"Then I'll be there."

"Does that mean you accept the job?" A noisy creak drew his attention. He stepped to open the door. "Lizzie."

"I wanted to tell you something and it can't wait," Lizzie blurted. Her musical laughter erupted. "I'm moving in a couple of months, near the grands in South Carolina."

"Oh, man. I'm going to miss you." He hugged the older

woman. "Thanks for warning me." He turned to Faith. "We've got a new member on our coffee team."

"Already?"

"I've asked Faith to help."

She put a hand to her chest. "Thank the Lord. I didn't want to leave you without a replacement. That gives me enough time to train her."

Caleb's mouth pulled to one side.

"I need it, Lizzie. Can I fix you a cup of coffee?"

Lizzie patted her hair and grinned. "To go, please. I'm going to the beauty shop to get my hair set."

Faith whipped around the counter and started the coffee making process.

"She's a very pretty lady, hon," Lizzie offered quietly, pulling on his arm. "It's been a while."

Coffee burned in his throat and his eyes itched. "Not long enough."

"You'll know when it's right. I didn't mean to be a nosey old lady."

"You're no—"

Lizzie interjected. "My wisdom hairs tell another story. Let me get my coffee and scoot. Thelma leaves the shop if I'm late." She stilled her focus on him. "But chew on what I said."

"I will." He brushed a kiss on her upturned powdered cheek.

Faith gave the nice lady her coffee.

"Thanks, hon." Lizzie left as the door flapped behind her.

"She's something." Faith shook her head. "So much energy in one petite lady."

"Agreed." Caleb flicked on the open sign and brushed a speck of sugar off the counter.

"I hear my phone." Faith held up a finger and answered. Her expression changed and her smile diminished. He didn't want to eavesdrop, but he'd always had superior hearing. Caleb eyed the door and noticed customers approaching. Curiosity waited.

During the next few minutes, he saw her pace back and forth. It had to be bad news. No expression, still. Caleb hurried with the orders, spilling hot coffee on his hand. Keeping a PG-rated word, which was inching onto the tip of his tongue, at bay, he rang up the order. Once the customer cleared, he put his firetruck-red hand under the water.

"You okay?"

Faith brows crinkled. It was cute.

Wincing, Caleb sputtered. "Stupid... rushing."

"Here, put this on it." Faith offered him a pat of butter.

"No, thanks."

When she rubbed it on the aching heat, he moaned.

"How did you know?"

Faith quirked a brow. "Chefs get plenty of burns." Faith touched his shoulder. "I need to tell you something." The softness of her hand over his shirt caused his muscles to tighten. "Tell you later, Caleb. Customers. It's pretty cool, though." She pulled on her lip with her teeth.

His heartbeat missed a few times as he stared at her mouth which seemed to be as soft as her hands and entirely too dangerous for a single dad like him.

"Be back in a sec." Faith walked to the counter.

His pulse returned to almost normal. *Too much caffeine.* Caleb scowled at his coffee mug. *I need to drink more water.*

"About that call," Caleb wiped the counter near Faith, watching the customers
clear.

"It was from my friend in New York. We worked together in the test kitchen. She said Erika is going to call me later."

"Erika?'

"Mmhmm. My former boss."

Caleb narrowed his eyes. "So, she let you go and now wants to call you."

"I know. It's weird."

Her phone rang. Another familiar number appeared on the screen, her former boss'. She groaned and turned the phone in his direction.

"Take the call. I've got the front." Caleb shooed her with a hand.

Faith hurried to the kitchen.

He raked his fingers through his hair and groaned. His footsteps dulled the shine on the floor as he paced alongside the bank of windows, unsure of what to pray. *Go. Stay. I'd miss her. Jack would too.* He'd leave it in His Father's hands, though sick at the lack of control he had over the situation. Frustration singed his thoughts, but knowing he'd not go this alone cooled the slow burn. For now.

CHAPTER ELEVEN

*E*rika's voice boomed over the earpiece. "It's been some time since we've talked."

"Hi, Erika, keeping bus—"

Erika interrupted. "Listen, I'm opening a bakery in the area. I'd like to see if you'd be a good fit as the project lead and head baker. I'd need you to be here by next Monday."

Faith gulped. Today was Thursday. That didn't leave her much time to plan, but her options were limited at this point. "That works."

"Make sure to bring your recipe file. My travel coordinator will be in touch."

Faith went into the coffee shop and signaled Caleb to come sit down and pushed back her hair from her face. Sighing, her hands shook from the release of adrenaline.

His face clouded over. "Good or bad?"

"She wants to interview me."

Caleb deflated in front of her, blowing out a long breath in . . . what? Surprise? Frustration?

She couldn't read him. "It's for a project lead position at a bakery she might be opening in the city. I'd need to be there by Monday."

"What are you going to do?"

"I feel like I need to hear her out. I'm not discounting your job offer, I'm just putting off an answer a little longer. I need to figure out what's best for my career and future. I hope you can understand."

"You need to go. It doesn't hurt to hear what she has to say. We'll be fine for a few days."

"I'll be back at work Thursday morning. And I always keep my word."

He leaned in and gave her a slight smile. "I'm counting on it."

Gasoline-tinged hot air whipped around Faith as she exited La Guardia Airport's baggage claim. Taking a moment to get her bearings, she grabbed some vanilla-honey lotion from her purse and slathered it on her desert dry hands. She sniffed the warm, cookies-baking scent wafting from her skin to block out the odious smells from the bumper-to-bumper traffic. Once she flagged down the taxi, the driver barreled out of his side door, offered a curt nod, and swiped the bag from her hand before stuffing it into his trunk. He waved his hand back-and-forth at the back door, gesturing to give the hint. Faith slid across the cracked pleather bench seat, giving the driver the hotel address in Mid-town Manhattan.

"Got it." He set his GPS and floored the gas, pitching and swaying her in the back seat as he rounded the pack of cars ahead.

Her stomach protested at the herky-jerky motion. Faith realized she'd forgotten to eat in her haste to get to the airport that morning. She'd have to remedy that when she arrived at the hotel—if she got there in one piece. In the meantime, she rummaged in her purse and found a stray piece of chocolate peppermint candy at the bottom. She unwrapped it and popped it in her mouth. The mint did its trick for the moment and calmed her rising stomach.

Nearer to the city, the tall buildings crested into view, and it was hard to not compare them to the beautiful, rolling, mist-covered mountains she had left only that morning. A jaywalker darted in front of the car at an intersection, and the taxi driver muttered an off-color remark, then glanced in his rearview mirror as if in apology. Faith already had enough to think about, she didn't want to deal with the driver's crude language. She turned her attention to her phone, first texting Jen, then Taylor, Caleb, and her parents to let them know she'd arrived safely. The Sunday traffic was light, and they made it to the hotel in record time. The taxi driver dove into an open spot at the front of the hotel and turned with a grimace passing as his smile.

"Seventy dollars."

Faith handed him her card which he quickly swiped through a card reader.

Without another word he got out and ran around to the back of the car to get her suitcase. Faith had barely set foot out of the car and he already had her bag deposited on the curb. Giving her a salute, he climbed in and sped off, his car melting away into the traffic.

Faith eyed the somber, tan-colored stone building as she wheeled the suitcase into the expansive entrance. It crossed her mind that Erika must be trying to butter her up. This hotel was swankier than the ones she usually stayed in. As she entered the lobby, she noticed the colorful yet refined woven rugs scattered on the wooden floors matched the vases of vibrant flowers arranged in the seating areas around the room. After checking in she went to the fifteenth floor and found her room. The subdued colors of grey and white calmed her as she unpacked.

Faith scanned her phone's contact numbers and called Jen, her friend from her previous workplace.

"Hey. I'm here. Are you up for going in a half-hour to Schmitz's Deli?"

"You know me, I'm always hungry. I can't wait to see you."

As she peered into the mirror, she ran her hands through her curls to fluff her travel-flattened hair. Her empty stomach began to argue.

Faith treated herself to a small package of almonds then she refreshed her makeup before leaving the hotel room. The searing heat and high humidity embraced her like a soggy woolen coat as she plodded down the crowded, grey-black side-walk. Faith popped into a grocery store and bought a bottle of water which she finished before reaching the next block. Above the din of traffic, her phone rang. She hurried to answer. It was her little sister. "Grace."

"Make it okay?"

"Yes. Aren't you supposed to be in school?"

"I get early dismissal since I'm a senior. Hope told me you might be moving to that little town. Why are you in New York then?"

Grace, her more direct sister, acting like their lawyer parents.

"Well, I wanted to see what Erika wanted."

"She let you go, and now she's wanting you back? Some-thing's weird about it."

Another call came through. Caleb. A ripple of delight tingled within her.

"Gotta go, I'll text you later."

"K, good luck."

Faith answered Caleb's call.

"How was the flight?"

"A lot less bumpy than the ride from the airport. Ugh. I'd forgotten how crazy some drivers are here."

"I remember. When I lived there, a driver of mine once drove on the sidewalk to avoid a line of traffic. All I could do was pray."

Faith gasped and stilled her footsteps as someone ran into the back of her. She sliced a glance toward the person, who passed around her with the intensity of a subway train. "That's awful. You never told me."

He chuckled. "Tried to forget. Excited to be back?"

"It's good." Faith dodged a kid on a skateboard. "I'm meeting my friend Jen for dinner. Any guesses where I'm going?"

"Pizza at Joe's?"

"No."

"Hot dog vendor?"

"No, close. Schmitz's."

Caleb groaned. "Turkey and swiss with a big dill pickle. I'm jealous."

"Don't be. The diner we went to near Briar Creek was just as good."

"Close. Hey, are you going to visit the Carluccis?"

"I texted Rose, she and Harold are on their 45th wedding trip to Hawaii."

"Good for them, they were an awesome couple. Hold on, son."

Faith heard scratching and voices over the earpiece.

"Jack wants to say something."

"Hi, Fay, are you coming over?"

A smile rose on her lips. "I can't, sweetie. I'm in New York."

"Be home soon? Wanger and I want some more spaghetti."

"You do?"

"Mmhmm."

Voice catching, she said, "It's a date. Spaghetti next week."

Chuckling sounds met her ears. "For me, too?"

"If I have to." She tilted her head to the side and grinned, which earned a smarmy smile from a man walking beside Faith.

Drawing her arms close to her body, she glanced away, wanting to shake off the wormy revulsion she experienced.

Caleb's comforting voice distracted her from the thronging, no personal space crowd surrounding her. "Only if you want to."

"I do."

"Hey, I hope you don't like your old workplace, and you turn Erika down. This is going to sound selfish, but I want you here as my manager."

"Thanks, I think? See you in a few days." Disconnecting, she secured the phone in her crossbody bag, a throwback from her former New York City days.

Spying the black and white marquee for Schmitz's Deli, Faith's steps accelerated and her anticipation rose when she opened the heavy glass door. Faith surveyed the small restaurant, and Jen's black razor-sharp bob caught her attention. Jen was engrossed in something on her phone screen and didn't notice Faith standing next to her. At the tap on her shoulder, Jen glanced up, a grin splitting her face as she bolted from the booth and captured Faith in her Pilates-queen arms for a brief hug.

"You look fantastic. All that fresh country air must be your secret."

Faith gave her friend an appraising once-over, noting the slim black dress and strappy sandals. "Ditto, you're as gorgeous as ever."

Jen smoothed down her already perfect hair. "Thanks, I had to make sure I dressed up for you. You always look beautiful."

Faith smirked as she sat. "Not when we tested the new broccoli soup recipe."

Jen snorted. "I wasn't the one who didn't put the blender top back on!"

Laughing, Jen slid back into her seat and Faith sat across from her friend. Jen wiggled her fingers at Faith with a half-smile on her face. "Green looks great on you. It sets off the red glint in your brown hair."

Faith rolled her eyes. "Not that kind of green."

Her friend screwed up her mouth and pinched her nose. Faith giggled.

Jen proceeded to catch Faith up on all that had happened around the office. To Faith's surprise, several more work acquaintances had been let go.

"After cutting staff, what would make Erika want to do something completely different like opening a bakery? Plus, she let me go a month back, why the sudden change of thought?"

Jen lifted a shoulder. "You know Erika, she makes rash decisions. As for wanting you back, you were the star baker for the company, and she's wanting to land her own baking show on one of the big channels. This would give her more credibility."

Faith sighed. "That isn't surprising. I'd heard in the past she's wanted to make a bigger name for herself in the culinary field."

"Enough about her. What have you been up to, Faith? You said you've got a temporary job?"

"At a coffee shop. I've been asked to be the manager. It's kind of strange though. He and I used to date when we both lived there."

Jen batted her lashes and leaned forward for more. "Interesting. It sounds like he's caught the Faith Fever."

"Hardly. He's a dad." The sunlight shone into her face from the window next to her. Heat crawled up her neck, and she casually picked up her hair to let the air conditioning cool her down.

"But he must be a good guy, or you wouldn't have dated him. You and kids, though."

"I know, not for me." Shame pierced Faith as she recalled the quick conversation with Jack. "Tell me all the latest, I'm sure you've got a guy."

Jen groaned. "There isn't one. The last guy liked the Mets, and you know me. I'm a die-hard Yankees fan."

Faith winked at Jen. "There's a Yankees fan out there for you. Just wait and see."

Jen propped her chin on her palm. "Thanks." She directed her chocolate brown eyes at Faith. "There's one for you, too."

Faith nibbled on her sandwich and looked away. As swarms of pedestrians trod by the window, Faith grimaced at the commotion and felt like a stranger in this sprawling, cacophonous city, meanwhile, the quiet of Briar Creek called like a siren's song.

CHAPTER TWELVE

A ring of fire encircled Faith's stomach as she entered Erika's corporate office building. Her insides writhed in a mass of disquieting chaos and rumbles. She threw her cup of coffee away, her third of the day, and straightened her shoulders, already battle-worn. Jen walked toward her, and Faith relaxed a bit.

"I'll walk you there." Jen's dark eyes crinkled at the corners with reassurance. "You can do this, Faith. I know you can. I've been praying."

"Thanks." Faith linked her arm with Jen's. "If I were any more nervous, I'd be running out of here screaming. I don't know what it is, Jen, but I've got an unsettled feeling about this whole thing."

"It's your nerves talking." Her friend snuck a side hug to her as they neared the door.

"Go get 'em." Jen winked and sped away.

Glancing skyward Faith whispered, "Lord, Erika's wounded me once. I'm scared it will happen again. Please protect me. Amen." She pasted a smile on her face and strode through the door. Daniel meeting the lion.

Erika's assistant offered her tea, which Faith declined. She glanced at the clock situated behind the receptionist, noting she was five minutes early. Faith fiddled with her purse, checked her lipstick again, straightened her necklace several times, and she still sat. Hairs spiked on the back of her neck. A shadow inched across her body, and she stilled. The lioness hunted her prey. Faith took a deep breath and gazed upward.

"Hello, Faith." Erika teetered on dagger-like stilettos. She kept steely-eyed focus as she approached.

Faith shook the lady's chilled outstretched hand. "Good morning, Erika. Thank you for inviting me."

"Of course. Come in." Erika swished into her inner sanctum. Once she perched on her chair behind her glass and steel desk, Faith lowered onto the edge of the closest chair.

Opening her portfolio, Faith extracted a resume.

Erika waved it away. "I don't need it."

Faith fought a shrug as she replaced it in her binder.

"Did you bring your file?"

"Yes."

Erika's eyes lit up. "We'll go into the test kitchen tomorrow." She evaluated her nails. "I know you know that place very well. You can make a sampling for me to try." Her gaze leveled on Faith.

"You should be happy to know your recipes used in the eateries are the most popular."

A heaviness weighted Faith's shoulders. "I'm glad to hear it. Of course, I'll show you some of my new ones as well." Their conversation moved to Erika's goals for the business and what was desired, at least in broad terms, from the person she was looking to hire. She hinted at her aspirations for the television series as well, preening and almost cooing as she spoke of it.

"That's all for now. I expect to see you tomorrow at 8:00 am sharp." Erika's red talon pointed to the door as she growled into her Bluetooth. From her heated tone, she'd found another victim to corner.

As Faith travelled to the elevator, the binding chains of discomfort fell away. Once the metal doors closed, and she was cocooned in safety, Faith inhaled. She'd escaped. Without one claw mark.

Faith met Jen in the cafeteria. She plopped in the chair across from her friend and munched on her salad, weariness oozing from every pore.

"Don't tell me. . . she did her whole interrogation-style interview."

Faith nodded.

"Yuck, sorry. I hope it didn't scare you." Jen sighed. "I've missed you being here."

Faith glanced around to ensure it was safe to speak without one of Erika's minions lurking and found none within earshot. "It was weird. She asked me to bake for her tomorrow and bring all my recipes. She spoke about her desire for a cooking show. I didn't know how to take her. Does she have any interest in me, or is it my recipes?" Without waiting for an answer, Faith collected her trash and tossed it in the can.

Jen followed suit. "I'm not sure. It's been a hectic morning for you. Go take a nap, maybe a hot soak in the tub, and then we'll go out tonight and have some fun."

"You know what, Jen? I'm going to stay in tonight." She hugged her friend. "I need to bring my A-game tomorrow. See you in the morning."

Faith walked next door to the hotel.

Wanting to hear her opinion before tomorrow's craziness, she dialed Taylor's number.

"Tell me how it was, Faithful. Was it awkward seeing her?"

"I made sure it wasn't." Faith ran a hand over the bumpy hotel comforter and smoothed it flat. "Oh, she tried to act like the boss lady with me, but I held my own."

"Perfect. I'm proud of you. So tomorrow's another interview?"

"Not exactly. She's having me make some of my recipes for her to taste. And, Tay, she seemed overly concerned about my recipes."

"I'd be, too. You're amazing. Caleb's bragged about your baking to the guys at the softball game the other night."

"He did?" A smile covered her face, and a glow lit her from within. "That's sweet."

"I haven't seen him like this in a long time."

"Like what?"

"He's into you."

Faith's heartbeat hammered. "Me? You think?"

"Definitely. Why else would any guy brag about a girl's baking?"

"He likes to eat?"

"More like he likes the one who made the food."

"Oh."

"Yeah. Jarod's calling for me. Love you, wish you the best tomorrow."

"Love you, too, Tay. Thanks."

Faith streamed a movie on her laptop, seeking noise in the sterile, quiet room. It made her feel less alone.

At bedtime she covered her ears with a pillow to block the loud siren screeches.

With less than a restful night, Faith gulped a bitter hotel cup of coffee, which wasn't as good as Hawk's Creek Coffee. She zipped into the small grocery store next door to buy the items she needed for baking. After flagging down a speeding taxi, she piled the groceries into the seat next to her. The driver stopped a block away from the office as the morning rush hour traffic seeped through the stoplight. She paid the fare and alighted onto the crowded sidewalk, her bags banging into pedestrians sandwiched on either side of her. She mumbled an apology, but engrossed in their confined world of technology, the people didn't respond. Faith carried the cumbersome shopping bags through the lobby and pressed the call button with her elbow. Jen met her at the entrance to the office, and she happily handed half of the bags to her friend.

"Good morning. You look ready."

"I am, though I'm still curious why she wants me. The job is more than baking a great dessert. Wasn't she paying attention all the years I worked here? She had a hand in choosing all the recipes you and I did for the restaurants."

Jen smirked. "Erika's picky. It's going to be fine."

The building pressure inside her body eased. "Thanks. I needed to hear that. I'm too skeptical. You know me. It's hard for me to trust people."

Jen held the door open to the test kitchen and gave Faith the rest of her bags. "You're choosy. Nothing wrong with that. We all are." She nudged Faith toward the kitchen. "Go get your new job."

A grin flashed across Faith's face as she skittered through the door. "I will."

The hours sped as fast as a racehorse on the Kentucky Derby racetrack. Several times Faith caught Erika stealing glances at the recipes on her iPad. When she wasn't reading the recipes, Erika was questioning how Faith had come up with the recipe. She then retorted if Faith used these in the "small, quaint beverage shop" and other unkind words. Erika's digs raised Faith's ire, and she muttered under her breath, "I'll give you quaint." She glowered at Erika's back when the queen swept from the room.

Erika breezed into the kitchen a couple of hours later with her assistant. "I can see you're almost ready. Will you give Anabelle some of your recipes? That way we can recreate them for the mock-show I'm doing on Friday. Let them see what will be made in my bakery."

Faith bit the inside of her cheek as angry heat slithered up her spine. "When will you have time to talk about what my job will entail? Your expectations of me?" She transferred her chocolate cake to a nearby stand.

Erika didn't assess the cake or pastries she'd made but came to stand within a few inches of Faith. The cloying perfume her former boss wore tickled her nose. Resisting the urge to step back, Faith lifted her chin as Erika spoke. "We could meet for tea downstairs to discuss that before you leave tomorrow." She held out a gold thumb drive embossed with the double "E" logo, her trademark for Erika's Eatery. "Let Anabelle put the recipes on this flash drive."

Faith swallowed, sucked in some much-needed air, and stepped away to get a napkin and plate. The knife eased through the moist cake. "I came here so you could try this. Would you like a sample?"

Erika huffed, put the flash drive next to Faith's computer, rolled her eyes, and inhaled a small forkful. She'd barely swallowed before speaking. "It's delicious. Like I knew it would be." Her plate clanked on the hard granite counter. Erika wagged the flash drive again in front of Faith's face. "Ready to download?"

What was the hurry?

Protests clung to Faith's throat. Her recipes were the result of many late nights of baking, experimenting, and sporadic failures. They were created for her own future business, no one else's.

What was she doing?

If she chose to share these, it would be with someone who cared about her, like Caleb. Not someone who wanted to use her for their own recognition. Straightening her spine, Faith squared off with the diva.

"Erika, I haven't agreed to any job." She snapped her computer shut and grabbed her bag. "My recipes aren't for sale and certainly not to you." Without waiting for a response, Faith exited the kitchen.

The sound of shattering dishes and strong expletives filled Faith's ears as the door closed behind her on the nonexistent opportunity.

Faith's steps grew lighter once she exited the building. With shaking hands, she texted Jen and explained what had happened.

"That makes me so steaming mad. If I didn't need my job, I'd tell her my opinion of her." Jen patted Faith's back. "I'm proud you stood up to the lady."

"Thanks. Me too. Wanna meet for dinner later?"

Jen put a hand on her hip. "Did you need to ask?"

"Don't change, friend."

"I won't. See you later."

Both left the building, Jen toward the subway and Faith in search of a taxi. Why not add more excitement to the day she'd already had?

Now only one person left to call, and he'd waited long enough for her answer.

CHAPTER THIRTEEN

*E*xhilaration clung to Caleb like his favorite workout shirt. Heart pumping, he clenched the paddle and pushed against nature's current. A strident vibration from his cell phone rattled his seat, and he dug through the churning water to a calm place beyond the swirling water caps. Unlocking the screen, he saw Faith's number. He pressed the phone screen as it slid in his watery hands. "Hey."

"Hi. I'm—"

As slippery as a trout, the cell phone fell from his hands. Shielding his eyes with a hand, he caught his cell phone at the last second. He pressed the answer icon. Nothing. The river began to run faster, small waves began to buffet the kayak. Stowing his phone in a pocket, the rising tempo of the river etched at his weathered nerves. Adrenaline rushed and his ears pounded from his thundering heart being amidst the swirling current. Man and nature collided. *I need to find out what she said.* He dug the paddles into the water and nosed toward shore. Alighting from the water's edge, he shook off his wet limbs and focused his energy on pulling the kayak farther on the shore. Removing the rectangular phone from his pocket, Caleb held it to the sunlight and gave it a shake. Darkness. How to dry it out? Glancing at the phone screen, he tried to type in a search engine. *No phone. Smart guy. What'd Jar say he did last time his got wet? He put it in rice overnight.* Caleb wanted to release the last effects of the draining adrenaline by seeing if Jarod was up for a game of basketball before Jack got home. He walked up to his river outfitters business after stowing away the kayak and placed a call from his office phone to Jarod. His friend quickly agreed.

Caleb drank from his water bottle and wiped the rivulets of sweat running down his face with his shirt. Then he threw the ball to Jarod. "I'm up by two. Show me what you've got."

Laughing, Jarod swiped past him, and the basketball swooshed through the net. As he bounced it back, he shrugged and walked away grinning. Jarod swigged his water bottle and asked, "What's going on between you and Faith? She helped you with Jack when you had that migraine. Didn't you two date?"

"Years ago." Caleb dribbled the ball and took a shot, it bounced off the rim, and he caught it in mid-air. "Aagh." He eyed the net and lined up his shot again. "Faith's a friend."

Caleb observed Jarod's smile fade. It seemed to him he was struggling to say something. "I've gotta ask if this is going anywhere. Have you mentioned Avery?"

The name was a dagger to his solar plexus. He didn't want to think of his late wife and what had happened.

"You know I don't talk about her. With anyone."

Jarod picked up the ball and forcefully threw it at the goal. "Believe me, I know. You've got to let someone in."

"I'm fine." Catching the rebound, he took a shot. Another brick.

"Neither Tay nor I want to see Faith get hurt."

Jarod's subtle warning was not lost on Caleb.

Though he resisted the idea with all he had, deep down, Caleb knew that Jarod was right. Faith needed to know. Worry and doubt warred in his mind. He could only guess at how she'd take it, and he didn't think he could handle any more pity. Caleb played a few more rounds with Jarod. Beating his friend somehow calmed him.

Jarod grabbed his gear and started to walk to his car. "Next time."

"I'll still win."

"Yup. We're picking Faith up at the airport tomorrow."

"You've got your Wednesday night youth meeting. I'll get Faith."

"Bring Jack to church. It's pizza and game night, he'd love it."

"I might do that."

"Drop him off at five. Take Faith to dinner. We'll bring Jack home, lover boy." Jarod wiggled his eyebrows at Caleb.

Scowling, Caleb swung his bag into his car. "Hardly. Later." Driving home, he opened all his windows, letting the clean air freshen his car's interior. He had time for a quick shower before meeting Jack at his preschool's open house. Throwing on a dressier shirt and jeans, he played ball with Ranger before leaving. "See you, guy. Don't give me the sad look. Go lay on your bed." Ranger skulked to his bed. Caleb's lips tilted up and he rolled his eyes. "Spoiled." Pulling into the Briar Creek Community Church lot, he nodded to several people as he walked into the preschool area. He panned the room for Jack and found him playing with one of his good friends. Caleb snuck up to him he couldn't resist joining in on the fun. "Can I play?"

"Daddy." He smiled and kept playing with his friend.

"It's good to see you, Caleb."

Stifling a groan, he used a social smile on Jack's teacher, Miss Tessa, who always seemed more interested in him than any other dad at these events. "Likewise. Jack is enjoying the butterfly cocoons your class is raising."

"We could talk about it over coffee sometime." As Tessa drew closer to him, he stepped backwards onto the corner of a tough, plastic building brick.

She was quick to jump in and try to comfort him at the pained look on his face. "Ow, that had to hurt. Do you need to sit down? I'll keep you company."

Caleb waved his hands in front of him. "I'm all right. Jack, why don't you show me some of your projects? I see some artwork hanging on the board over there."

Miss Tessa's face fell.

"Come see." Pulling Caleb's hand, Jack led the way to the opposite side of the room and gave Tessa a parting shrug which she didn't notice. As he looked back, he noticed her rapt attention centered on another male. *Must be the new single dad and his daughter Jack told me about the other day. Poor victim.* Jack pointed to the family drawing he'd created of them and Ranger, a short and tall set of lines standing with a hairball on the ground.

Scrambling for positive things to say, he blurted, "Nice art, buddy. I love Ranger's fur. It looks like him."

"Love Wanger."

"He likes you, too."

Out of the blue, Jack summarized Caleb's feelings to perfection. "I miss Fay. She's good. Read me a story and cooked."

"She did."

"Fwiend, Daddy?"

An image filled his mind, Faith sleeping on his sofa that night, her reddish curls covering her pretty—no, beautiful—face. A subtle shift in his feelings, as gently as the leaves blowing in a light wind, filled his whole being. Friends? Maybe. But paired with something more, which stymied him. She was an unsolvable puzzle, and he couldn't wait to see her the next day.

CHAPTER FOURTEEN

*F*aith breathed a prayer for a safe flight. Heat from the late-afternoon sun hurt her eyes. As she adjusted the shade, the undulating cloud patterns were reminiscent of the Black Hawk River's motion and a certain river rafting guide.

As the tires of the plane screeched on the tarmac, she intoned a thankful prayer. Faith wove through the throngs of people and headed to the baggage claim. Waiting for her luggage to tumble off the conveyor belt, she felt a warm hand touch the back of her arm. She whirled to find Caleb standing behind her. "Caleb? You're my ride? Where's Jack?" Faith glanced around, a slow burn from the hang up yesterday fighting to surface.

"He's with Taylor and Jarod at their youth meeting."

She bent to get her luggage, but Caleb beat her to it, grunting as he offloaded the heavy bag. "You packed for a week, not a few days."

"You never know what you might need." She glanced at him and shrugged. Faith began to head toward the door.

"Wait up. This monster's hard to roll."

"I can handle it." She grabbed the bag from his hand and forced it to move.

"What's going on?"

The suitcase wheels ground to a halt. "You hung up on me."

Caleb's mouth drew into a line. He motioned for her to pull aside.

Wheeling the luggage next to her, she waited for a response. Faith's air hovered in her lungs, and thunder trembled in her chest.

"My phone fell into the water." As he took the phone from his pocket, a kernel of rice dropped to the ground. "That's where it was overnight. In the rice. I couldn't call you back."

"Oh."

"So, about New York?"

"I'm staying."

"You're moving to New York?"

"No."

"What happened?"

"Erika." Holding back any sign of sadness required more effort than her tired body allowed. She sniffed. "She wanted to *steal* my recipes."

"I don't know what to say. Sorry doesn't help."

"Listening does."

"You'll get a job soon."

"I'm sorry I accused you of hanging up."

"No worries. I'd think it, too, if I were you."

They arrived at his car, and he wrestled her large bag into the small trunk. Faith noted the collection of books he'd pushed aside. "Same ones as before?"

"New ones— a library book sale. Did you go to a bookstore in New York?"

"Il Libro."

"My favorite."

Faith pulled a bookmark from her bag and laid it on the car's console. "For you." It was a photo of a bi-plane landing on the runway with New York City's skyline as a backdrop.

· "Cool, a World War II airplane. Speaking of those, there's a book on them in the backseat if you want to borrow it."

She masked her grimace behind a smile. "If I need it, I know who to see."

Heading out to the carpark and out through the toll booth, they spoke about Briar Creek happenings and what went on at the coffee shop during her absence. Their talk subsided to a comfortable silence as Caleb navigated the heavy rush-hour traffic outside the airport. She was lost in her musings and barely heard Caleb's words.

"This traffic won't let up for a while," he said. "Are you hungry?"

"Starving." Her stomach flip-flopped as he scrutinized her face.

"Dinner then."

The chatted as they wound around the roads. The green darkness of the tall trees beside the road was interrupted by a beacon of bright light. A neon pink sign glowed ahead as they drove through a sleepy little town. Faith said, "Look at this adorable place. I've always wanted to go to an old-fashioned diner."

After parking, they entered through the narrow doorway and into a rectangular dining room. The hostess led them to a bubblegum-colored vinyl booth, complete with a shiny, shocking pink and black Formica-topped table with its own miniature jukebox.

Faith fished out fifty cents from her wallet to play an Elvis song. She tapped her toe along with the beat on the black and white terrazzo floor, sipping a cherry cola in pure contentment.

Caleb glanced at her, wearing a hint of a smile. "I wasn't sure you'd like this place until you shouted."

"I voice my pleasure." Faith dragged a fry into her pool of

ketchup. "There's not flaxseed or a piece of kale anywhere in here."

Caleb bit into his grilled chicken sandwich, then stole the fry from her fingers and popped it into his mouth.

"Hey!" Faith reached for one of the tomatoes from his salad and he playfully pushed her hand away. As he scooped the roundest tomato on his spoon and offered it to her, Faith leaned forward and accepted his offer. The juicy summertime taste whetted her appetite for more, and she picked the nearest one from Caleb's plate. Before he could protest, she'd put a fry near his succulent lips, and he bit into the potato and smiled. Going in for a second bite, his soft lips brushed her fingers. Faith's eyes widened. Caleb's expression was flat, his eyes shuttered. The only telling evidence of his attraction was his pulse thrumming in his throat. *Say something.* "I'll need to find a place to live."

"There's one for rent down the road from me and Jack." Stealing another fry, he popped it into his mouth, and when finished asked, "Have you met Sylvia Danton at church yet?"

Faith's curls bounced with the shake of her head.

"She's a realtor. I'll text you her number." He glanced down and worked his fingers over his keyboard.

Frustration with herself boiled inside. *Way to ruin a romantic gesture.* A strident buzz alerted her to his message.

"Text her. It's still early." Caleb smirked and stole another fry.

Fingers flying over the keyboard, she pressed send in the same moment the wait person extended the check to Caleb. She grabbed it. "I'm paying."

"Not with me." He stood and casually pulled his platinum credit card from his wallet. Faith slid the receipt to him.

"Next time I'll pay." Faith gathered her bag and extricated herself from the sticky vinyl bench. Her declaration was met with silence.

On the drive back to Taylor and Jarod's, they chatted about their siblings, sharing war stories.

"My younger brother Dylan will be working for me during summer break next month."

"I'd like to meet him. When my family comes to visit you can meet my sisters, Hope and Grace."

"Are they coming anytime soon?"

"Maybe when I rent a place." Faith glanced out of the window at the whir of trees in the forest. "Tonight was fun."

"We'll do something outdoors next time. I could teach you to kayak."

Dinner churned in her stomach. *Not me.* "I saw 'The Rock' has a new movie coming out soon."

"If the weather's bad, we can go."

"Mmhmm." *I'll pray for a storm to roll through.* Faith downplayed her enthusiasm for ditching the river ride. "I remembered that you like action movies."

Caleb questioned. "And you don't. Why a movie?"

"Hot buttered popcorn."

"Tempting. I might reconsider."

As Caleb pulled into the driveway, Faith's eyes searched his face and her hands grew damp. While walking to the front door, their hands brushed one another's as they stepped in sync. She put her schoolgirl clammy palms to her pants and wiped them when he looked away. The yellow bug light softened the hard planes of Caleb's face as they stood on the porch.

He leaned over. Faith's knees jelled, in expectation of a kiss. She glanced to her side. *My suitcase.* She whipped her head around and conked his mouth with her forehead.

"Ouch!"

"Sorry, my bag." Remorse filled her as he walked away rubbing his lips.

"Fay." Two little arms hugged her waist.

Faith stooped down to be eye level with him. "Hi, Jack." She gave him a little hug. Her floral suitcase rolled beside her. Veering her gaze up, she noticed Caleb's dimpled smile. *Handsome.*

"Hi, son."

"Daddy." Jack shifted his allegiance to his father as he gave him a squeeze. "I had fun."

Taylor and Jarod came from the house, and Sugar soon followed, barking and wagging her bushy tail.

"Someone had two pieces of pizza tonight." Jarod pointed to Jack.

"You were hungry."

Taylor came closer to Caleb and Faith. "We cut a small piece into two."

"Smart. Thanks. I'd better get this pizza boy home." Caleb scooped his son into his arms while Jack kicked and giggled. "Watch out for my mouth, please. It's already been punched tonight."

Cupping her hands over her mouth, Faith shouted to Caleb's back. "I didn't mean to hit you."

Deep laughter stilled the cricket's night song. "Bye."

Tay pulled on Faith's arm. "This I've gotta hear."

"It was nothing—an accident."

Jarod strolled by Faith. "How was dinner?"

"You knew about it?"

"I suggested he take you out."

The luster from the wonderful night faded. "It was your idea."

Tay glanced at Faith and Jarod and held out her hands. "I've seen the way he looks at you. He's interested. Jar presented the idea, but Caleb wanted to do it."

"Yeah." Jarod padded from the room.

"He did have fun until I hit him."

"I don't think you physically punched Caleb."

Faith hid part of her face in her hands and shook her head.

89

"He leaned closer to me, and I hit his mouth with my forehead. Ugh, I'm so clumsy."

Tay chewed on her lip and tapped her foot. "You made an impact, that's for sure."

Faith groaned. "Not funny, Tay." She stretched as a yawn tumbled from her mouth. "I'm headed to bed. Night. Sleep well." Stepping out from the room a light glowed from her phone. It drew her attention to the screen. *Caleb.*

"I had to ice my mouth."

"No. I'm sorry."

"I wanted to call and let you know that everything's okay since you tend to dwell on things."

As her mouth opened, the heat in her middle increased, and surprise caught her unaware. Faith had no idea he remembered little things about her. "You're right, I do. That's very thoughtful of you."

"One of my more virtuous qualities." Faith's glance catapulted to the ceiling. Her lips made not one solitary comment. "See you tomorrow. Jack's handing me my cape. Book time."

"Night, Superman."

As he chuckled, the phone vibrated her cheek. She held a hand up to it and rubbed.

A sweet, sleepy voice said, "Night, Fay. See you at party."

Wrapping her arms over her middle, a whisper of a smile appeared. "You will. Night, Jack." The phone clicked. She slid the present for Jack into the gift bag and fluffed the tissue paper. Picking up a pen, she bit her lip and wondered which name to use on the card: her real one, or Jack's creation. Scrawling her nickname, she sealed the envelope, drew a few balloons on the front, and tucked it into the bag. She was looking forward to going to her first kid's party, something years before she'd never have imagined.

CHAPTER FIFTEEN

*W*rinkling his face in concentration, the hard cookie began to slide down his face. Caleb swiveled his glance to Jack, whose nose was wrinkling like a bunny.

"You got it, Jack," one of his son's school friends said.

"Who's gonna be the cookie face?" Caleb's Mom asked, laughing.

"Me," declared Jack.

Giving his son another glance, his head cantilevered too far to the side and all he wore was a cookie path of crumbs across his face.

Dusting the trace of defeat that decorated his face with a hand, he said, "Nice job, buddy."

Mouth working overtime to chew his prize, Jack bared his victory grin and displayed more than a mouthful of pearly whites coated in chocolate.

He handed Jack a water bottle and whispered. "Swish with this, champ. You got a little something in your teeth."

"'K, Dad." Jack swallowed a mouthful then grinned.

During all the activity, Ranger began to howl at the sound of the doorbell.

Jack started for the door.

"I'll get it." Caleb gave the cookie package to his mom. "Jack, who's playing next?"

Dylan, Caleb's younger brother got into the fun. "I'll play with two of you. Jack, you choose."

Raised hands shot in the air around the group.

Pointing to a dark-haired boy near him and a red-haired girl, Jack declared, "Zach and Caitlyn and Uncle Dylan."

Caleb sprinted to the door. As it widened, his heart picked up speed.

"Ready to play a game?"

Faith stepped through the doorway. Her lips wore a tilt of a smile. "Am I going to get messy?"

"No. Why?"

Snapping a picture of him on her phone, his skin prickled when Faith showed him his face, still covered in the remnants of cookie.

"I'll go get clean."

"And I'll follow the giggles."

Turning on the bathroom light, he leaned into the mirror and groaned. Dots of crumbs covered the side of his face like a confectionary mask. Splashing water on his face, he hurried back to the party, not wanting to miss any of the fun ahead.

Rounding the corner to the large family room, clusters of people were spread throughout. She stood in place looking for either the birthday boy or his dad.

"Miss me?"

"More than you know. There's a lot of guests."

"And more to come. Some are going to be late, like Jar and Tay, since they're at the youth meeting."

Caleb introduced her to some of Jack's preschool friends' parents who were very nice and chatty, which made her feel at ease.

"Be back in a sec, the cake's here." Caleb walked toward the new arrivals, a man and an attractive woman.

Noticing the cake box in the lady's hands, her mouth dried. *His late wife's sister.* Faith went to the present table and dropped off hers. Busy fluffing the lackluster tissue paper in the bag, she sensed someone behind her and turned. The cake lady.

"It doesn't have to be perfect. Jack's going to tear into it anyway."

"True." *She's very to the point.*

"I don't think we've met. I'm Lauren."

"Hi, I'm Faith."

"Friend from church or school?"

"Neither."

Lauren's eyebrows climbed. "You work for Caleb?" Her eyes scrutinized Faith harder than an airport security person as they wandered top to bottom.

"Yes."

"Gift shop?"

"Coffee shop manager." Shifting position, Faith willed herself to stand straight and not hunch like she wanted to do.

"How long have you known him?" She tapped her fingernail against flawless, smooth skin.

"A while."

"And Lizzie's the manager."

Lizzie had impeccable timing as the kind lady sidled next to Faith and put an arm around her shoulders. "I'm moving, Lauren. Out of state. Isn't Caleb fortunate to have Faith to replace me?"

93

"Excuse me. I haven't spoken to Jack yet," stated Lauren before abruptly walking away.

Relaxing her posture, Faith gave Lizzie a hug. "Thanks."

"I had to bust in. She'd make an Iron Maiden look cozy."

Faith silently agreed. "Did your hubby come?"

"No, Lucas is not a kid's party kind of man. But he did make a present for Jack in his woodshop. A wooden whistle… not that Caleb will like it."

The two ladies laughed.

"Maybe he'll love it," offered Faith

"Speaking of Lucas, I've wanted to ask if I can get your raspberry twist recipe? My sweet-toothed husband loves them."

"Sure."

"You know, you and I have a lot in common." Lizzie rocked back on her heels, and a grin widened her ample cheeks. "I used to own a bakery myself."

"Really?"

"On Beech Street, downtown, near city hall. Gosh, I closed it down three years ago." She shook her head, her dangling gold earrings sounding like a windchime. "I can't believe it's been that long. It's still vacant for some reason."

"That's a shame."

Miss Lizzie pulled down her glasses as she looked at Faith. "Our town needs a bakery. The lard buttercream the grocery store puts on their cakes is close to a sin." Tinkling earrings sounded. "Pure junk compared to a homemade frosting. I'm sure yours would be as tasty as your raspberry twists. Ever think about opening a bakery?"

"It's my dream." Panic jackhammered inside her, and she wished she could eat the words that danced from her mouth.

Lizzie crowed. "I knew there was more to you, girl." She gave a vise-like squeeze to Faith's arm, and Faith tried not to wince. "You told me the other day you'd spoken to a realtor. Get them to show you my old place. It's probably looking like a dog that rolled in a mud puddle, but it'd clean up well."

Caleb approached them. "I caught the end of what you said, Lizzie. You're not talking about me, are you?"

"Caleb-boy, your ego is as tall as you. Good thing you can live up to it. We were talking about dreams, weren't we, Faith?" Lizzie smiled and went to greet Taylor and Jarod who'd finally arrived.

"What's your dream?" Caleb reached out a hand and lightly touched her shoulder.

"I'll tell you someday." Faith nodded to the door. "Tay and Jarod are here."

They walked over to their friends and spent time chatting together as happiness skittered in Faith. *A chance at a bakery of my own. Wait until I tell Tay.*

Jack ran to his dad and decreed, "Cake, peeze."

"Everyone," announced Caleb, "it's cake time."

Lizzie gave her a quick smile. "Next one could be from your own bakery."

Faith noticed an older man across the room with the same coloring as Caleb.

She whispered to Lizzie, "Are those Caleb's parents?"

"You've never met them—"

"No."

"You will now." Lizzie wound around the milling people and Faith followed.

Reaching the couple, Lizzie said, "Good to see you two. It's been a while since you've been to the coffee bar."

The striking couple smiled.

Dry-mouthed, Faith plastered a smile on her face.

"Steve and Georgia, this is Faith. She's Caleb's new manager at Hawk's Creek Coffee."

Faith returned his parents' handshakes. "Nice to meet you both."

"Great to meet you, Faith." Caleb's mom's dark eyes met hers before she turned her attention to Lizzie. "Caleb mentioned you were leaving. We'll miss seeing you." She gave Lizzie a hug.

Caleb's dad grinned, and Faith saw where Caleb had gotten his dimples.

"Caleb said you were a chef." His dad lowered his voice as he spoke with Faith. "Can you teach my son to cook so my grandson won't starve?"

"I can try," said Faith, working to withhold a smile.

"That's a relief. His mom keeps giving him care packages when he and Jack come to visit." He tilted his head. "He's almost thirty. A man needs to know how to cook for himself."

Caleb's mom shook her head. "I'm still waiting on you to learn. Can you teach two men?"

Giggling, Faith nodded.

"I've tried and given up. Who puts water in their eggs?"

Faith leaned toward Caleb's mom. "Caleb."

Three ladies laughed. And one man didn't.

Three candles reflected Jack's radiant smile as he blew the flickering time markers. Everyone cheered as his cheeks puffed, and an evident whoosh of air was accompanied by a whoopie cushion sound. Laughter crowded Caleb's over-sized kitchen as his son dug a finger into the thick frosting on the superhero's cape, courtesy of former sister-in-law, Lauren.

Caleb ruffled his son's hair. "I'll go cut the cake. You'll get the first piece, birthday boy."

"I'll help." Lauren came over to the island and began to lay out the paper plates.

"Jack loves his cake." Lauren's stare lingered on Caleb. "I'm glad my parents aren't here to see your new girlfriend."

"My what?" He focused on slicing the cake and not on the bug-under-the-microscope feeling he was experiencing.

"Your new manager. Didn't take you long, did it?"

The knife barked on the cake dish. "We're. Not. Dating." Caleb straightened his spine and matched her gaze. "My parents are getting along with my manager. With Faith." He pushed a slice onto an awaiting paper plate. "I'm twenty-nine. I'll eventually date." He hefted a shoulder. "Don't you think Jack needs a woman to help raise him?"

"He has me and his grandmothers." Lauren whisked a plate from the island. "Aren't we enough?"

Sweat beaded on his upper lip. He was cornered.

Dylan came into the kitchen and tension eased from Caleb's body.

Lauren gave Dylan a quick hug before leaving the room.

"I'm glad to see you, little bro."

"Lauren getting too prickly?"

"You could say that."

"Before I take some cake, who's that hot girl next to mom and dad?"

Dylan had seen everyone before except Faith. Jealously sizzled beneath his exterior.

"Faith."

"Your new manager? You've told me about her on the phone. Introduce us."

Caleb navigated around his former family and willed a smile for Faith. "Having fun?"

"Yep." Her eyes sparkled like jade as she looked at him. "Who's with you?"

"My brother, Dylan."

Faith turned to smile at his brother.

Caleb's innards churned.

She's a friend. Calm down.

Dylan wrapped Faith in conversation as Caleb handed her a slice of cake and inched possessively closer to her.

"Looks good." She put a forkful in her mouth.

Caleb's eyes followed the path of the fork. He resisted a fervent urge to swipe the spot of buttercream from the corner of her petal pink lips. "You've got a smudge." He gestured to the spot. A burning need to shelter her from embarrassment freight trained across him as she reddened and swiped it with a napkin. Happy she understood his signal, he belted out. "You got it." Several heads swiveled in his direction. His stomach dived.

Dylan smirked and walked toward the cake.

Faith shook her head. "Soccer dad."

"Not yet." People tittered around the kitchen and went back to conversing. "Clever one, Belle." *Where did that come from?* "Faith."

"Dylan's nice. Is he going to work with you or me?"

"Me."

"You know who else I met?"

"No."

"Your parents. I didn't know your mom was a high school culinary arts teacher. That's cool." Her expression shifted. "And I met your sister-in -law. Is she usually so inquisitive?"

Heated, he grabbed a cup of water and drank in one gulp. Once cooled, he spoke. "Er. No."

"She wanted to know how long I'd known you. It seemed very. . . territorial."

A trickle of sweat cooled his heated skin. "Oh, you know family." Leaving the end of the statement hanging was Caleb's tactical ploy for Faith to change the subject, before he did.

"I do. Hope and Grace acted like they're the big sisters when I lived at home and had a friend over."

"Three girls," his voice dropped. "Bless your dad."

Putting a hand on her hip, Faith huffed. "We were very well-behaved, kind of like your son."

As he swung his glance in the direction of scattered giggles, his jaw slacked when he saw Jack standing on the coffee table and wearing the reading cape.

"I'm like Daddy." Like a matador with a red cloak, Jack flapped it to and fro.

Laughter erupted.

Holding his hands in front of him, ears on fire, Caleb winced. "Alright, alright. I wear it when I read Jack's bedtime stories."

More glee-filled noises rumbled through the crowd.

Jarod strolled by and clapped him on the back. "Bring it to softball practice next week. The way you're hitting, you'll need it."

Caleb grunted.

Hopping off the coffee table, Jack ran to the other room with his friends. "Movie, Daddy."

"Faith, could you bring the small bottles of water from the fridge?" He didn't dare glance at her, as he could hear the snuffles of laughter already.

Grabbing the little bags of popcorn, he went to start the movie. When he bent over to begin the streaming, he felt a soft touch caress his back. Perplexed, he turned to see his son attempting to Velcro the cape onto his back. Caleb ripped it off and handed it to Jack. "You can wear it while you watch the movie."

"Cape is hot." Jack's bottom lip hung nearly to his chin as he tried to pull it off his little body.

Caleb unfastened it, tossing the cape onto the chair nearby and gave the popcorn to the happy partygoers while Faith followed behind with the waters.

He crossed the room and stood in the doorway perusing the room.

To his surprise Faith sat on the floor and crisscrossed her legs in front of her.

Caleb squatted next to her and spoke softly. "You don't have to stay. We're all in the next room."

"I haven't seen this movie since forever." She patted the short beige carpet. "Sit, relax."

Sinking into the softness of the flooring, Caleb enjoyed the vanilla cupcake smell wafting from Faith as he readjusted his position. Jack came and sat between the two of them, putting a hand on each of their legs. Caleb was content and peaceful next to his son and friend. A few minutes into the movie, more adults came into the room and sat next to their kids. By the close of the movie, more adults were watching than their doe-eyed three-year-olds.

"Jack, your friends are looking sleepy." Pushing off the floor, Caleb extended a hand to Faith. Jack grabbed it and flew into his arms. Caleb pretended to stagger as he held him until Jack wiggled down. He reached his hand out once again to Faith, and she took it, bouncing from the floor, but dropping it quickly when their friends entered.

Taylor said, "We're going. Are you staying, Faith?"

"Going. See you later." Faith hugged Jack. "Bye, birthday boy."

"Fanks, Fay."

Caleb said as the ladies each gave him a parting wave, "Night, you two. Thanks for coming."

Four little sets of hands tried to swipe their treat bags from the box he held as more of the guests exited.

Dylan high-fived Jack and play-punched Caleb.

"What's that for?" asked Caleb.

"Guy," Dylan stood nearer to his brother and half-whispered, "Faith's into you."

"Huh?"

"She didn't mind you standing next to her like a second-skin earlier."

"The room was crowded."

"Tell yourself that. Not me. I saw what happened. See you two later." Dylan took a treat bag from Jack's outstretched hand and exited.

"Are you sure you don't need help cleaning up?" His mom held a paper towel in her hand.

Caleb hugged her and took the towel from her hand. "You and Dad have a two-hour drive ahead of you."

"Tax season ended a few days ago, and I'm exhausted." His dad winced and clapped his back. "Come on, hon. He's right, we've got a long drive ahead."

His mom gave Jack one last hug.

"I like Faith. She's a smart young lady and pretty. We'll talk tomorrow after Dad and I get back from church."

Palms slicking, he waved as the car pulled away. *Wonder if I can avoid that subject tomorrow?* Sighing, he closed the door. Quiet. One little boy he could handle. Four or more, a bit harder to corral. *It's almost bedtime.*

He swiveled and knocked over a cup of tea perched on a side table. *Gonna stain.* Running to the kitchen, he stepped in the way of a bobbing balloon which reared back and bopped him on the face.

Once he peeled it away and got into the heart of the kitchen, his eyes widened. Piles of leftover food on the counters, scattered popcorn on the floor, and Ranger.

Ranger's paws were propped on the counter. And his big, slobbery snout edged toward the cake.

Caleb snapped his fingers. "Ranger, move."

Whimpering, he skulked to the floor. Caleb got a dog treat from the pantry and gave it to him before leading him outside. First, he snagged a paper towel and the spray cleaner, then he ran into the family room to erase the spill.

Walking back into the kitchen, he took a sample of frosting and sighed.

"Me too."

He put a minuscule piece on a paper plate and presented it to his son. "Enjoy."

Jack ran to the table.

"Did you have fun?"

Poking balloons tied to his chair and the biggest blue frosting grin gracing a little boy's mouth was his reply.

"Nice." Sunlight had shifted beyond the trees he could see from the large breakfast area windows. "Go play with your toys, I'll clean this mess. Then shower and bed."

"Have to?"

"Yes." He held a brewing laugh inside as Jack drooped his shoulders and dragged himself from the kitchen. Moments later whirs and buzzes and giggles lightened the home.

The scent of lemon sunshine mixed with watermelon surrounded his son as Caleb wore the obligatory red cape and read Jack a new book, courtesy of Faith. "And the dog found a home with the family who loved him. The end." He closed the book and put it on the shelf. "Time for prayers. Who's on the list tonight?"

Jack folded his hands and closed his eyes as he recited all the guests from the party. Except one. Faith.

"What about Faith?"

Jack pulled a crayoned masterpiece from under his pillow. "Made it for Fay."

As he smoothed the crumpled paper, his eyes widened and his throat seized. "You made her a heart?"

"She's a fwiend. I give it to her."

"After school tomorrow."

Jack turned on his side and burrowed into his covers. "Night, Mommy and Fay." His long eyelashes kissed his cheeks as his breathing slowed.

Caleb bussed his son's forehead and gently took the picture from his clasped hand.

The band closing his throat persisted as he looked at the

photograph beside his son's bed. Laughter and cuddles flooded his memory. He could hear his wife reading the stories to their son and feeling the love in her voice just as the memory vanished. Averting his gaze away from the frame, he stood, and the picture created from Jack's affection floated to the floor.

A misshapen heart. His.

Wetness leached from his eyes.

Soft snores shattered his concentration, and fleeting pain pinged his soul. Could he love someone else? Silence engulfed him as he exited the room. Another night. Alone. In an ocean masquerading as a bed.

CHAPTER SIXTEEN

*C*lip, clap, clop. Faith halted cleaning and turned to view her next customers. With a smile as bright as the neon green shirt he wore, Jack trotted in front of his dad.

"Afternoon. Great shirt! It reminds me of a Florida beach and the crabs that pinch your arms." She gestured with her fingers, opening and closing them and playfully grabbed Jack's hand with the "pincers."

Running away and laughing, Jack went to investigate the display of cookies and other treats. "Daddy."

"You wanted to give Faith something?" Caleb held something behind his back, then waved it toward his son.

"Yeah." Skidding to a stop, Jack held out a hand to his dad. After a thorough inspection, he gave her the manila-colored paper.

"What is it?" She bent down to Jack's level.

Caleb's grin matched his son's intensity. "He made it at school."

Smoothing the paper over her knees, she turned it to the front. An over-sized red heart. A catch in her throat halted words. Feeling the waxy shape as she ran a finger around the paper, she hoped her next words fit the specialness of Jack's present. "I love it. Thank you." She gathered him in her arms, and the filtering sunshine warmed her upturned face. Happiness enveloped her. "I'll put this on Tay and Jarod's fridge until I get a place of my own." Rising slowly, as not to bump Jack, she put the artwork carefully on the table beside them and eyed it one more time. Precious.

"Heard from the realtor?" asked Caleb.

"As a matter of fact, Tay and I are meeting Mrs. Danton Saturday."

"That house I mentioned a while back is still for rent." Caleb ran a hand over his face. "You'd be close to Tay and Jar, too."

"True. And Jack." Faith reached out to softly pretend to pinch Jack, who smiled and raced back to the counter. "Can he have a small cookie?"

Flicking a glance at his phone, he exhaled. "It's fine, dinner's going to be late. Work out night. Jack gets to see his friends in the kids area."

As Jack's eyes grew larger, his little body drooped. "Tired."

"Buddy, we talked this morning. It's only an hour."

"I'll watch him and feed him dinner."

"You're sure..."

"Positive. Taylor and Jarod need a break for a few hours." Faith glanced skyward. "She was pretty excited about going to look for a place for me. But not more than me. I like my space."

"We'll help clean, then we can go to the house. I'll leave from there. You're awesome." Caleb's hand lingered on her arm, and a bottle rocket whizzed up her limb. She looked away, not wanting him to see any telling emotion on her face.

Last dish cleaned and the door locked, all three left for their cars.

Faith called, "Be there soon." Pulling away, she waited to belt out a tune until she was out of earshot of Caleb. While the vocal abilities of her family were pleasing in tone, she squeaked like a rat.

On the drive to Caleb's, she stopped by the old building Lizzie had mentioned several days earlier and walked up to the place. Lizzie was right—it did have character. Faith's gaze lingered on the building. The setting sun cast a serene glow on the windows and gave a beauty to the well-worn appearance. Curiosity got the better of her, and she stuck her face near the soiled glass. Faith was pleasantly surprised to see nicely finished floors and sturdy wooden shelves on the back wall. *Better get to Caleb's.* As she stepped off the curb, an unbidden pang settled in her midsection. She turned to take another glance. The building seemed to beckon to her—despondent that she hadn't stayed. A stronger emotion crept into the periphery. Hope.

For the rest of the short trip, she planned what things she'd sell in the bakery.

Double-chocolate brownies.

Raspberry twists.

Mini-cheesecake bites.

So tangled was she in her thoughts, she missed the turn. Whipping around in a safe spot, she arrived at Caleb's and parked in the driveway.

"Forget where I lived?"

"No, lost in an idea." She half laughed.

Caleb opened the door for Faith and Jack. "I'd like to hear. Jack, you can watch the Dog movie for a bit, and the pizza's coming soon. After that no more tv."

"Yay!" Jack ran into the family room, as Ranger padded behind him.

Catching her tongue between her teeth, she inhaled and spoke. "I'm thinking of opening a bakery."

"You're leaving?"

"Staying." A smile tickled her lips.

A PROMISE FOR FAITH

"Staying?" Duo dimples emerged on Caleb's lean face, and he enfolded her in a hug. The scent of leather, vanilla, and something spicy—intriguingly masculine, like him—wafted around her.

"Permanently."

"I wanna hear more about this bakery idea." Caleb plopped on the sofa and patted a hand on the adjacent cushion.

Sliding into the seat, Faith pivoted toward him, the intensity of her heartbeat pulsating in her chest. *Breathe.* "At Jack's birthday party, Lizzie mentioned owning a bakery before and how the town needed one. It made me realize how much I wanted to own a bakery, in Briar Creek." Faith put a hand on his taut arm. "That'd mean you wouldn't have a manager."

Caleb moved closer, and Faith's breathing stopped.

Staring off into the distance, a memory trailed of them in New York. Walks in Central Park, holding hands and kicking the crisp, new-fallen leaves, sharing a hot chocolate and him kissing the whipped cream off her lips. The stubble of his morning-before shave. Faith put a finger to her lips. They were cold and untouched. A past reality. She shook her head.

"So, you don't want to see my business plan, Faith?"

"What?"

"I've been talking for the last couple of minutes and you didn't say anything. Everything okay?"

"Fine." Curls spilled over her shoulders as she shook her head and smiled. "I'd like to see your business plan."

Caleb glanced at her again and sprung from the seat. "I'll get it." Faith picked at her nails and waited. She ran over her bank account on her phone, the college fund leftover would take care of part of the payment. The rest would have to come from a bank. *Hurry up, Saturday, the building is waiting.*

As the doorbell rang and Ranger barked, Faith jumped from the sofa and went to answer it. Pulling it open, she came face to face with Lauren. "Uh, hi."

Lauren's leopard shoes matched the huntress narrowed eyes staring at Faith. Stepping into the doorway, her gaze veered around Faith. "Caleb here? I brought dinner." She motioned to the cookware carrying bag she held.

"He's here, so's Jack."

Caleb came into the room. "Lauren, didn't know you were coming."

Faith observed the quick mask slip onto Caleb's face as the air ignited with tenseness.

"So, Caleb, your manager cooks for you too?"

"Faith was invited. She's watching Jack while I go work out. I have pizza coming. Thanks for bringing this."

"I'll take it to the kitchen." Lauren's heels popped on the wooden floor. Faith looked up at Caleb whose posture was straighter than an arrow ready to spring from a bow.

"I didn't know she was coming," he muttered.

Faith rejoined. "I could tell."

She and Caleb walked to the kitchen. Faith steeled herself for another barb from the not-so-friendly Lauren. *Be nice, she's his family. Jack's family.*

Her attention was waylaid by a young runner.

As the air gushed past, she noticed how his hair was parted into combed rows and scented of bubble gum.

Jack flew into his aunt's arms. "Hi, Lolo."

Lauren smoothed his hair back and kissed his cheek. "Jojo, I brought your favorite, spaghetti and meatballs."

"Yay! Hungry." He ran toward the table.

Caleb said, "We're having pizza tonight. It should be here any second." As if on cue, the doorbell pealed. "Spaghetti tomorrow, Jack. Excuse me, ladies." Watching him jet from the kitchen, Faith hated to see him leave.

Lauren marched to the refrigerator, rearranged a few things, put the dish inside, then she fixed her jade eyes on Faith. Loop-de-loops twisted Faith's innards.

"Don't think you can replace my sister. First you become the manager, then a dinner date." Lauren's lips shrank into her over-filled cheeks as they puckered.

"I'm a friend," said Faith.

Holding the pizza boxes in one hand, he slid them onto the counter. Garlic and cheese paired with the cloying stench of Lauren's dark-amber perfume made Faith cough.

"Enjoy your pizza. See you two later." Before she left, Lauren slid a kiss on Jack's cheek and sashayed from the kitchen.

"It looks like I barged in on something."

Faith shrugged and pushed the hair from her eyes. "Nothing I can't handle. Let's eat, it smells great."

"After Jack goes to bed, I can show you the business plan."

A flash of excitement trilled inside. "Sure."

Waiting in the family room while Caleb finished putting Jack to bed, she strolled around the family room. Photos of baby Jack were on the bookshelves. One photo behind the others was of a woman holding the baby and smiling into the camera, blonde and model perfect. *Avery.* Looking in the mirror she felt like she was the exact opposite. She pulled on a walnut-brown curl shot with crimson, a gift from her part Mediterranean bloodline. Faith sighed. *Why do I care? We're friends.* Her eyes darted to another photo on the mantle; Caleb and Jack. Sadness and happiness commingled, pulling Faith closer to the photo. She could have given Caleb a child if they'd married. *Dangerous thought.*

"Jack's down. Ready to look at the business plan?" Heat radiated from Caleb's body and contacted her cold skin and his breath teased the hair covering her ear.

Leave. "No, I'm suddenly really tired." Covering a pseudo-yawn with a hand, she snagged her purse from beside the sofa.

"We didn't talk about Lauren. I know she said something to you."

Hello, Pandora's Box. "I didn't pay attention to her. See you

STACY T. SIMMONS

tomorrow." Closing the door behind her, she willed the snap-
shot of father and son to clear her mind. *Can't wish for what
didn't happen.* Doubt teased her thoughts. She'd have to pray
harder on the bakery decision. Living in a town with her past
might make for one difficult future.

CHAPTER SEVENTEEN

*S*towing the computer on the desk by the bookshelf, Caleb's glance was drawn to the photos as it often was. *Crooked.* Putting them back in place, he saw the particles of dust had shifted. *Not Jack's doing, they're out of his reach.* Brain attempting to solve the mystery, he moved to the mantle, square with the photo of him and Jack. *She was staring at this picture.* Why did she leave? *She didn't look tired.* Scattershot pain zinged through him. *She loved me. We could have been a family.* Horror crawled into every pore. *I wouldn't have Jack. Or have had Avery. It was meant to be this way—maybe not me alone, but to have had my loves. Including the one I left in New York.* He flicked on his phone and paused a thumb over Faith's number. Apologize for leaving eight years ago? She'd think he was insane. Lightness flared within his soul. She was staying. It felt right.

A lone owl hooted in the night, keeping him company in his bedroom as he read another book and drank another cold glass of water. He inched a foot to the empty, icy sheets on the other side. Gathering the comforter close to his body he exhaled. Bitter sadness left a steel-bladed tang in his mouth. Glancing to his silent phone on the bedside table, he said, "G'night, Faith," and doused the sole light in the room.

Fresh perspective with the morning, Caleb tackled his early morning workout. Once finished, his sleepy son had awoken and shuffled into the kitchen as he made their breakfast. After a bowl of oatmeal was given to his son, he poured a cup of coffee and brought it to his lips. Caleb paused and reached for the honey on the counter. He put a liberal squeeze into his coffee and a shake of cinnamon. Breathing in, he smelled Faith. Muscles tightened and he stopped to rub his arms. *Must've worked out too hard this morning.* One last swig and he caught the door opening as he headed to the shower.

"Morning." Mrs. Settles hurried inside. Her eyes widened. "Hope you're not going to work like that."

Glancing down, Caleb noticed the sloppy mess of his state of clothes. "Good morning. No, heading to get ready. Jack'll be out in a sec."

Mrs. Settles stepped toward the kitchen. "Time to grab a quick cup before we leave."

"Try it with honey."

"Caleb, don't you drink it black?"

"Most of the time. A friend told me to try it." Caleb waved back to the kind older lady. "It was good."

"Another time. Not sure what's got you in a happy mood today, but it's nice." Lifting a shoulder, Mrs. Settles headed toward the kitchen.

After dressing, he put on an extra spritz of body spray and raked some styling product he found in the back of his cabinet through his hair. He was ready for the day. While searching for his keys, he saw Jack's backpack still on the island. Another pour of coffee into his travel mug, and Jack's pack thrown over a shoulder, he ran to the car. As he pulled hard into the parking spot minutes after, he shot from his car to the reception desk and explained what had happened. Several clucks of the receptionist's tongue later, he was awarded a visitor magnetic badge. Once he slid through the double doors, a chorus of voices led his steps to Jack's class in the large playroom.

Quicker than a racehorse, Miss Tessa appeared beside him, revealing one hundred teeth from a curtain of shiny, over-plumped lips. "Caleb. Mr. Gaines. It's good to see you. Did you come to join our dance party?"

Backing away, he held Jack's backpack toward her like it was a ring of garlic to ward away a vampire. "No, he forgot this at home." Hoping for a pint-sized interruption, he searched for Jack in the throng. His son was too busy to notice. "Late for work." Putting the pack down next to him, he strode from the frenetic room and to his car. Settling in the seat, he flicked on some soft music and nosed the car away from the school and headed to someone he'd like to see. Someone who was as natural as she was beautiful.

His chance to see Faith came later in the day. A morning rush of spring breakers turned into an overbooked afternoon on the rapids. His team did a fantastic job of directing the awaiting rafters to the coffee shop and others to the gift area. With his rafting trips finished, he sauntered to the coffee shop where Ryan and Faith were juggling the orders.

"I'll help." Caleb stepped around the stream of people and moved behind the counter. He wanted to brush back the pieces of hair that had escaped the loose ponytail she wore. "Where do you need me?"

Ryan gestured to the coffee maker. "Make this order." He scooted the computer screen forward a page, "Then this one."

"Don't add cinnamon." Faith glanced at him and his heart picked up speed.

"I'll do honey instead."

"You hated it."

Flicking a silver pitcher under the steam wand, he spoke louder to be heard. "Not anymore." He was charmed when her perfect mouth rounded. He came to his senses abruptly as hot milk bubbled onto his hand. "Ouch."

"Run it under cool water. I'll be there in a minute." Faith took the frothed milk from his hand, and he watched her pour a perfect heart into the espresso.

As the human tidal wave ebbed, Caleb went to the kitchen and ran a stream of water over it to ease the throbbing red line forming on his left hand. Murmuring a groan of ecstasy, he looked around to see if he'd been heard.

Faith appeared in the kitchen suddenly. "I thought my cookies made people happy." A twist of her lips followed the remark. She laid a hand on his and began to rub the burn cream gently onto his skin, then covered it with a bandage.

Vanilla and cinnamon with a hint of coffee haloed her. He breathed in as deeply as he dared. "It's better now." Caleb wished his hand could linger in hers. Unhappiness covered him as he pulled his hand from hers. He couldn't tell what her expression meant, but he noticed the quick lick of her lips. *She's nervous.* "I brought my laptop. Want to look over the business plan after work?" He accidentally hit his burn on the side of the counter and groaned.

Her curly hair brushed his arm as she bent toward him. "You okay?"

His hand ached but he wanted to look invincible to her. It was merely a second-degree burn. "I'm great." Flicking the moisture from his hands he moved a piece of her hair away from her face. *Those eyes.* Their gazes must've stayed on one another longer than he realized as Caleb heard a throat clear behind them.

"Need you up front, Faith." Ryan walked back to the coffee shop area.

To his chagrin she tucked the strands into her bun. Caleb had been itching to touch more of her silky hair. "Later."

"Yeah." When she left, he winced and shook his affected hand before Faith darted into the room.

"Cookies," she pulled a tray near where he was standing.

He moved his hand behind his back.

Before leaving the room, Faith advised, "I know that hurts. Put more butter on it."

Her concern reached a parched, dusty place. One he'd folded into a compartmentalized box and hidden from others. A chink developed in the steel-trapped box of his heart.

CHAPTER EIGHTEEN

*K*nots filled Faith. *He's in pain.* She glanced at the bone-white hash marks on her arms. A story of a souffle left too long in the oven, the other charred brownies when she was a preteen. She rubbed them as a faint remembrance of pain awakened. *Caleb belongs on the water, not in a coffee shop. Goodness knows, he's not great with coffee.* Faith looked over to the table where Ryan and Caleb were refilling the containers of creamers and sweeteners. With his attention elsewhere, Faith admired the dimples marking his cheeks as he smiled.

A strident voice brought her back from her adoration.

"Mocha toffee iced." A teenager tapped on her phone screen and slid a credit card across the counter. "You'd have noticed me earlier if you weren't staring at Captain America over there."

Don't argue. "Coffee's coming up."

"I work at his kid's school part-time. Everyone drools when he comes to pick up his little brat." The young woman's nose wrinkled.

She's not staying. She switched the mug in her hand to a to-go cup. Her mood boiled as lava-like as the steam rising from the coffee maker. *Hold your anger.*

"I'm staying."

Faith gave the coffee to her along with her credit card. "We're closed. Coffee's on me."

Turning on her heel, the customer snapped her wallet closed and walked as slow as thick honey by Caleb.

He didn't notice. Faith couldn't help but feel a tiny bit happy. *Jack's not a brat! He's a wonderful little guy.*

"What's got that smile on your face?" Caleb had his elbows on the counter. "It's because Ryan's going to close the shop so we can talk, right?"

"I'm not sure Ryan's thrilled about it."

"When he hears he can go home early next Friday, with pay, I think he'll change his mind."

"Getting the cleaner now." Ryan raced to the storage room whistling.

Clicking off the machine, Faith shook her head. "Bribing an employee? Real nice."

"Employee incentive, not a bribe." Caleb pulled out a chair. "It's all in your perspective. Have a seat."

Too surprised to argue, she sat down and leaned toward the table.

Caleb pulled a folder along with his laptop out of his backpack. "I made copies."

Joy rushed over her. "That's great! I can look these over later." She put them aside and focused on the laptop's screen.

Caleb scrolling down the long list made Faith's eyes blurry. She rubbed them, hoping to clear her vision.

He pointed out his spreadsheet figures to her. "This is how much the coffee shop outlay was at the beginning. It might be similar to opening a bakery."

A marching line of zeroes behind the number twenty-five refocused her attention.

"I thought it'd be less." Her chin fell to her chest.

"Lizzie's old place was a bakery before, so maybe less to remodel."

She lifted her head. "Sounds reasonable."

"I'll be praying for tomorrow."

"Thanks. It's scary." Glass shards poked at her middle.

"I was petrified when I opened the outfitters."

"You?" She ran a finger over the wooden table and frowned. "You don't get scared."

"I had a wife and a newborn. I was *the* financial support system for my family. If that won't rock you to your soul, nothing will."

"Brave."

"Me, brave? Cocky. Filled with determination to prove myself. Wall Street investment broker coming back home, like I couldn't cut it." Caleb shifted his chair's position and laced his fingers behind his head. "Truth was, I missed it here. No honking cars, lots of trees, neighborhoods. And being on the water. That's how I got the idea for the outfitters." He closed his computer. "I'm yammering on, probably boring you."

"No, I haven't seen you this excited since, well, a long time." At her admission, she felt exposed, so she avoided eye contact.

Caleb scratched his face. "So, I mope, like a sloth?"

"Not always." Grinning, Faith put her pointer finger and thumb close together. "Sometimes."

Caleb's brows raised. "You'll see me smile all the time now." His lips curled into a cheesy smile.

She held her hands over her face. "Not like that. It's creepy." Shooting from her seat, she moved toward the counter. Warm hands covered her shoulders, and she turned toward him.

"I can be creepy." He laughed in a low-throated way.

Instinctively, Faith curled up into him, giggling. She heard his galloping heartbeat underneath his polo shirt as his arms wrapped around her. Lifting her head, she smiled.

Caleb tucked a piece of hair around her ear as their feet moved to silent music.

He's a dad. He's your boss. His heart seemed to beat to her questioning. Torn between laying her head on his all-too-manly chest or running away from this completely crazy situation, she ducked her head back near his heart and finished the dance to their song.

An alarm sounded in Caleb and Faith's vicinity.

"Late for something?" she mumbled into his chest as an easy smile crossed her face.

Caleb stepped away and flicked on his phone. She read the concern on his face by his lips pulling down.

"Got to get Jack." Brushing a finger down her arm raised bumps on Faith's skin and it left a trail of warmth where his finger had traced a path. "Save another dance for me."

Poker-hot fire shot through her face. "I will."

As the distance between them grew larger and the door closed behind him, a fleeting sadness visited Faith. Another opportunity to grow closer had danced away with his departure.

CHAPTER NINETEEN

*F*aith pulled into the small-town, meandering traffic and drove like a well-seasoned NYC cab driver. Her nervous energy propelled the car toward the realtor's office.

"You're not in New York any longer. Slow down, I'm pregnant." Tay motioned to the speedometer, then her middle.

"You are? Congratulations, this is fantastic!" She reached over and squeezed her friend's hand. "Sorry I sped, slowing down now."

"Appreciate it. Morning sickness is not a joke."

Turning into a space and hopping from the car, she outpaced her friend to the door. Remembering to exhibit manners, she held the door open for Taylor.

At the reception desk as an ebony-haired lady waited with an expectant look.

Faith said, "Hello. We have a 2 o'clock appointment with Mrs. Danton."

The kind looking receptionist scrutinized her computer screen. "Faith Fuller?"

She nodded.

"I'll let Sylvia know." She tapped on her computer keyboard. "She'll be with you shortly. Please have a seat."

Minutes later a petite, sandy-haired woman entered the waiting area. She wore a finely tailored turquoise dress and neutral pumps. A demure smile graced her attractive visage.

"Hello, Faith. Good to see you, Taylor."

Faith smiled and shook her hand while Mrs. Danton gave her friend from church a quick hug.

Mrs. Danton glanced at her tablet. "Did you get the property list and schedule I emailed?"

"Yes."

"Ready to go?"

Both ladies nodded.

"Good. We can all fit in my car."

Her receptionist handed them each a bottle of icy sparkling water as they were leaving. They climbed into her luxurious SUV as soft strains of jazz music filtered through the speakers.

"We'll go to the storefront first."

Faith's excitement mounted as she saw the smudged store windows before her. The sparkle dimmed when her eyes trailed to the front of the building where time had taken the shine off the brass-plate on the door. A few bricks were chipped, and debris collected on the sidewalk.

Mrs. Danton's keys jangled as she turned the door lock. "Let's go inside, it's charming." She held the door open for the ladies to enter.

Tay whistled as she pointed out the beautiful crown molding and wide-plank mahogany floors to Faith.

While the other two ladies were talking together, Faith wandered away and headed to the kitchen. Her joy turned to dismay as she noted the antiquated condition of the appliances. Her money would only stretch so far. She ran a hand over the marble-topped table island, which seemed to be in perfect condition. Faith imagined all the dough she could roll out on the expansive top.

"This kitchen." Taylor walked in behind Faith, ran a finger over the dusty marble and frowned. "Do you think the appliances work?"

"I'd have to check with an electrician." Tapping a finger on her chin, she questioned, "I can't help but wonder what it'd cost to replace them."

"How much do you have?" her friend asked. "It looks expensive to me."

"Hopefully enough." Faith rifled around in her bag, found a box of Altoids, and popped one in her mouth. She relished the cool sensation on her tongue and hoped it would appease her agitated stomach.

"Faith, we need to go." Mrs. Danton's voice travelled to the rear of the building.

"Coming." She took photos of the wood trim and front area as she went to the door to help remember the space and do some planning as well.

Faith left a fragment of her heart in the shop as Mrs. Danton closed the door behind them.

They traveled a few minutes down the road and stopped in front of a house.

Mrs. Danton swiveled her arm towards the picturesque yard. "This rental home ought to go quickly. It's well-maintained."

The two-story home, with its Wedgewood blue siding and wooden-railed porch hugging the front, held Faith's attention. Her thoughts turned to how cute a small table set or a swing chair would look on the ample porch. The trio made their way through the multi-paneled door and into the foyer. As they toured the home, everyone remarked on the shiplap-clad dining room which opened into the gleaming kitchen filled with granite countertops and plentiful storage spaces. And in the master bedroom, Faith held back a whoop of joy when she saw the New York City apartment-sized closet with enough space for her shoe collection. *Heaven.* Sauntering back through the kitchen, Faith opened some cabinet doors to imagine where to put her numerous pots and pans.

A squeak drew her attention. Mrs. Danton opened the back door. "Wait until you see the backyard."

Faith walked to the back of the yard, and she felt like dancing. A sliver of Briar Creek wound through the edge of the property, just enough to wet her feet on a scorching summer day.

Taylor put a hand on Faith's arm and whispered with a gleam in her eyes, "Caleb lives a few doors down."

Faith cut her eyes toward Taylor. Her heart rat-a-tatted inside her ribs, and she raised her face to the warm breeze and breathed in the fresh air. *This could be my new place.*

Every other home they saw that day wasn't as enchanting to Faith as the blue cottage. Either the closets were too small or the kitchen too outdated. And none had a creek in the backyard or the temptation of a handsome neighbor nearby.

Faith promptly pulled into the coffee shop parking lot by seven o'clock. Opening the door, the scent of chocolate teased her senses.

Ryan popped his head around the kitchen door. "Morning, how'd it go?"

"Hi." She fumbled with the ties on her apron from a lack of having no morning jet-fuel-in-a-mug.

"Let me get it." Ryan pulled the strings together into a loose knot.

"I really liked this one house."

Rocking back on his heels, he asked, "Near Caleb's?"

Shunning his glib words, Faith declared, "You should see the kitchen. It has yards of cabinet space and a great cooktop." She began to assemble ingredients for the cookie of the day in a stainless bowl. "Plus, the view."

Shaking his head, he flicked on the mixer switch and yelled over the din, "Of your neighbor."

Faith swatted his arm with a kitchen towel. "He's four or five houses away. I couldn't see him." Folding the towel, she put it back on the hook by the sink. "A trickle of Briar Creek cuts through the yard. *That* view."

Faith winced as she heard an inharmonious beat box mix of wet pool float and an MMA metal mixer cage match.

CHAPTER TWENTY

ollowing the noisy racket to the kitchen, Caleb ran his fingers through his wavy hair and found it sticking up like porcupine quills. After batting it down, he blotted his face with the towel around his neck and rubbed his water-logged eyes. When his vision cleared, he saw . . . Faith and Ryan. He looked down at his dripping t-shirt, sodden shorts, and the transparent puddle at his feet. Caleb's face scalded. He half-turned, ready to leave the room. *Maybe she didn't see me.* He glanced back at her. Faith's beautiful eyes got lighter and her lips twitched. *Caught.*

"Forget to do something?" Her finger pointed to the towel.

Caleb noticed the flash of mischief cross her lips.

"I thought Ryan was the only one here." Caleb's Adam's apple bobbed as he choked on air. "My foot slipped on the deck and I fell in the river."

Faith grinned and tugged at the towel on his shoulder. "I don't want to fill out an accident report. Dry the floors, please."

Taking the towel from his shoulders, he put it on the floor and retraced his steps. Then he hurried back to the kitchen to speak with Faith and Ryan.

"Finished." He pushed the towel to the corner with a foot. "How was house hunting?"

Faith gave Caleb the highlight reel from Saturday.

"So, you saw the blue house?" He heard Ryan sigh.

"It's the house with a view, right, Faith?" Ryan smiled as he carried a full tray of scones to the coffee shop.

Puzzled, Caleb asked, "What view?" Cold chills ran over him, and he moved closer to the oven, absorbing its heat.

"The creek," answered Faith.

Scratching his jawline, he reflected. "It's more of a trench of shallow water. Ranger and Jack splash around in it on a warm day."

He noticed her expression change, and he held back a grimace.

"I think it's charming." She busily rolled the dough and put it on the baking sheet. "I'm renting the house."

Hello, neighbor. Sneaking closer to Faith, he commented, "The creek's not bad. I think I've heard it gurgling now and then when we get rain." *Oh, brother. Lay it on.*

"We used to jump in the puddles when I was growing up. That'd be fun to walk in the creek in the rain."

He looked at her face's rising color and her lips sweeping in a grin. *Beautiful. I'd dance through the rain with her.*

"I need to get to the oven."

Taking the pan from her, he held onto her fingers and thunder rolled through him. Before he could bobble the pan, he turned and put it in the oven.

As her brow lowered, a hand ran over his arm. "You've got goosebumps. You need to go get changed."

She noticed. No one's looked out for me for a long time.

He didn't argue when she put her hands on his back and walked him to the door.

"Grab a coffee on the way out."

A PROMISE FOR FAITH

"Muffin to go with the coffee?" He felt her hand lift off his back and heard her quiet exhale.

"Good thing you own this place."

He took the muffin. "What about the bakery?" Warm hands touched his back and he felt a light push.

"Later. My meeting is tomorrow."

"Bye." *Persistent. One of the things I like about her.*

Driving home, one of Jack's songs came into rotation. As it continued to play, Caleb recalled the fishing trip together as he and Jack sang and Faith listened. *She baited her own hook and released the fish.* He touched his damp hair. *She cared for Jack when my migraine pounded.* Eyeing the remains of the muffin on the car seat he considered. *Her eyes lighting up when we cooked together. Like Avery and I did sometimes.* Caleb swallowed and clutched the wheel. He ran a finger over the slight divot where for six years the eternity band circled. Enmeshed in memories between time-spaces of past and present, a singular idea over-shadowed. *She's more than a friend.* The seatbelt dug over his heart. *I need to let go. It hurts. But Faith's worth it.*

CHAPTER TWENTY-ONE

aith's insides pitched as she entered the bank lobby and checked in at the kiosk in the waiting area. She pressed the portfolio onto her legs as she sat. It bunched her skirt and created a spiderweb of black polyester tunnels right above the bend of her knees. After three interminable days of creating the business plan, she wasn't going to chance it being misplaced.

A man approached Faith. As he neared, his florid cheeks rounded with a smile. "Ms. Fuller?"

Faith nodded. Her voice was disabled by a sandpaper-dry throat.

"Good morning. Jim Knapp. Great to meet you." He shook her hand. "Let's go into my office." He pulled out a chair for Faith then sat at his desk. "Did you bring your files and business plan?"

Finding her voice, she answered, "Yes." Handing her paperwork to him, the sound of his concentration was discernible as papers were rifled and tapping computer keys pervaded the quiet air. Minutes trudged past. Faith silently prayed.

Friendly concern etched the brackets around his mouth as

he leaned forward in his chair. "Your bank account looks fairly healthy." He paused to wipe his glasses. "Looking at the figures, I can offer you a small loan. You don't have the assets we require for a larger business loan. In fact, no financial institution would lend a sizable amount of money to you with your smaller assets."

A chill arrowed down her spine. "How much would I qualify for?"

He turned his laptop screen for her to view. Faith's eyes widened, and the blood rushed out of her head as she read the paltry amount. Her heart ripped in two, but she remained calm through the maelstrom of emotions. Faith pushed her chair back and stood. "I'll get back to you." She clamped a hand onto the back of the chair.

"Absolutely. Let me know if we can be of help." He stood and handed her a printout of what they'd discussed along with the business card. Coming around his desk, he gave her a smile and held out his hand. "Have a good day."

She wrested her hand from the chair and shook his, her mind more on the numbers than being able to put one foot in front of the other to get herself out the door. "You too."

Faith kept her churning pain inside until she got into her car and shut the door. She closed her eyes and prayed while scalding tears of disappointment poured down. He was the only one who could help. She couldn't do this on her own.

After some minutes she took a deep breath, exhaled, and pulled out of the space, heading the fifteen miles to Hawk's Creek. Arriving she swerved into an empty spot, shoved her gear shift into park, and glanced in the rearview mirror. Faith closed her eyes for several seconds, attempting to erase the crimson lightning bolts in her eyes. She checked again. No change. Faith threw on the Hawk's Creek ball cap and bolted in the side entrance and rammed straight into Caleb.

"Hey, watch . . ."

Crevasses arose between his eyebrows. "What's going on?"

Her breathing hitched. "Bad news."

He wrapped his arms around her and rested his chin on top of her cap. "Wanna talk?"

She shook her head in his chest, but breathed deep as tattered, raw places eased in her heart. "Not now. I can't." Faith pulled away, put on an apron she'd found hanging on a hook by the door, gave him a watery smile, and started for the front.

As she walked away, she heard his voice call. "I'm here if you want to talk."

"Thanks, I'll remember." She kept on walking through the door, afraid to say more in case the threatening tears spilled.

An hour later Faith's phone rang.

Taylor asked, "How did your meeting go?"

"Not as expected."

"What happened?"

"I'll tell you tonight. And since Caleb called you, can he and Jack come over for dinner?"

"How did you —"

Faith snorted. "C'mon. We've been friends for a long time. If you didn't already know that I was upset, you'd have been all 'Oh, I'm sorry, Faith. Is there anything I can do, Faith?' And wheedled it out of me."

"Am I that transparent?"

Faith laughed. "No. You're just that good of a friend. And I love you for it."

"Love you back. You're not mad about Caleb calling?"

"Not at all."

"Before you ask, Caleb's coming by the house tonight to hear what went on. He's worried."

"If I believed in that stuff, I'd think you had mind reading skills."

"Just knew what you'd want to do. Sheesh, planning time's over. It never lasts long enough. Later."

"See you."

The mid-afternoon rush kept Faith and the crew busy, and she didn't see Caleb all afternoon which surprised her. Faith and Ryan went over the list of baking for the next day, and she noticed a shadow on the computer screen. She pivoted her glance. *Caleb looks too good to have worked all day. I'm a hot-mess-Hannah.* Faith ran a finger down the waterfall of hair on her shoulder and flipped it behind her. She pointed to a recipe on the screen, hoping Caleb hadn't seen.

Caleb half-waved and turned to leave. "I'll come back."

Ryan shook his head. "No, boss, we're finished. You two talk." He sauntered toward the coffee bar.

Caleb turned to Faith. A flash of a smile appeared. "How're you doing?"

"Better. Tay called."

Caleb leaned against the counter. "I knew she would."

"So, you two are coming over tonight?"

"Affirmative. I've been thinking about you all day."

"You have?"

"I didn't like seeing you upset."

"Oh."

"See you tonight?"

"You got it."

Caleb sprinted toward a group of people standing outside. Before going through the door, he winked at Faith.

Faith tracked his exit and saw his shoulders shaking with laughter at something one of the people said. *Those dimples and broad, muscular shoulders.*

A masculine voice caught her attention nearby. "Faith, can we review tomorrow's baking list? You didn't agree. Did you hear? What's going on out there?"

She turned to face Ryan. "Admiring the scenery."

"I bet." His black brows met in the middle.

"What'd you have in mind?" She forced her eyes to meet

Ryan's. He went on about a new recipe as Faith half-listened. Someone outside was far more entertaining.

CHAPTER TWENTY-TWO

*C*aleb glanced through the window, checking on Faith. He half-listened to his customers' rafting stories as worry for her took precedence. *What can I do to help?* He excused himself from the crowd and made an appointment for the next day with the local banker, Mr. Knapp. As he drove to pick up Jack from school he ran over the figures for his businesses. It'd be tight. He'd have to quit his master's program and tighten his finances for a long time. Heading home, he and Jack sang to the tunes from his son's playlist. Glancing at the empty seat beside him created a tug of longing for Faith. Prepping for tomorrow, while Jack ate a light snack, his stomach lurched. The coffee shop was taking a downturn from a few months prior. If he couldn't get it to turn around, tomorrow's bank appointment would be for nothing. He held his head in his hands and prayed —for the coffee shop business and a good outcome from the bank.

"Daddy, me ready." Jack held Faith's birthday present in his hands. "Fay can read it to me."

Putting a hand on his son's shoulder, he replied, "I bet she'll love it." Caleb glanced at his grungy clothes and he sprinted

STACY T. SIMMONS

from the seat. "I'm gonna get ready. Let's put on the reading show you like."

Jack ran to the sofa as Ranger barked beside him.

"Shh, Wanger."

Ranger obeyed.

Skitter-beats pounded in his chest when Faith came to the car. Her hair curled on her shoulders, and the pink dress showed enough leg to catch his attention.

He alighted from the car. "You look beautiful."

"Thanks." She twirled a finger in her sunset-bathed hair.

His mouth dried. Pointing to his car, Caleb reached in and unbuckled Jack.

"Fay, I brought the book."

"You did. Do you want to go read it?"

"Sure."

Walking into the house, Caleb was touched by two of them entering the home together.

Jack turned and waved. "Hurry, Daddy."

Stepping faster, he followed in their wake, his nose catching the light sweet scent that trailed behind her. *Feminine and subtle. Like her.*

Dinner finished, Caleb and Faith took clean-up duty. He glanced out of the kitchen window and noticed Jack playing with Ranger out in the yard while Taylor and Jarod watched nearby.

Switching his gaze from the yard to her across the room, he remarked, "We didn't talk about the bank meeting today."

"No. It's not something I want to think about."

He saw her shoulders sag. The hairs on the back of his neck stood soldier straight. Her tone echoed hopelessness. Caleb's heart plunged. "I'm going to the bank tomorrow."

"For your business?"

134

"No. Yours."

He could feel the fire from her flaring look.

"I'm asking my parents. Tonight."

Walking next to her, his voice softened. "Let me see."

"Why?"

Silk waves wove through his fingers. He blurted, "I want to help you."

Pulling away, she put a hand on her hip. "I didn't ask for it."

No, but I want to do it. "I know."

"That kind of money would come with an obligation."

"What do you mean?" Jarring notes sounded in his head.

"You'd still be my boss."

"Business partner." Pulse pounding, he released a slow breath. "Big difference."

"I wanted to do this on my own. I'll see what my parents say."

"I'm going tomorrow."

"Wait."

"I'll be the back-up plan." *Not the most romantic thing.*

"What are we?"

"We?" A trickle of sweat tracked along his neck.

Faith pointed to him. "You. And me."

Say it. "Aren't we in l—"

His sweaty son entered and interjected. "Tired, Daddy." Jack's eyes barely stayed open.

Flicking a quick glance to his phone, he noted the hour creeping towards Jack's bedtime. He cast an apologetic glance to Faith. "We'll go. Bye, Faith. Jack, let's say goodbye to Tay and Jarod." Stepping outside, they thanked their friends. Swinging back through the kitchen, he waved to Faith and wished he could admit what was burning in his heart and mind, as his son came before his own needs. Family first.

CHAPTER TWENTY-THREE

*C*ontrolling her breath, she returned to cleaning the last pan. *What was he going to say? It began with an . . . L. Does he love me?* Bubbles popped in her face, and the splat of water met her ears. Turning the water off, she leaned into the counter. *Is that why he offered to help? I know I bake well, but money of that magnitude? It's coming from a place far more precious than his bank account.* Hugging the dish towel close to her body, she gave in to the happiness floating like the iridescent soapsuds popping around her.

"Faith?"

"Huh?"

Her friend motioned to her shirt. "You're wet. Hand me the towel."

Faith complied. "I look like Caleb did earlier."

"Okay."

"He came into the coffee shop dripping wet. And his shirt was…" her voice trailed.

"Faithful, don't tell me. You've fallen for him."

Wipe any evidence from your expression. "No." *I'm hanging onto the cliff and ready to dive headfirst, though.*

"Has he shared with you about Avery?"

"No."

"I don't want you hurt."

"He's too nice."

Taylor's brows quirked. "Be cautious."

Is that why he wants to go into business with me? Doesn't add up.

"Yes, Mom. Speaking of her, I need to call them."

"You've got this, it's going to be good." Her friend gave her a quick hug and left the room.

She went upstairs and sat on the edge of the bed, heart in her throat as the phone rang. Faith's dad's deep voice brought instant comfort but also shook her newfound determination.

"It's ten-thirty. Are you okay?" her dad asked.

"Everything's fine."

"Can we talk tomorrow?"

"I'm thinking of opening a bakery," she blurted.

"In Tampa?"

"No. Briar Creek."

"Let me get your mom."

"What's wrong? We were going to head to bed." Her mom's scissor-sharp voice showed irritation.

Faith gave her the news.

"Why didn't you tell us the last time we spoke?" Cat, the lawyer-lioness, threatened to appear. "Is this the job you were speaking about?"

Faith pulled the phone away from her ear. "No."

"Why there? What made you want to do this? How can you afford it?"

"You and Dad have always known I wanted to own a bakery. Tampa already has dozens."

"I'm not convinced this is the best idea. You need to think this through. Hold on, your dad's motioning to speak with you."

Dad's voice came over the earpiece. "Make sure this is the right decision."

"It is."

"I'm of the same mindset as your mom."

"That's a relief."

"What happened?"

Faith gulped and caught a quick breath. "I had a meeting with the bank. It was awful."

"As in?"

"My money from my leftover college fund? It's not enough. The man said it would—"

He hurriedly broke in. "You should have asked for our advice instead of rushing into this."

Shrinking into the bed she uttered, "I realize that." Stomach in knots, she put a hand to her midsection. "Are you two willing to help?"

"How much?"

Faith gave him the number.

She heard the hiss of air in her earpiece. Her midsection ached.

"We're putting a lot of money into the house." Her mom's voice rose. "So, unless we were business partners and held you accountable for every dollar and cent...." Her dad's deep laugh barked in her ear. "I know you well enough to realize that this wouldn't fly."

Rubbing her forehead, she sighed. "Touché."

"You have a job."

"Yes."

"Regroup. I'd love to have helped. Your mom and I will be praying. Keep us posted.

"Thanks."

The call disconnected.

How was she going to do this? She typed a list on the phone. Each grasping, desperate, idea more preposterous than the next. Though she had enough money to keep herself afloat with the manager's job for some time, it was miles away from opening a business. Pride, ugly as it was, had blinded her to the truth. She needed her heavenly Father's *and* Caleb's help. Admitting it to him tomorrow was infinitely harder than asking her parents for money. Glancing at her phone, she considered calling him. Tears burned her eyes, and she forcibly kept it from trickling down her face. Both the tears and her phone would stay put. She'd handle her talk with Caleb tomorrow.

CHAPTER TWENTY-FOUR

*W*alking from the building with the papers in his hand, Caleb climbed in his car and drove to downtown Briar Creek and parked in front of the old building. Getting closer to the dirt-scarred windows, he could see the sturdy building in its prime. Lizzie's bakery was always filled with townspeople. He remembered bringing baby Jack to Lizzie's and getting a brownie to take home for himself and Avery. He pulled on the taut dress-shirt collar and loosened the tie. Was this a smart idea? Did it come from his heart or his mind? *I'm giving up another dream of mine—an MBA— to grant Faith hers.* He uttered a sharp word, climbed back into his car, and drove to the coffee shop to give her the news.

Plucking a yellow rose from the bush near the entrance of the shop, a thorn pierced his skin. Darting the injured finger to his mouth without thinking, he tasted the salty remnant perched on the tip. Stomach rippling in revulsion, he entered.

"Your face." Faith came toward him. "Don't tell me. Plan-B fell through."

"No, nothing like that. I've got to get a band aid."

"I'll get a band-aid. What happened?"

"I got it from this." Feeling like a besotted teenager, he produced the flower.

Taking it from his hand, she put her face near the blossom. "I love it." She must have remembered the band aid as she scooted quickly to the back and returned soon after. "It's perfect."

Peeling the layer of paper, she wrapped the band aid around his finger.

His minute wound ceased aching as he sorted the word blob stuck on the tip of his tongue.

"Before I start, are your parents helping with your business?"

He saw a petal escape the bud in her hands.

"They've sunk all the money they can spare into their home remodel." Her bottom lip reddened as she bit her lower lip.

"Oh."

Silence filled the air.

"Let's sit in the corner." Caleb walked toward the table.

Faith gestured to the coffee bar. "Work."

"It's not busy. Ryan's got it."

A look of expectation, or maybe caution, crossed her face. Caleb couldn't fully read her feelings as he sat adjacent to Faith. "Mr. Knapp assured me that we could purchase the place together. There's not much left for renovations, though."

Faith's smile lit his heart. "For real?"

"Yeah. I sweet-talked Mrs. Danton into letting me borrow the keys, and I checked it out before my meeting. Looks pretty good. But I want to see what you think it needs to get it into shape. After work."

"I like that idea. Later, we'll have to hire a lawyer to draw up the paperwork." Faith flew from the seat. "Lists need to be made of what to order. Caleb, do you know what this means to me?"

Dimples framed his smile. "I've got an idea."

"Are you bringing Jack to see the place? He can be a sous-chef whenever he wants."

"Tonight, it's you and me. Dylan's in town for spring break, so he's watching Jack."

"I can't wait."

His eyes shot to the lengthening line.

Faith rose from the chair. "Neither will the customers. Later."

"At six."

"I'll be there."

For the first time in many days, hours, minutes, he felt connected. He had a business partner. Someone he trusted and cared about. Tonight he'd show her how much.

CHAPTER TWENTY-FIVE

*P*ulling into the space next to Caleb, Faith pulled in a calming breath of air. In front of Faith was her future... with Caleb. Pushing the door open, a bell alerted her arrival. Scanning the front, she noticed that Caleb wasn't around.

"Hello?"

"In back."

Her heels struck the aged wooden floor, and she smoothed her coral dress as she walked. Pulse tickling her throat, she rounded the corner. Caleb had changed, too. He wore a sport-tailored inky-blue dress shirt, which complimented his tan, and a pair of dress pants. She held in her breath, taking everything in, head to toe. *He looks so handsome.*

"You're gorgeous."

"So are you." Faith giggled.

As he walked closer to her, she noticed his hair's dampness and that the earlier stubble was gone. Her hand immediately went to his cheek.

"You shaved."

"I thought the occasion called for it."

"I like it."

"Better than my usual every-other-day shave?"

"Equally."

Caleb seemed to stand taller with her compliment.

"Tell me what changes you see for this kitchen."

Faith pulled out her phone and began to read from a list she'd made Saturday. After ten minutes of non-stop talking, Caleb ran a finger down her arm.

Fine hairs on her arm electrified. Sparks ignited. Glancing at him, she saw his eyes had darkened.

"I know I talk a lot. I'm excited."

"We'll do as much as we can to get this running. The other will come later." Caleb leaned in. "Let's seal our deal."

"I don't see a contract."

Inches from her he whispered, "Not that kind."

Faith's mouth rounded. "Oh."

Caleb's breath was warm on her lips. A rapid pulse pressured in her veins. She waited. Seconds seemed like hours as they stood close enough for Faith to see the flecks of yellow dotting his sea green eyes. His warmth surrounded her chilled body. Their lips came together in a rush, her hands played with the muscular lines on his strong back, and she felt his fingers go through her hair. Realizing what was happening, she stepped back. Looking at him, she saw he was breathing heavier and his lips bore a stain of peach lipstick she wore.

Caleb took her hands. "Faith, the love I had for you years ago doesn't compare to what I feel now."

Warmth suffused her. "Love?"

One quick kiss later, he answered. "Love. I want to see where we go. In business and in life." He shrugged and smiled. "It's fast, I know, but I couldn't wait to tell you once I figured it out myself."

"The time's right." Gathering her nerve, she continued. "Something's bloomed inside me, from a place that's been barren. And I love you more than I have words to say." He folded her in his arms. She felt at peace, secure, cherished.

"You'll have to see the other side of my outfitters and go kayaking with me. It's like falling in love. That rush is kind of what I'm feeling for you." He held her at arm's length, and Faith felt his focus on her. "Even though I've never seen you in a boat, I don't think you're scared of them, are you?"

A metal tang permeated her mouth. Her hands shook in his. "What's wrong?"

Through shuddering breaths, she confessed. "I haven't been completely honest with you. We might be a while." Swiveling a glance around, she said, "There's no place to sit."

Dusting off the island, he gently placed her atop and joined her there. Taking her hand again, he gave it a fast squeeze.

Taking a deep breath, she put her other hand on Caleb's arm. "You're wrong. I'm terrified of them and I do anything and everything to not be near boats. Well, I . . ." Faith swallowed, and her gaze drifted to the ground.

Faith relaxed in Caleb's strength as he put an arm around her.

"I haven't been on a boat since I was fourteen. My grandfather and I were on a fishing trip on the bay. He'd baited my hook, and I heard a splash. When I looked over at him, Grandpa had slunk over the side of the boat and one side of his face was in the murky water. I pulled and pulled until I got him back into the boat and put my jacket under his face. I used my cell phone to call 911." War drums beat in her chest, her mouth cottoned. "The marine paramedics came, but he didn't make it. He'd had a severe stroke. I've been petrified of boats ever since."

Caleb's arms wrapped around her and he murmured, "I'm so sorry." He pulled away. "Aagh, I talked about kayaking. I won't ask again. Forgive me?"

She gently pushed away, and her heart squeezed when she saw the moisture in his beautiful green eyes. Faith stiffened her

spine. Her voice was stronger now. "You couldn't have known."
He raised his head as she pointed a finger to his heart. "Caleb,
you love the water, and I love it, too. In a different way, like the
beach or in a pool. It doesn't mean I'm not willing to try. I trust
you."

"We'll go on a paddleboat. Start off on something calmer.
Jack would like it, too."

"I know where we can go. Price Lake. Would that be okay?"
She noticed his color fade to a bleached white, and he glanced
away.

"That was the place where I proposed to Avery."

Faith gasped. Her chest tightened as she tried to gather her
thoughts which scattered like dandelion seeds. "Oh, Caleb, I
didn't realize. I'm sorry." Her gaze remained on his face, and she
touched his arm.

Caleb cleared his throat. "She . . ." He cleared his throat
again, his voice sounding heavy and thick to Faith. "A drunk
driver hit her car as she was coming home from the hospital.
She was a nurse there. We'd been married five years."

He met her less than a year after he moved here. "I can't imagine
what you went through." She ran her hand down his arm and
put it on top of his hand, squeezing. He picked it up and kissed
her fingers.

"Jack barely remembers her. He was almost one when she
passed. "It's weird to be in love, to be honest." I wasn't sure if I
could feel." Touching his forehead with hers, a grin shadowed
his face. "I'm happy it's you." Soft kisses followed.

"So am I."

He put her down on the ground, and they finished their
inspection holding hands and giggling.

To Faith it felt natural, like the seven years between then and
now vanished. Where only now and being together mattered.

"We'll have to find a lawyer to draw up the papers." Caleb
kissed her fingers. "And Mrs. Danton needs an answer."

"Mine's yes." Sparkles lit Faith as she surveyed her new bakery.

"Then it's ours."

Falling into each other's arms they laughed, kissed, and finished the last part of their dance. It felt like nothing could wreck their happiness.

CHAPTER TWENTY-SIX

A week later she put her copies of the business documents to the side and commenced with the plan to surprise her friends with a celebratory dinner. She gathered the spices for the chicken marinade and swiped her phone's main screen to click on her music app. She paused, looking at the photo of her and Caleb in the soon-to-be bakery on their special night. Laughing, she turned on the music and began to sing along to a popular Christian song. The music stopped mid-chorus as her phone vibrated on the island. Faith pulled at the towel on her shoulder—chef style—wiped her hands and answered.

"Miss Fuller, this is Pete Carruthers. I was inspecting the building today. I found something I think you're going to want to hear about. I tried to call Mr. Gaines but couldn't reach him."

Her throat closed, and dread settled like a fiery pit in her stomach.

Faith sunk into a chair, pushing the words from depths she wasn't sure she'd possessed. "Go on."

He cleared his throat. "The building needs a new foundation. It's shifted and is entirely unstable. My guess is it will be almost as much as the cost of the building to repair it. Maybe more."

"It's that badly damaged? It looks great from what I saw."

"Unfortunately, you can't see foundation issues unless you know what you're looking for. I'll email you my estimate of repairs in a few days. Let me know what you two want to do. I'm sorry for the bad news."

"Okay, once we look it over. We'll do that."

At the end of the call, Faith scanned his message. Mr. Carruthers' numbers glared in bold, dark soldier's lines. Sadness flowed in wandering trails from her eyes, but not one to crumble at bad news, she wiped her eyes with her shirt sleeve, leaving a dark stripe of mascara on the yellow blouse. She ignored it. Faith exhaled and sat straighter in the chair, then started to text Caleb but decided that telling him in person would be better. Before she could head out to find him, she heard someone coming in the door.

"I'm home. Where are you, Faith?"

She mumbled, "Here."

Taylor dropped to her knees beside the chair. "What's going on? Faithful, tell me," she crooned.

Faith gave her friend a tenuous smile and blew out a puff of air. She spoke haltingly. "I got a phone call... Mr. Carruthers... the building inspector and contractor said . . . the foundation..."

"What did he say?" Taylor continued rubbing and patting Faith's back.

"It's irreparable. There won't be any bakery." She threw her hands in the air then glanced at Taylor. Her need for sympathy outweighed an ardent distaste for melodrama.

Taylor touched Faith's hand as it rested on the arm of the chair. "Oh, hon. I'm so sorry. Jarod and I will be praying." She patted Faith's hand. "Let's talk it over while I fix dinner."

Faith forced a smile onto her bone-dry lips. "I started it before the call." She ducked her head.

"Help me finish. You're a better cook than me, and the baby's hungry."

"Twist my arm." She attempted to smile with her joking words, but it wasn't quite there.

Dinner that night was quiet. Faith wasn't in the mood to talk nor were her sympathetic friends.

Abruptly Sugar yipped at the sound of the doorbell and startled Faith. Faith jumped from her chair to answer the door, grateful for the interruption. Opening the door, all oxygen deserted her. Caleb held a gorgeous bouquet of pink peonies, peach-kissed tulips, baby blue hydrangeas and white tulips. He handed her the vase. The heady aroma wrapped around her. She stood on tiptoes to give him a quick peck on the cheek. At the last moment, he turned his head and her lips landed on his soft mouth. Flustered, she bent over and sniffed the lacey peonies in the bouquet. "Mmm, they smell like the orange trees that were in my grandparent's yard. They're gorgeous. Thank you."

Caleb's hand slid down her arm, and his breath tickled her ear. "Not as gorgeous as you."

Warmth suffused her body, tinging her cheeks. Faith's eyes softened as she glanced at him. "Charmer."

"Only to you."

Her gaze fell on the dimples that framed Caleb's full, kissable lips. His finger pulled gently on a curl near her face. *Say something.* "Where's Jack?"

"Mrs. Settles is watching him. He's got the summer sniffles; must be something in the July air. I wanted to drop these off to my new business partner."

She fixed a smile to her face. "Let's go show off these beauties to Tay and Jar." Faith took his hand as they entered the family room. "Tay look at this."

"I think they're beautiful. Jar and I will put them in your room for you." Taylor pulled Jarod out of the room.

"Can you sit for a minute?" She motioned to the chair next to her. Caleb sat and folded one tall leg over the other.

"You feeling okay? You got quiet. Did you get Jack's cold?"

It would be simpler than what I'm going to say. "Remember Mr. Carruthers?"

"Mmhmm. What's going on?"

"Did you get a voicemail message?"

"Why?"

Balling a fist in her lap, she forced out the words. "It needs a new foundation which is too expensive to repair."

Softly speaking, Caleb asked, "How much?"

Finding the page on her phone, she turned it toward him.

Caleb seemed to crumble into the sofa cushions.

"Half of the building's cost." He groaned, then exhaled. "How are you doing?"

"Wrecked."

A lone tear trailed down her face and Caleb wiped it away with the pad of a finger.

"We can find a new place."

CHAPTER TWENTY-SEVEN

"*I*n Briar Creek?" Sourness threatened her next words. "Where? I haven't seen another empty building."

"Mine."

Leaning in closer, she questioned, "What?"

"Hawk's Creek Coffee."

Her mind stilled. A gasp seeped from her mouth before she uttered, "I know how much that place means to you." Faith sifted rubber fingers through her curls and thought aloud. "The kitchen is perfect for the coffee shop. For a bakery though?"

Caleb lightly touched her shoulders. "There's space behind the shop. We can add on."

As she glanced out of the window, she noticed the skies were threaded with orange-yellow rays of light. Their radiating fingers of heat seemed to fill Faith. "It might work. Do we have the money?"

"We had it to rebuild a bakery."

"True." Faith brushed a kiss across his cheek. "You're incredible."

"No, in love."

Faith peeked around Caleb's back.

"What're you doing?"

"I wasn't sure if you were wearing a cape."

Deep laughter rumbled.

"Hardly, Belle."

Caleb held up his phone. "Mrs. Settles." He moved to a spot by the doorway and spoke in hushed tones. A short time later he walked toward Faith.

"Everything okay?"

"It's good. Mrs. Settles needs to get home, it's close to her bedtime."

Brushing a kiss across his knuckles, she smiled. "Take some food home with you, that way you don't have to cook tomorrow night."

"Is my cooking that horrible?"

Faith tugged on his hand. "Come help." Spooling shiny foil over several plates, Faith stood back and surveyed what else she could add to the pile. "Bran muffins with chia seeds."

She felt a tickle on her ribcage.

"Wait, chia seeds?"

Faith lifted a shoulder. "Who knew they tasted like poppy seeds?"

"I did."

Giggling as he nuzzled her neck, her knees felt weak. She reached out a hand to hold onto the counter and accidentally put it into the bowl of mashed sweet potatoes. Faith squirmed.

"What's wrong?"

Raising her hand, an orange blob dripped to the floor. Sugar scrabbled to the spot and slurped up the remains. Faith washed her hand in the sink as Caleb wrapped his arms around her.

"Maybe I should leave." Taylor backed out of the kitchen.

"I'm going." Caleb gave Faith a kiss on the cheek. "Walk me out?"

Standing next to his car, Faith played with the collar on his shirt. With each touch, his unique scent of vanilla and an exotic spice was released, making her forget what she'd wanted to say.

Caleb slapped his arm.

"Bugs are out. I don't want you getting bitten."

Weed-eater noises buzzed near her ear and she jerked away. "See you tomorrow?"

"First thing."

One quick kiss. Leaning in, he met her halfway, and more than a few moments later, he pulled out of the driveway. Faith waved and her stomach sank to her toes. *I miss him.* Dipping her head down, she caught the scent of Caleb that clung to her shirt like an invisible hug. Phone vibrating in rhythm to her rampaging heart, she clicked on the message.

Caleb texted, *I love you.* She quickly texted back and hugged the phone to her heart. Faith peered into the phone screen. *My mom. Wonder what she needs?* Finding a quiet place to sit, she answered.

"Hi, Mom. Are y'all okay?"

"Fine, how are you?"

Ever-formal Mom. "Well, thank you."

"How did the inspection go? Wasn't it today?"

She remembered. "It was terrible."

"In what way?"

"The foundation is shot, and will cost way more than I have, or Caleb has, to repair."

"Caleb?"

"My boss."

"He's backing you?"

"Mmhmm." Faith played with the frilly leaves of one of Caleb's flowers. "We're going out."

"This is news. His name's familiar, how long have you known each other?"

"We dated in New York, so a while."

"Now he's in Briar Creek?"

"Yes."

"I see. Your dad and I had a discussion, and we've agreed we can give you a small loan to help start your business."

Faith blurted. "Hands off?"

"Yes, no interference. Surprised you, didn't I?"

More than you'll ever know. "I'm happy."

"I'll have the bank wire the money to your local account."

Didn't set it up yet. Slipped my mind. "Wait, please, a couple of days. I'll let you know the bank account then. Thank you, Mom."

"Your dad and I don't say it as much as we should. We're proud of you. You are seizing an opportunity you've wanted since you were young. Love you."

"Love you. And thanks."

Disconnecting, she texted Caleb, and for the next hour they spoke about their thoughts for the business, which made Faith's heart happy. Head bobbing near the end of their texting, Faith bowed out from the conversation. Heavy-lidded eyes were the last thing she remembered as she drifted off.

Jitters riddled her body as she approached the bank door. She pulled open the smoked-glass barrier and stepped inside. A smiling face greeted her at the kiosk, and before she could say no, she was seated in front of the man who'd rejected her, Mr. Knapp.

"Back again, Ms. Fuller?"

"I wanted to open an account."

"Very good." He peered over his hard frame glasses. "Are you and Mr. Gaines—Caleb— going forward with the business? I can get your papers ready."

Cheeky. "Not yet. We'll let you know." She noticed his pithy smile took on a more pinched look.

"We're here to help you when you're ready. Let's start with the banking information."

Faith recited her New York account as his fingers bounced over his keyboard.

"Excuse me." Swiveling, he muttered into his phone. Glancing up, he motioned to the door. "Come in, Lauren."

Couldn't be. A swish sounded in the office as the person entered. Pushing her head higher, Faith met Lauren's eyes. Caleb's former sister-in-law. Quashing a mewl of protest, she pressed a social smile onto her face.

"Lauren, meet Faith Fuller."

Lauren leaned on the desk and lowered her eyes. "We met. Recently."

One bushy brow raised. "Oh, excellent. Can you take over? I need to head across town for a meeting."

"Of course." Lauren folded herself into the chair and threw a glance at Faith. "How are you, Ms. Fuller?"

Willing herself to remain still, Faith managed to verbalize, "Well, and you, Mrs…" Unable to recall her last name she stayed quiet.

"It's Wilcox." Adjusting her seat away from Faith, Lauren began to enter information into the system. "Getting cozy with my brother-in-law?"

Faith scooted toward the edge of her seat. "Ask him."

Lauren's eyes rounded. "I will." Lauren rose and gave Faith a print-out. "Mr. Knapp will be glad to help you with anything else you might need in the future."

Subtle. "I'll remember that." Walking away as fast as she could, Faith had a hard time shaking the cold reception from Cruella de Vil's doppelganger.

Driving to Taylor and Jarod's the long way, she passed by Caleb's house. Out of nowhere a black and white ball ponged across the street in front of her car. She pressed on the brakes, eyeing the yard to make sure Jack didn't dart out. Faith pulled to the curb and cut the motor. As she opened the door, it bounced back toward the car. A spotted ball caught her attention on the curb next to her car.

"Lose this?"

Holding Ranger's leash in one hand, Jack waved. "Fay, mine."

She rolled the ball to him, and he kicked it across the yard and ran to catch it.

Caleb lowered his sunglasses as he came closer. "You look beautiful."

"You're sweet. "Eyeing her pedestrian outfit of jeans and a back of the closet blouse, she rolled her eyes. *I didn't know I'd see him today.* Through her dark sunglasses, she viewed his strong legs and arms, showcased in athletic shorts and a ratty old t-shirt. *Even wearing that, he's hot.* She put a finger on the middle of his shirt as a smile sliced her face. "I like your dino tee."

Pulling it away from his chest, he grinned. "It's pre-historic."

Faith curled up a corner of her mouth. "No more dad jokes."

"Promise."

Faith flicked a glance at his tan arms and couldn't resist putting a hand on one and giving his muscles a quick squeeze. "Do I get a reward for saving the ball?"

"This."

Their lips met in a furtive, stolen kiss. Faith felt like she'd reached the end of her favorite book. It left her yearning for more. Staring into his eyes and seeing the schoolboy-like smile skim his face, she thought he might feel the same.

CHAPTER TWENTY-EIGHT

*L*egs less than solid, Caleb met Faith in the bank lobby. A trail of perspiration cooled his legs beneath his dress pants. Licking his lips and tapping a foot, he scanned the bank for Lauren. *She's not here.*

"Nervous?"

He felt the heat from her palm on his arm and saw the quiver of her mouth in her smile. *Be strong.* Taking her hand, he laced his fingers through hers, and waited as his rampant heartbeat slowed. Seeking to comfort her, he ran a finger over the back of her hand. "I'm nervous, too."

Faith leaned into him, and her pink-kissed lips formed a smile.

"You're okay with my parents giving money toward the renovation?"

"Does it mean we'll get that contraption where it speeds up the cooling process?" *Real romantic, Gaines.*

As her brow wrinkled, Caleb had a catch in his midsection. *Even her brows are cute. I'm hopeless.*

"Yes, it's called a blast chiller. I don't even want to show you the price tag on that equipment."

"Thank you. I feel like this is what my dad calls a 'Yes, dear' moment. When my mom says something and his face turns red."

Planting a quick kiss on his cheek, Faith laughed.

"Glad you're both in good moods." Mr. Knapp smiled and motioned for them to come into his office.

An hour later, they exited his office. With a satisfied noise, Caleb took Faith's hand, and they walked right past Lauren. *Don't look, maybe she'll not see.*

"Hi, Caleb."

Too late.

Willing his eyes to meet hers, he forced a smile across his face. "Lauren, didn't see you earlier."

"Off my lunch break. What're you both doing here?"

"Faith and I were signing papers."

"Oh, for what?"

"Caleb and I are going into business together."

He heard the sharp breath Lauren inhaled. Momentary schoolboy guilt swarmed down the length of him.

"Congratulations."

"Thanks, we're happy."

Lauren's brown eyes narrowed.

Caleb gulped.

"I'll have to find out more about this. Can I come by your house after Jack is asleep tonight? Me and Tanner?"

Reinforcements.

"Fine by me. About eight, then."

Lauren pushed the door harder than necessary, it sprung back toward them, and Caleb muscled it to keep it open for Faith to exit.

"Do you need me to be there?"

"No need, thanks. I can handle it." He twirled a piece of her irresistible hair around his finger. "Tanner knew about it. He didn't want to have to deal with his wife's temper." Twirling stopped, he opened the car door for Faith and brushed a kiss over her soft cheek. "Let's talk about something else. How will we celebrate?"

"Before or after my move?"

"After. The move's in a week."

"Okay. What are we doing?"

"I want to surprise you."

"It's not kayaking?"

"No water until you say so." Caleb went to his side of the car and sat down.

Peace settled in Faith. She reached over and ran a hand down his arm and played with the sprinkling of dark hair on his arm until he pulled away.

"Ticklish."

"I'll stay on my side."

"Too lonely over here."

When he took her hand, Faith wished that she could crawl over the seat to snuggle with him. Within the angles and planes of his sportscar, the air became humid. Faith pulled the air vent toward her.

"Hot?"

"Mmhmm."

After ten minutes of winter frost, Faith had enough. Shivering, she flicked the dual thermostat on her side down to low.

"Didn't take long."

Pinpoints emerged on her skin where his hand trailed down her arm. Clusters of heat melted chilled places wherever his fingers touched.

Honk!

She smothered a giggle as Caleb sped through the intersection and openly admired a flush of color on his sun-tanned face.

Depositing her at the door a few minutes after, Faith blew him a kiss as he pulled from the driveway.

Stepping over Sugar as her tail whooshed on the tile floor,

Faith stared at her moving list on her screen and began with number one: double check with the movers in New York. Praying for patience, she pressed the number on the screen. Her moving adventure would soon begin.

CHAPTER TWENTY-NINE

$\mathcal{F}$aith clicked through the last page to e-sign her home rental documents. Calmness settled deep within as she left Mrs. Danton's real estate office. She checked her phone before starting the car and saw a text from Caleb.

Come to Hawk's Creek.

Confused by his message, she called. "Work?"

Caleb let out a rumbling laugh. "No. Hurry."

"Be there soon." In a few short moments, her car swerved into the parking lot of Hawk Creek Outfitters. Faith's heart swelled as her jaw dropped when she looked up to the deck. A "Welcome Home" banner was doing a jaunty little flap in the breeze, and a crowd was milling on the deck. Excitement percolated within, and Faith couldn't wait to join the party.

Caleb spotted her below and dashed to the car. She climbed out of the car laughing. "Surprise." His whispered breath tickled her ear. He lightly put his hand on her back as she climbed the stairs.

Though exhausted from all the changes the last few days, Faith's adrenaline kicked in as she made her way around the deck to greet her friends, tiredness forgotten. Her stomach rumbled, fully approving of the table filled with platters of food. Nearby, another table held a stunning chocolate cake painted with artistic swirls of white chocolate. Her mouth watered.

Ryan came over and gave her a one-armed hug. "Congrats. Hope you like the cake I created."

Faith raised her eyebrows. "It's gorgeous, thanks. I'm happy you'll be joining me at the bakery."

"Thanks. We could feature it in the bakery if you want."

"Definitely."

Caleb whisked a kiss across her cheek. "Back in a bit. I want to say hello to someone."

She conversed with Ryan for a few more minutes until he excused himself. Faith wasn't alone long as a familiar arm came around her shoulders.

Taylor gave her a kiss on the cheek and held onto her growing bump. "We're so happy for you. Having fun?" Faith nodded. "Jarod's bringing one last surprise. It should arrive any moment." Taylor moved away and pulled a camera out of its bag.

"What did you two do?"

"Look over there." She pointed in the direction of the parking lot. Faith noticed Jarod's truck pulling into a spot. He jumped out of his truck and held the door open for someone. Several other persons alighted from the truck, and the group hurried to see her. Faith's eyes widened, as her whole family stood before her. Their sweet presence was the icing to this wonderful party. She cut a smile to Taylor and Jarod who stood behind them, grinning.

Her mom smoothed a fly away from Faith's face. "Hi. Surprised?"

Faith kissed her mom's cheek. "Shocked."

Her dad grinned and gave her a peck. "Congratulations." They chatted for a bit and eventually Caleb walked up with two plates in his hands.

Faith introduced Caleb to her parents.

"Good to see meet you, Mr. and Mrs. Fuller." He tipped his head toward Faith's sisters. "Hope and Grace." Her sisters gave him the once-over, and by their delighted looks, liked what they saw. Hope and Grace left after the small talk turned to business.

After a few minutes, her dad glanced back to the plates Caleb still held. "We'll talk later. Go eat. Cat, let's get some cake, it looks too good to miss." He took his wife's hand and headed toward the dessert table.

Caleb and Faith found two unoccupied chairs near the river. He handed her the man-portion plate he'd been so thoughtful to make for her.

Faith took the plate from Caleb. "You got a bit of everything at the table."

"I did. I thought you'd be starving."

"I am." Faith swiveled in the seat to face him. "I can't believe my family is here. Did you know?"

Caleb nodded. "Taylor spoke with them last week and they moved some things around to be here."

"I'm glad they're here." *Surprised they put work aside for me. Maybe things are changing.* A relaxed smile formed on her lips. Contentment rested inside.

He pointed to the smaller shoreline dock some feet away. "Speaking of family, Dylan and Hope look like they're getting along."

Dylan was showing off his rock-skipping skills to Hope while Grace was enamored with something on her phone's screen.

Faith shielded her eyes with a hand to get a better view. "You're right. They're all alone together on the dock. What will my parents say? I thought I was overprotective of my sisters, sheesh." She brushed a finger over his arm and grinned.

"Me, overprotective? I never get to talk to him when he's

away at UNC; he's so busy with his junior year pre-law courses and socializing."

"Hope's the same way, like a red-headed butterfly flitting around on campus, and just as hard to catch. Unless it's by a cute guy."

"Speaking of a handsome guy."

Jack ran and stood in between Faith and Caleb. He reached over to his dad's plate and took a piece of cheese.

"Son, you ate right before Faith got here."

"Hungwy."

"Sit over here. I'll feed you if your mean old dad won't." Faith scooted over as Jack snuggled next to her.

"Old?"

"Who's old?" Mr. Gaines questioned.

"Daddy is, Gwanpa."

"Not as old as us." Caleb's mom motioned to herself and her husband. "We're pre-historic."

Mouth agape, Faith pointed to Caleb. "It runs in your family."

Caleb winked.

"Help Gigi get some cake. I'll get one for you, too."

Caleb's mom wrapped an arm around her grandson as Jack jumped out of the chair.

"Fanks."

Caleb pulled up two extra chairs for his parents. Returning with full plates, they sandwiched themselves between him and Faith.

Mrs. Gaines swiveled in her chair. "Faith. I didn't get to ask you at Jack's birthday party. How are you liking it here? It must be quite different than living in New York."

"It is. I'm loving it. People are more relaxed in this area, not as hurried as in New York. Plus, it's gorgeous here, and I'm living in the same town as my best friend and her husband. Caleb's been phenomenal . . . he's a great friend, too."

Mr. Gaines' blue eyes lit up. "He's a pretty good guy and smart enough to know who to choose as a business partner. He's told us about your delicious baking. Did you go to culinary school in New York?"

"I did. When I graduated, I went to work for the company where I'd interned."

After a few more minutes of conversation, Mr. Gaines stood up, smiling. "I apologize. We arranged to meet some of our friends for dinner in Asheville. The traffic's going to get worse if we don't get going."

His mom's eyebrows peaked. "We'll have to continue our conversation soon." She gently elbowed her son in the ribs. "You need to bring her to Asheville for dinner."

Caleb glanced skyward. "I will."

Before they left, Mrs. Gaines produced a card from her handbag and handed it to Faith. She noted Caleb's green eyes matched his mother's as did his big, welcoming smile. "We're so happy for you, Faith. I know we'll be seeing you soon." His mom turned to him. "See you later, son." Caleb dipped his chin.

"Thank you. It was so nice to see y'all. I'll look forward to it." She tucked the card into her bag. Caleb and Faith watched as they exited the deck after speaking to Dylan.

"Your parents are sweet." She glanced up at him, grinning before she sat back down.

Caleb dropped into the seat next to her. "She behaved herself today. Usually she's much more inquisitive." Faith giggled and pulled the envelope out of her bag, balancing her plate on her lap. He leaned in closer. Faith pushed her chair nearer to his. "We'll read it together."

On the front was a picture of a pretty cottage with flowers and trees below the words "Welcome home." Her spirit danced. "*Home.*" She kept reading. The inside contained a sweet, hand-written message. A comforting warmth blossomed.

"Please give them my thanks." She tucked it away in her

purse. Looking up and beyond Caleb, she noticed Ryan approaching.

He presented them with two slices of cake. "Let me know what you think."

Faith put down her still-full plate and reached for the dessert. She wet her lips and took a forkful. The heady richness of milk chocolate hit her tongue. She eyed the layers of white chocolate swirls on the cake's side. "Fantastic. Thank you."

Caleb flicked a thumbs-up sign and stated, "I agree."

Jack wriggled next to his dad and dug into the frosting. "Mmm."

Running a finger through her slice's frosting, Faith popped it in her mouth, which merited a deep giggle from Jack.

"Who's this cutie?" Her mom's perennial red lipstick lips moved to a smile.

Caleb put a hand on his son's arm. "This is my son Jack."

Exchanging a look between them, her dad squatted to Jack's level and stuck out a hand. "Nice to meet you."

The same hand which moments before was covered knuckle-deep in frosting reached out to Faith's dad.

Her midsection stiffened and she stopped breathing. Wanting to glance away, yet spring to Jack's rescue, if need be, Faith focused on the unfolding scene.

Not flinching, her dad took Jack's sticky hand in his.

Elation rang in Faith.

"Good grip, young man. Ballplayer, Caleb?"

"Not yet. In the fall he'll be signing up for soccer or basketball."

Turning to his dad, Jack mimicked shooting a hoop with his hands. "Like Dad."

"I used to play back in college."

Cat took her husband's arm. "Let's get the girls, darling. We've had a busy day, and tomorrow will be busier."

Amid a round of hugs, her mom whispered to her, "You

know he could go on forever about his glory days. That little man is precious."

Pulling back from the hug, Faith spied a light shining in her mother's hazel eyes.

"He is."

Tapping her on the shoulder, her mom parted with surprising words, "You never mentioned he was a hunk, Faith."

"Mom, really."

"He is. Might be a good man for you."

Her dad gave her a hug. "Seems like a smart guy."

Faith was shocked. They'd never liked anyone she'd been interested in. None. Ever.

CHAPTER THIRTY

*S*unlight warmed her face, gentle, yet insistent on waking Faith from a rock-hard slumber. Wiping her eyes, she grumbled to herself at the earliness of the hour until the fuzz lifted from her brain. *Moving day, I've gotta hurry!* Faith threw back her covers and changed. She crept downstairs and into the kitchen to make a quick breakfast before her friends awoke.

Faith brewed hair-raising, strong coffee once she heard their footsteps moving around above. Bleary-eyed, both Tay and Jarod slumped into the kitchen, eagerly accepting the mugs she handed them. When someone knocked on the front door, Sugar scurried out of the kitchen barking. Faith waved a hand at Jarod's seat as he stood. "I'll get it." Peering through the glass sidelight, her heart gave a little flutter. Faith whipped open the door to deliver Caleb a small bear hug, careful to not spill her drink on either of them. "Morning." She held up her mug. "There's more of this if you want."

"If Jarod made it, I'll pass. His brew is too bitter."

"I did, and it's stronger than his usual he-man dark coffee."

He wrinkled his nose and patted his stomach. "Thanks, but

no. I value my digestive system. That stuff could probably burn through steel."

"Maybe so, but I'll drink it anyway." She took a sip as they went to the kitchen. Taylor and Jarod greeted him. They quickly finished their breakfast, excusing themselves to get ready. Faith pulled out the leftover party cake from the fridge to offer some to Caleb.

He eyed it with longing. "No, thanks. I already had a Kale and strawberry smoothie. After we finish your move, I might be tempted, though."

Before Faith could reply, the doorbell rang. She stopped cutting the cake and glanced toward the foyer.

"I'll get it." Caleb got up and answered the door.

"Thanks."

As Hope and Grace entered the room, their eyes lit up as she served some of the cake along with big mugs of vanilla mocha.

Hope met her halfway in the kitchen to help. She muttered under her breath, "Grace and I think Caleb is hot."

"Hot?"

"As in, I don't know, like a movie star. Muscles, dimples." Hope hip bumped Faith. "His little brother's not so bad, either."

"What happened to that guy you were dating? Tyler, Nolan?"

"Not anymore." Hope bounced over to their sister and gave her the smaller helping of cake.

Grace's mouth turned up and she looked like a younger version of their mom. Ink black hair, chocolate bar eyes. Both resembled the ever-adorable Audrey Hepburn.

"She's working on her next victim."

Hope slid Grace's cake plate closer to her.

"Mom."

They still act like they're little kids. Always fighting over dessert.

Her mom entered the kitchen along with her dad. "Girls, don't fight." She quickly made some seat adjustments, and her sisters quieted.

"Cake, Dad?"

"Sure."

Faith served a giant wedge to her father until she noticed her mom give her dad a hard stare. He made a shrinking gesture with his finger and thumb. The room erupted in laughter as her mom put her hand over his and made his hand shrink even smaller.

"I'll have the same size piece," said Taylor as she strolled back into the action, followed by her husband.

"Not me, I'll take Mr. Fuller's original size," Jarod bluffed, puffing out his chest and holding his arms as if he were a heavy-weight lifter.

Moments later Dylan sauntered into the room and snagged the mammoth chunk of cake out from under Jarod's nose, settling in at the table next to Hope.

Not to be outdone, Jack sat next to his uncle with a smaller piece of cake and a glass of milk.

Faith enjoyed seeing her sisters talk with Dylan and Jack.

Grace reached out to wipe Jack's mouth with her napkin, which brought a wreath of smiles to both her parents' and Faith's faces.

"Fanks." He took a sip of milk and lowered the glass. Grace wiped his milk mustache away.

She was always the more capable one around kids, more so than Faith. *Maybe it is time for me to learn. I might be a part of his life for some time to come.* The thought brought a smile to her lips.

Caleb reached into a tall moving box and pulled on some accordion-folded packing paper. The jagged box edge trapped the paper and its contents came out of his hands, smacking the tile kitchen floor. Faith ran into the room. "What happened?"

He held up the tattered ribbon of paper, and his eye trailed to the mosaic-pattern of china scattered on the beige floor. "I'm sorry, it stuck to the box. I'll buy you a new one."

She let out a whoosh of air. It was the ugliest platter she'd owned, a hideous yellow and green vine pattern. She'd bought it at an antique store for a '70's church party the previous year and kept it tucked away in a back corner of a cabinet. Faith clenched her teeth to keep from laughing.

"It was an accident." Caleb tried to sweep up the shards with his hands. "I bet it's a family treasure."

Faith touched his shoulder. "It's replaceable. Nothing a trip to an antique store together wouldn't solve."

His Adam's apple bobbed. "We'll go. I've never been antiquing; it might be fun."

Her dad passed by them carrying a box. "You could say that."

"Dad."

He laughed and left the room.

Faith held out her hand, and Caleb took it in his free hand. "It'll be an adventure."

"I'm sure it will." He grinned and brushed her knuckles with his thumb.

Dylan, Jack, and her family came into the family room.

"Anyone hungry?"

Her dad said, "We're pooped and we have an early flight tomorrow. Raincheck?"

"For Thanksgiving or Christmas?"

"Christmas, if you want us here?" her mom asked.

"I do." Faith hugged her mom and then the rest of her family before they headed outside.

"I'm bailing. See you." Dylan walked outside with Faith's family. "Jack, wanna go with me?"

Big brown eyes focused in Caleb's direction.

"There's half a chicken in the fridge, if you want to take it with you."

"Got it."

Faith got the remainder of the cake from the fridge.

"Can they have this?"

"Why not? Small piece, Dyl."

Waving, he and Jack left.

"Pizza?"

Caleb raised his eyebrows and nodded. "In a bit? I've got to rest my tired feet."

"I feel like dipping my feet in the cold creek. It might do us both good. I'll get some water bottles and meet you out back."

Faith disappeared into the house and returned with two cold, sweating bottles of water. Sitting down she peeled off her socks and tennis shoes and stuck her feet in the icy cold water. Their persistent pounding and throbbing ceased. She handed Caleb a bottle.

"Thanks." In less than a minute, he, too, had his feet in the water, gently kicking them around. "Ahh." Caleb shifted his position to kiss her hair. "You're smart."

She raised her shoulders to her ears and winced, rubbing a sore spot on her right shoulder. "Desperate. My feet were killing me."

"Do you need a back rub?"

Her stomach fluttered, but she nodded. Her guitar-string muscles loosened under his strong hands. She sighed and relaxed into him, not caring that his shirt was grimy. After a few minutes of his relaxing ministrations, she knelt behind him and kneaded his shoulders. Faith admired his strong, chiseled muscles underneath his thin cotton t-shirt. *All that rowing.* Faith probed her fingers around to find a knot, then applied gentle pressure on his ropy muscle. Caleb sighed.

Giggling, she continued to rub his back. Her fingers ached, but she was enjoying the feel of his hard muscles under her fingers too much to stop. Fingers numb she had to give in. She halted and shook her hands, moving feeling back into them.

Caleb turned around and lifted her fingers to his lips. "I'm going to have to take a pass on dinner. I'm exhausted and I've got an early morning tomorrow." He stood and extended his hands. As Faith reached for his grip, he pulled her to her feet.

She balled up her socks and stuffed them in her shoes. The green blades tickled her feet, so she ran until she reached the concrete patio.

Caleb hopped on one foot as he put on his shoes. "Hey! Wait a sec." He sprinted past her into the house and put his empty bottle in the sink.

Catching up with him, she poked a finger into his chest. "Overachiever."

"It's one of my weaknesses, being too competitive." Caleb's easy grin faded but his twinkling eyes remained. "Ready for your surprise in a couple more weeks?"

"Any hints?"

He lowered his head to hers, and Faith drew in a breath as his lips found their mark. All too soon they separated.

"There might be some of that."

"Anything else?"

Caleb looked up at the sky. "Moonlight."

She gifted Caleb with a small grin and a quick kiss on the cheek. "Romantic."

"Fire."

"Go on."

"No more. I'll see you in a few days. Yell if you need me."

After another goodbye kiss, Faith was ready to yell for another one.

It was too tempting to wait another day.

CHAPTER THIRTY-ONE

*F*aith double-checked her new outfit in the mirror. The slim jeans accentuated all the right places, while the cute plaid top covered the missed-a-few-workouts areas. Phone buzzing, she checked the door alarm. Her stomach flip-flopped like she was on an amusement park roller coaster the closer she got to the foyer. Giving her hair a quick once over in the foyer mirror, she opened the door.

"Hey, Caleb. You look great."

"Thanks. So do you." His green polo shirt fit nicely across his muscular shoulders and arms. Those dimples. The smile. "Ready?"

Faith shut the door and locked it, swinging her keys in her hand. Caleb touched the dip in her back as he opened the passenger side door. She felt the heat coming from his palm.

He spoke in little more than a whisper. "Tonight's going to be great."

As she got inside the car, Faith inhaled his sweet scent. A bright flame settled in her chest. "Care to share any more hints? There's moonlight, and later I'd think a kiss or two, so romance. Where's the fire?"

Caleb laughed. "You'll see."

As they rumbled down the road, Faith asked him questions.

"I won't tell, so wait." Caleb grinned. "What's your favorite book?"

"Too tough to pick. I usually read three at a time. What are you looking for?" She noticed him panning the field next to them as they turned off the highway and onto a country road.

"A dirt road." He clicked on the left signal and turned through an open gate, driving onto a grassy field.

Anticipation swelled as her gaze alighted upon a hot air balloon. The red and blue swirled pattern shined as it glowed its dragon's breath fire in the inky sky. "Spectacular."

Caleb met her on the passenger's side with both their jackets in hand, his mouth agape and his eyes fixed on the balloon as the burner blasted in the still country evening. He took Faith's hand and urged her toward the luminous balloon.

Growing closer, she felt the warmth from the fiery bursts. Faith dropped his hand and shielded her face with her arm. The balloon undulated in the light breeze as the crew held it in place with thick cords. The pilot introduced himself as Michael and asked them to hold one of the ropes steady while the balloon finished filling. She pulled on the sturdy cable alongside Caleb, his nearness making her feel secure at the feet of this goliath.

Captain Michael climbed into the gondola. "Step onto the stool and climb in." He held onto her arm and she hopped into the compact basket, Caleb following behind. Adrenaline surged through Faith in anticipation of what was to come.

As the ground crew dropped the ropes, Caleb drew closer to her, and she saw that his eyes mirrored the glowing flames. "Glad I'm with you."

Faith's gaze slid to his face. "Me too. I'm so excited. It's hard to catch a breath." The balloon hovered near the ground, and a gust of wind bolstered the firing burner, carrying it higher into the air. She shifted her stance and grabbed onto the edge of the gondola as it swayed in the light wind. In the distance, a filmy, blue-grey haze circled the Smokey Mountains, capturing both Caleb and Faith's attention. The swaying gondola drifted over the Black Hawk River, the cool wind raising bumps on Faith's arms. She fumbled with her jacket in the cramped space.

"I've got it." Caleb put the inside-out sleeve to rights.

She returned the favor and helped as he put on his jacket. His fingers touched her face as he brushed a lock of hair away. Faith felt exhilarated from both the ride and nearness of Caleb.

Caleb pointed below.

Faith pushed back the pesky strand that refused to stay put. "It's beautiful. You should be proud."

"I am. And I'll say again how beautiful you are, Belle."

Captain Michael said, "Would one of you like to fire the burner?

Faith's eyes met Caleb's. "Do it. I'll take a picture."

Captain Michael handed Caleb the thick, soot-stained leather glove.

Flecks of firelight sparked in Caleb's eyes as he pulled on the handle, and the orange flames licked the balloon's interior. Laughing, Faith snapped a photo. Caleb maneuvered around the captain and back to Faith.

"I'll take a picture of you two."

Caleb handed Michael his phone.

He enveloped her in his arms. Faith's breath caught in her throat as Caleb brushed a kiss on her lips. The afterglow from the kiss heated her face more than the firing burner. All at once Caleb released her and pointed to a bird soaring in the currents above them.

After a few more minutes soaring through the sky, Captain Michael landed with little more than a gentle bump. He threw the ropes to the awaiting ground crew who scrambled to secure the balloon.

Emboldened, she brushed a fleeting kiss on his cheek. His lips swerved upward.

A crew member pointed their way to a van, and they settled into the seats and talking while they waited for Michael to drive them to the launch site parking.

He sat down behind the wheel and his seat creaked as he turned to speak. "I hope you two enjoyed it. Nice to have you aboard."

Faith's words bubbled out. "It was magical."

Caleb nodded.

Captain Michael saluted them once he parked. "Thanks for flying."

Caleb popped open the van door. Faith climbed out, stretched, and then turned to walk toward Caleb's truck. She only made it a couple of steps before tripping awkwardly over the stony ground. Moving quickly to her side, Caleb wrapped his arm around her for support and helped guide her to more even terrain.

"This is going to sound corny. Thank you for making one of my dreams come true."

"Welcome." Caleb maneuvered the vehicle out of the bumpy field and onto the smooth country road.

"Where to next?"

"You'll see."

Noticing they were heading into a familiar area, Faith glanced over to Caleb.

"Are we going to the coffee shop?"

"Good guess."

Nosing into the empty lot, he ran to open the door and flick on the lights.

A crooked arrow created in crayon and effort was taped to the floor.

"What?"

"Jack made it."

Stepping around the art, she walked with Caleb to the kitchen.

"Close your eyes."

Pinching her eyelids shut, she felt him gently move her to the kitchen's center.

"Open them."

Prying one eye open and then the other, she began to dance at what was before her.

"An industrial stand mixer and a marble topped island. How? I was only away from work for a few days."

"Turns out the church softball team does more than not score runs."

"We were going to pay for this together."

As he walked his hand down her back, quivers rioted with each ounce of movement.

"I had to go big on it."

"You did." She took his face in her hands and stared into his gorgeous eyes. "I love you."

"I love you, too. It seems like I made the right choice."

Faith gave him another kiss. "You did. I can make all kinds of delicious things with the stand mixer." As she ran a hand over the cool marble, Caleb's hand covered hers. "What would I do without you?"

"I don't want you to ever find out."

Their lips closed over one another's and her heartbeat accelerated. Sometime later, they broke the kiss and hugged.

Caleb nuzzled her neck. "Can we do this every day?"

"I wouldn't get any work done."

"Maybe not, but it'd be fun."

"It would be." Faith brushed her hands across the island to cool her warm hands. *I wish I could put my hot face on the marble too. His kisses heat me more than the oven over there.*

Caleb said. "I'm glad you like the island. Will the island be big enough for our picnic?"

"Picnic?"

"Tay made this for us." Caleb pulled out a feast from the fridge and laid it out on the island, then popped the cork on some fruity bubbly juice and poured it into two red plastic cups.

After Faith got hers, they clinked "glasses" and dove into the repast.

~

Caleb walked Faith to her door, and in the nimbus of the porch light, they hugged and kissed. When her chin felt burned from Caleb's stubble, she backed up.

"I'd better get in."

"Wise decision." He winked.

"Thanks again."

"Welcome."

"Night."

Faith eased the door shut and trod through the foyer, hooking her bag on the newel post. From the recesses of her messy bag, her phone squawked.

Faith flicked the screen to take the call. "Hi."

Taylor jumped right in. "What did you do? Did you have a good time? Was he a gentleman? Huh, huh, huh? Tell me everything."

"What's this? A prisoner interrogation?"

"Well, I did promise your mom I'd keep an eye on you."

"Oh, you did, did you? Funny, she never mentioned it to me." Faith laughed. "Hold on a sec. At least let me sit down. He took me on a ride in a hot air balloon. It was beautiful."

"Oh, my chips and salsa."

She giggled at her friend's reaction and decided to enjoy the night once again through her retelling. Faith wiggled into the comfortable couch cushions.

"We went to dinner afterward at a cute little diner. The Dew Drop."

"Aagh, that's so romantic. Tell me about the ride."

"I was a little scared when I first saw the balloon but decided to go for it. It was like riding on a cloud. Very quiet and serene." Faith continued, describing the landscape, the pictures, their kiss, all of it.

Taylor yawned in the earpiece. "Sorry, it's late. But tell me all the rest or I'll have trouble sleeping."

"You won't. I'll tell you more tomorrow. Night."

Humming to herself, she readied for a night of sleep. Peeking at the phone screen she realized she'd missed a call from Caleb. Curling up in her bed she pressed his number.

"Were you asleep?"

"No." Scrubbing a hand over her face, she fought back a yawn.

"After church, why don't you and I and Jack go paddle boating?"

"Um."

"Slow water, promise. We'll be there with you."

"I'm game."

"Tomorrow."

"Yes."

Making kissing noises into the phone, Faith's mind reeled. She'd faced one small fear tonight on the balloon ride. What loomed tomorrow was far fierier and more mammoth in nature than the nylon balloon she'd rode with Caleb into the stars. Cold, hard fear encased in a metal monster. A boat.

CHAPTER THIRTY-TWO

*C*aleb rubbed sunscreen on Jack's face to ready his skin for the afternoon of paddle boating.

Peering into the mirror, Jack grimaced.

"I'm a funny cowr. I wanna to look like you." Jack pointed a finger into his chest.

"Rub it in. Your tan will show again." Inspecting his face in the bathroom mirror, he asked, "Can you fix me up?"

He handed the bottle to Jack as a frisson of anxiety wove up his spine. "Hold on a sec."

Caleb threw his shirt on the towel rack. "Go for it."

Pale blobs covered the tan tile floor, and one cold splat decorated his left foot. Caleb looked at the mess, then his son. Both giggled together. When he glanced in the mirror, he held back a cry of alarm, his face was as pale as tissue, two green eyes providing the only color.

"Let's go." He threw on his shirt, and as Jack left the room, he wiped off the sunscreen and pitched the evidence.

With less than two minutes of Jack's favorite song played, they pulled into the driveway.

Nearing the door, Caleb heard a sound which made Jack

hold his ears and pretend to scream.

What was that? Is there a feral cat loose in her house?

Putting an ear to the door he was able to make out the words. "Don't you be afraid of giants in your way, with God you know that anything's possible . . ."

Rubbing his ears didn't help. That wasn't Francesca Battistelli's beautiful voice. Faith was tone deaf. His heart hurt along with his ears at her lack of musical talent. Despite her moaning, mournful voice, she was beautiful and kind. *And she should never sing in public. Not even karaoke in an empty room.*

On tiptoes, Jack pressed the button. When the door began to creak, Caleb placed a smile on his face.

"Hi, you two. You didn't hear my singing, did you?"

He noticed her feet shifted back and forth on the concrete.

What to say? *I can't lie.*

"Fay sing bad."

"Jack, don't say that." His shoulders slumped at Jack's slight. When he glanced back at her, he noticed her wiping moisture from her eyes. Heavy hearted, he reached a hand in comfort to her. Overhearing snuffles, he patted her shoulder.

"I'm not crying."

When she flicked the hair from her face, he could see a smile cross her face.

"It's true. I stink." Faith hugged his son. "Thanks for being honest, even when your dad was floundering like a fish in a net."

"I wouldn't say that."

Feeling the stare from both Faith and his son, he raised his hands in apology.

"I didn't want to hurt you."

"Nice, but truth wins every single time. Let's go."

On the drive to Wildcat Lake, only Jack sang while Caleb held back joining in voice in quiet support of his gorgeous, albeit utterly non-musical, girlfriend.

Caleb stepped out of the car and tipped his head back,

letting the invigorating sunshine heat his face. He eyed the scattered yellow birch trees that dotted the landscape and noticed the gleam of the still lake beyond them. Glancing at Faith he couldn't read her expression.

"You want to do this?"

"I have to."

"Let's go." Caleb took her hand, and the trio walked to the small rental building. He pointed at the paddleboats. "You two get to pick."

There were only three to choose from.

Both Faith and Jack went closer to the bobbing boats and seemed to scrutinize each one, pointing out the merits of the watercraft.

Caleb whistled and stomped his foot in mock impatience.

A laugh bubbled out from Faith. "The one in the middle. Jack and I like the blue stripes on the side."

Caleb squinted an eye at the chosen boat. "It'll –"

"You folks ready?" the shop clerk interrupted, popping his head out of the framed open window. After ringing them up, the clerk gave them life jackets, and Caleb fastened on his son's first and then his own. While he said a prayer for calmness for Faith, he noticed her shaking hands as she closed the life vest buckles.

Faith took off her sandals, and breathed a prayer and grabbed Caleb's outstretched hand, boarding the rocking white and blue boat. When it dipped, the cool lake water dampened her feet, sending shivers of trepidation up her spine. She shook her wet feet off on the side of the boat after she sat down beside Jack in the three-seater boat. Caleb's nearness and quiet command of the little boat comforted her enough to enjoy the peaceful surroundings.

Jack screamed, "Turtle!"

All Faith noticed was the flat arrow-tail of the turtle as it dove underwater.

Jack's lips turned down.

She patted his arm.

"We'll see another one."

"Look over there." He pointed to a tortoise-shelled turtle bobbing to the surface. Caleb leaned over the side of the boat, dipped his hand into the cool water, and splashed some on her bare legs.

"Hey!" She whipped her head back toward him. "Two can play this game." Faith's fingers locked over the seat edge as she leaned over the boat's side. Her insides matched the wavy reflection of herself she saw in the water. Faith reached out her fingers to the surface of the water. With the change of position, her wet feet slipped off the pedals. She snapped her body back in the seat, forgetting about splashing Caleb. Faith's instincts were to panic, but she slowed her breathing and focused on the clear water.

He put a steadying hand on her shoulder. "Doing okay?"

"Getting better. Thanks."

"We'll keep it nice and steady, no more splashing."

"Okay." As she relaxed, Faith glanced over at Caleb. He was leaning back in the seat, slowly pedaling as he tilted his head back and smiled. Happiness trickled through her as she blatantly stared at him. When he straightened, she glanced the other way and pretended to see something in the water.

During their fifth lap around the lake, the hot sun began to scorch Faith's arms. Her legs grew weary, so she stopped paddling. "Let's head in. I need some water. What about you two?"

Concern for Jack's red face hit Faith. She pointed to Jack to show Caleb.

"Agreed."

He steered them towards the dock as they both paddled to finish their excursion. The little boat bumped the rubber fender, and the rental shop clerk came running out to throw Caleb a dock line. Caleb caught it with a confident swipe and tied the strong cord to the paddleboat's cleat. He jumped onto the dock and kept one foot on the front of the boat to steady it as first Jack, then she, alighted.

Faith pushed off from the front of the boat and hopped onto the dock. "I'm not used to all that exercise. My legs feel like rubber." She stretched her legs out for a few moments.

"Got your land legs back? Let's go get some water. I saw some at the rental place."

Faith flitted a shy smile up at him.

Caleb kissed her cheek, and they began walking to the rental building.

Jack ran ahead as Caleb unscrewed his water bottle. "See fish, Dad?"

"All right. Okay with you, Faith?"

Eyeing her dark shorts, she stated, "Sounds fun to me."

Grabbing her hand in his, Jack pulled her toward the grassy spot ahead.

"Come on, Fay. Hurry."

Pretending to jog to match Jack's shorter stride, they soon settled near the edge of the lake.

Jack peered in the clear water. When he leaned over too far for Faith's comfort, she reached a hand to pull him back. *Caleb's the parent. Not me.* Instead of guiding Jack, she scanned the water beyond and noticed a duck flapping and wetting its dun-colored feathers.

"Look, Jack."

"Duck. See, Daddy?"

"I do. It's swimming like the fish we just saw." Caleb put his hands beside his face and puckered his lips, making a popping noise.

Copying his dad, Jack covered most of his little face with his hands and made his own fish mouth.

He's a great dad; funny, silly, kind. How would he be with our kids? Wait, me a mom? The one who feared the kids in the church nursery as a teen? A two-time babysitter, and only when paid more than the going rate? Must be all the heat.

Overhearing words being spoken brought her to the present. Caleb was beside her while Jack still looked at the lake a step from them.

"You were brave."

"I felt safe with you. If anything had gone south, you were there to help me. And Jack's narration of the wildlife helped, too."

"He's good at that, you ought to see him at the zoo."

"I bet he has a ball."

"Yeah."

Caleb put his arm around her. Leaning her head on his shoulder, she held a sigh before it released.

"You'd make a great mom."

"Me?"

"Don't look shocked. Jack loves you. Ever want any?"

All traces of moisture left her mouth. She turned to reach for her bottle on the ground and saw Jack's foot slide into the mud at the water's edge.

Caleb followed the line of sight to his son. His legs had already slid thigh deep into the water.

"Dad!"

Blood pressure skyrocketing, he raced to Jack. Faith beat him by a second and swooped him from the water.

Giving his son a head to toe once over, his adrenaline level dropped when he saw how Faith had cuddled him.

"Glad you're good." Faith rocked Jack back and forth. " I know it's scary, hon."

He rubbed the sweaty hair away from Jack's forehead. "You okay, champ?"

"Fay saved me."

"True, buddy." He swiped his hand over her hair. "Thanks."

Jack burrowed his head deeper into Faith's shoulder. Under the covering of her beautiful reddish hair, one brown eye peered at him.

It made him smile and his heart ache. *Avery held him like that. Look at the future. At the two of them. Both wet and muddy, and to Faith all that matters is Jack.* Rays of sunshine and the portrait of love he was witnessing melted his own fears of a permanent relationship.

"Let's go home, the two of you need to clean up."

Driving home the car was quiet, as if the interaction between the three of them deeply satisfied one another and a new bond was forged over the water.

Faith scooted into her house after a quick kiss.

Eyeing the backseat, he noticed Jack's head lolling to the side and a line of drool on his shoulder.

Soap bubble clean later, Caleb tucked Jack into bed and read him Faith's story at the insistence of his son.

During prayers Faith was mentioned first which gave Caleb a catch in his throat.

"Love Fay, Daddy?"

"Yes."

"Me too. Her can be my mommy." Bright brown eyes closed, and a flashing smile fell from his son's face as he slept.

Leaving the room, he padded to the family room as Ranger clopped next to him. Watching mindless entertainment kept Caleb from thinking about the words his son had said. He hadn't been sure he'd ever find a person to replace Avery. *Not replace. This is new, different. She was incredible. It's a miracle I found someone else to spend our lives with. How do I find out if she's ready?*

Caleb looked at Ranger. "Any ideas?"

Thump, thump, thump. Ranger's backside swiveled against the sofa.

Why'd I ask my dog? Ridiculous. Covering up in his bed, Caleb closed his eyes and prayed. He needed advice from his Heavenly Father, knowing he couldn't figure this out on his own.

CHAPTER THIRTY-THREE

*U*nfurling the bright red ribbon together, Faith swiped a glance at Caleb. A grin bisected his face.

Mayor Sherry Roberts gave the couple a soft smile. "Congratulations, Faith and Caleb, on your grand opening of Briar Creek Bakery. We'll cut the ribbon and you can say a few words afterward."

Faith was the first to respond. "Thank you, Mayor Roberts."

Caleb followed with dip of his head.

One of the chamber of commerce members handed her the oversized ceremonial scissors. Caleb's warm hands covered her trembling grip on the heavy scissors. The mayor and chamber president both gave a short speech and held part of the ribbon as she and Caleb snipped through it. Cheers rang out from the crowd. She blinked against the bright flash of light when the local newspaper photographer took a picture.

"Best wishes, you two. I'll come back with my kids soon." Mayor Roberts gave her shoulder a pat and shook her hand. Other chamber members added their remarks before leaving.

She saw Taylor and Jarod moving toward them, threading their way around small groups of people who stood chatting.

Faith laughed and hugged them as Caleb pulled out his phone and took a picture of the happy friends.

"Let me take one of you and Caleb." Her friend gave her a knowing look and grinned.

Faith sidled over and put her arm around him. He gave her a buss on the cheek, heating her face.

"Later I'll give you a real kiss." Caleb flashed his dimpled grin.

His flippant comment threw her off balance. Faith felt a tug on her sleeve and pivoted around.

"We're swamped," Ryan yelled over the din.

"Take a raincheck on the, um, kiss." Faith wiggled her eyebrow and grinned.

"I'll remember that." He laughed and shook his head. Caleb sauntered over to join his parents and Jack at a table. Smiling, she turned and disappeared into the crowd of customers.

"Congratulations, Miss Fuller. I've brought my staff to come celebrate your grand opening," Mr. Knapp grinned. "It seems we've made a great investment by the looks of the crowd."

Shaking his hand, Faith looked at the small group from the bank behind him. *No Avery.* "Let me know what I can get for you, and if I remember correctly, you've got some kids at home."

"Three, and they'll be coming back with me soon to try your place out."

Motioning for Willow, their new bakery assistant, to come over, Faith stated, "Let's pick out some things to take home for your family. Willow will help you with it."

"You know, Miss Fuller... Faith. I wished from the beginning I could have helped you out when you came in for that loan."

Meeting his eyes, she smiled. "Honestly, me too. But look how this turned out. The Lord had better plans for me than both of us together."

"That He did." Mr. Knapp took the box from Willow's outstretched hands. "Thank you, see you soon."

Before helping another customer, she managed to say, "Welcome, thanks for coming." Turning away to blow an errant strand from her eyes, she pivoted around to help the next customer. Lightning flashed and her insides roiled. Her.

"Seems you did it."

Caleb came and stood next to Faith and put an arm around her shoulders.

"We did it. Here to get something for you and Tanner?"

"When the bank manager says for us to go, we go. And, you're still family." Tossing her blonde hair over her shoulder, a smirk more than a smile graced her face. "What's delicious?"

"Everything. Faith and Ryan are outstanding bakers."

Standing taller, Faith willed her voice to speak in a kinder fashion than her heart wanted. "We'll pack up some small cakes for you and your hubby. Maybe someday you could share your birthday cake recipe with us? It was really good."

Stepping away from the counter, Lauren's eyes wouldn't focus on Faith.

"It's a family recipe. I am not sure if I can or should share it."

"Jack and I are family. I co-own this bakery." Caleb's stance shifted. "It is one of the best cakes I've tasted, Lauren."

"In that case, sure. I'll email it to you."

"Thanks, and I'd like you to come over when you're free for coffee sometime soon."

Not missing Caleb's double-take, Faith's mood relaxed. "We need to get to know each other. We both live in the same town and care about the same people."

"We do. I'll let you know when I'm free." Taking the box, she nodded and left the bakery.

"You are incredible." Caleb brushed a kiss on her temple. "Staring down the dragon and winning."

Nudging him with an elbow, she glanced up and smiled. "Remember, I did work for Erika. Those two are similar."

"Happy that's behind you."

"Me too."

"Looks like our cookie monster wants a refill."

Our. Quiet, settled happiness warmed Faith. Jack indeed was their cookie monster.

As the crowd ebbed, Faith moved to the rear of the shop and grabbed a present. Walking toward the table, her heart stung when she saw Jack's heavy-lidded eyes. *He needs to get home.*

Sweeping into the seat next to Jack, she whisked an arm around his small shoulders.

"A grand opening isn't finished until someone gets a present."

A sparkle returned to his brown eyes, and he put a hand on Faith's outstretched palm.

"For Dad?'

Faith shook her head.

Bouncing in the seat, Jack's voice raised. "Me."

Bringing the yellow bag from behind her and placing it on the table, joy rushed through her.

Tearing through the tissue paper, Jack soon found his special present.

Jack put the small chef's hat on his head, which had their Briar Creek Bakery logo embroidered on it.

"Look again." She pointed to the bottom of the bag.

Digging his hands inside, Jack pulled out another wrapped present. His fingers danced above the wrapping.

"Open it."

Ripping apart the gift wrap, Jack threw it to the ground.

"Hand it to me, please."

Jack deposited it into his dad's awaiting hands before he tried on his second present.

"Superhero shirt."

"Mmhmm."

Jack dug his head into her ribcage, which pinched, so Faith

moved to ease the jab in her middle before squeezing him tighter.

"I hope you like them."

"Yup."

"What do you say, son?"

Hat tilted toward his eyes and the shirt bunched up on his body, he was precious. Faith muffled a sigh.

"Fanks."

Eyes swerving to her business partner, she motioned with a head tilt. "Someone's tired. Take him home and the rest of us will clean up."

"We've got it, you two," Ryan interjected, "Willow and I will do this. Head home. Five o'clock baking tomorrow, right?"

"Don't we have a few things leftover?" Taking a tour of the bare kitchen, her shoulders slumped. "I see your point, nothing's left. So, yes, see you at five tomorrow. Night."

Holding the door open for both her and Jack, Caleb asked, "How about we go to my house and watch a movie? Have popcorn for dinner?"

Jack cheered.

"Son, you ate enough here at the bakery. A cheese sandwich, then bed."

"Aww."

"I'll make it, Jack, and put pickles on the side for you."

"Kay."

"And the popcorn," she placed a kiss on Caleb's cheek as she crossed the threshold. "It's my pick. Your Goji berry popcorn is… interesting."

"One step ahead of you. I bought your buttery stuff at the store the other day in case we had a movie night."

Faith said, "You are what my mom would say is a 'keeper.'"

Caleb laughed.

After pulling into his driveway, Caleb ran to open her car door. On impulse, she touched his face with her fingers. He kissed them as they trailed past his lips. Faith was glad the night sky concealed her heated and tingling face.

Caleb picked up the tired little boy in his arms and flicked on the lights in his house as they headed into the kitchen.

Faith made a small grilled cheese with extra pickles on the side as Caleb took charge of his son's shower.

Two bites into the sandwich, Jack's head bobbed.

"Bedtime."

"Night, Fay." Jack waved from his vantage point over his dad's shoulder.

"Sleep well."

Caleb's low voice carried into the kitchen as he read Jack's story.

Smiling at the rise of animation in his voice, Faith cleared the dishes from Jack's dinner. While putting the cheese slices away in the fridge, she looked at the papers held by magnet on the stainless-steel front.

Baby Jack in Caleb's arms at the hospital, another photo of the boy's recent birthday party. Taking a second glance, she saw a postcard with a college insignia on it.

Looking around, she turned the card over and read the message. Her stomach dropped as she read the words, "not enrolled" next to the MBA program course listings.

Why?

A kiss whispered along her neck.

Fire heated her midsection. Caught.

"See something interesting?"

Quickly putting the evidence under the magnet didn't absolve her from her crime.

"I shouldn't have looked."

"No."

Toe to toe with Caleb, she saw the rise and fall of his chest and the scowl on his face.

"Can I ask why?"

"You're more important to me than paper."

"Wait. What do you mean?"

"Our business. I put my tuition money into it."

"No, Caleb." She stepped around him and paced, mouth bone dry.

"My choice."

"It is." She held her hand over her heart. "We'll make sure you are able to take the classes someday."

"Oh, it's we now?"

Delightful ribbons of peace covered her. "We."

Any other words were silenced by the meeting of their lips as his strong hands played with the hair cascading down her back.

Lips vibrating, they separated, but her heart was still seconds behind, locked in the kiss and enjoying the circle of arms around her.

"You did Jack's dinner, I'll do ours."

Once the hum of the microwave began, Caleb gathered her in his arms for a moment and held her there. Faith enjoyed the warmth of his circle and the homey feel of their surroundings. It was as if they were a married couple, in their own place, enjoying a movie night. Her midsection buzzed with a thousand fireflies at the closeness. *I could get used to this.* As her phone sounded on the counter, she sighed, and unwrapped herself from his arms. Noting it was Ryan, she answered. A quick conversation cleared up his question about a new recipe.

Caleb pulled the steaming bags out of the microwave, and Faith rummaged for two bowls in the cabinet across from the fridge.

As she handed them to him, she picked up one of the berries and popped it into her mouth, wrinkling her nose at the tart, bitter taste. "Don't go sneaking any Goji berries in mine. But you're welcome to some of my artery clogging butter if you want it."

He scowled as he poured the popcorn into the bowls. Joke-ster that he was, he turned up his nose and waved his oily hands at her before washing them off. "As if I'd ever eat this stuff. Gross."

"Buttery, just how I like it." She took the bowl from him and waltzed into his family room. Caleb followed and eased onto the sofa next to her.

"You sat through two hours of my favorite World War II movie as I drooled over the planes. It's your turn tonight."

"I'm in the mood for Sci-Fi."

"Done." He pressed his remote to start streaming the online menu. Faith pointed at the screen when the cursor landed on one of her old favorites and she snuggled into Caleb.

When the creature on the screen appeared from an airway above the characters, she jumped and jostled her popcorn. As she picked up the scattered pieces off the floor, Caleb bent down to help, stealing a kiss in the process. Faith could taste the Goji berries on his lips. *Can he taste the butter from mine?* No more popcorn mishaps but more stolen kisses later, the credits rolled on the screen.

Caleb clicked off the television and rose from the sofa. "Walk you to your car." Faith took his outstretched hand and slipped past him as he opened the front door. Ranger tried to shimmy through, but she gently pulled him back.

"Thanks, he's been trying to do that a lot recently." Caleb patted the dog's head.

"If I were him, I wouldn't leave. He has a great owner and friend in the both of you."

"He is spoiled."

Conversation quieted in the chilly night. Faith willed the shivers to stop and rubbed her arms together. Caleb pulled her to his side and wrapped his arm around her shoulders as a soli-tary owl's song cut through the quiet air.

Faith fumbled with her keys, distracted by his nearness.

Chuckling, Caleb took them from her and unlocked the door, swinging it open.

"See you soon, beautiful. Sweet dreams."

Bubbles of joy floated inside Faith. "Goodnight, handsome. I love you."

He tipped her face farther up with a finger and gazed into her heart with his eyes. "I love you, too." Caleb folded her into his arms and gave her a kiss before walking away. "Night."

As she pulled from the driveway, Caleb waved and smiled.

Faith grinned back.

Her heart thrummed in her chest, and a twinge of sadness pinged inside at her leaving. *We won't have to be apart like this someday soon. If our relationship keeps building, there'll be some wedding vows said in the future.* A grin crossed her face at the delightful thought.

CHAPTER THIRTY-FOUR

*C*aleb pulled Dylan's suitcase out of the trunk. "Good to see you." He clapped his brother's back. "Got you all summer?"

"Not all. I'm going to FSU before heading back to UNC."

Eyebrows lifting, and curiosity stirring, he asked, "New development?"

"Hope. We're seeing where it goes. She's in Florida, and I'm in North Carolina." Dylan slung his backpack over a shoulder. "I could say to you, bro, how's Faith? But I'm not butting into that."

Swinging the door open and stepping aside, he retorted, "For now."

Between Jack's happy laugh and Ranger's excited bark, neither could speak. Caleb pointed upstairs, and Dylan nodded. Reaching the guest room, and a modicum of peace, Caleb exhaled. *I'm going to have a crazy summer ahead.*

As he made his way back downstairs, he heard the doorbell ring. Before he could answer, Dylan threw open the door.

"Got company."

"Who?"

Stopping mid-track, his glance shifted between two sisters.

Once Faith had given a hug to Dylan and a high-five to Jack, she stood next to him. Heat stung his face. He looked at his old workout shirt and shorts. *Nice.*

"Look who's surprised me."

"Hey, Hope. Nice to see you." Caleb extended a hand to Faith's red-haired sister.

"Hi Caleb."

Caleb hid his grin as he bent down and kissed Faith's cheek.

Dylan's reaction reminded him of when he'd get a gift at Christmas or his birthday. Jumpy as a jumping bean and all smiles.

"What're you doing here?" Dylan asked. " Don't you have class?"

"Not now, I've got a weeklong break until summer classes. Can we go someplace and talk?"

"I don't have my car." Dylan turned to his big brother. "Can I have your keys, Caleb?"

He fished in his pocket and dangled them in front of Dylan. His brother snatched them from his hand. "Okay, I've gotta change and go to work anyway." Caleb looked at Faith. "Can you give me a ride? I don't want to send for a driver."

"Fine by me. I'm meeting Lauren for coffee."

"Need me there to referee?"

"No, I'm fine."

"I'll be ready in fifteen. Jack, why don't you and Ranger take Faith to the family room? You can show her your new trick you taught Ranger."

"Come on, Jack, show me."

Holding hands, they went into the family room as Caleb ran to the back to get cleaned up.

With Mrs. Settles arriving, Caleb left a few instructions for the day for her and Jack and brushed a kiss across his son's face.

"See you, sport."

"Bye."

Riding in the SUV with Faith made Caleb's pulse quicken. The tan length of leg showing from her shorts and the scent of something floral coupled with her NASCAR performance driving were the causes for his reaction, he reasoned.

"You smell good." He leaned over and buried his lips in her hair. "Like summer and flowers. Delicious."

"Don't distract me. Your sitting near me does that enough."

"Same." Caleb pointed to her legs. "I like those shorts."

His insides clenched when he saw the blush on her cheeks and the subtle shift in her seat.

When she swerved into a spot, Caleb held onto the door and smirked. "Remind me to never go to Germany with you."

"I've always wanted to speed along the Autobahn. You can go over a hundred miles per hour there. Pure bliss."

Under his breath he said, "Terror for me."

Leaning toward him, she gave him a kiss before alighting. "I like it when your eyes glow. It's really hot."

Maybe that drive wouldn't be so bad.

"Text me when your booking is over. I'll drive you home, really fast." Faith's slamming of the door matched the ka-thunks of his heartbeat. Glancing one more time at her departing form, he grinned at her swinging hips. *Happy man that it's July, more hot weather to come.* Turning his eyes inside the coffee bar, he saw Lauren. The smile fell from his face. Facing her would be like facing class V rapids at their ultimate. Impetuous and unpredictable.

CHAPTER THIRTY-FIVE

Spotting the blonde in the corner facing away from her, Faith grabbed a cup of caffeinated courage behind the counter.

"Hi, boss." Willow's smile sprang from her freckled cheeks. "Didn't think you were coming in today."

"Hey. I'm meeting someone. Prayers are welcome."

"Will do. Are you taking her order to her? I've almost got it ready." Steam rose from the wand as Willow ably frothed the cream for the cappuccino.

"Of course, and I'll give her a strawberry cookie in case she's hungry."

Walking toward Lauren, flashes of the photo of her sister Avery flitted in Faith's vision. *They look so much alike.* She took a sip of coffee, and the burn from the brew scalded her tongue. Fighting back a wince, she put a smile on her face.

"Hi, Lauren."

"Hello. Is that mine?"

With a nod, Faith placed both items in front of her. Lauren picked up the mug and inhaled. "Mmm, I love the smell of coffee."

Faith sat across the table from Lauren.

"Anytime you want to stop by, you're welcome."

"It's weird to see you with my brother-in-law. With Caleb."

So, this is how it is. Be nice.

"Look, I've never been in your shoes and lost a loved one. Well, not a sister." Reaching out a hand, she quickly changed her mind and took it from Lauren's area. "It's got to hurt."

"We were close. Same town, married around the same time. She beat me to having kids." Lauren touched her midsection. "I don't know why I'm telling you all this. Jack's going to have a cousin in a few months."

"That's great. He'll be thrilled and Caleb will be too."

"I'd still like him to be this little one's cousin."

"You're family."

"Why are you being nice to me?"

"Aren't we supposed to be kind to others? Isn't that in the Bible?"

"It is." Lauren wiped a tear away with a finger. "Sorry, I was scared you'd take Jack from me, or turn him from me."

"Jack loves you. I'm not anything but Caleb's business partner."

"No, you're more than that." The edge of the cup teetered near Lauren's blush lipstick. "Even I can see that."

"Oh."

"I love that stubborn, aggravating man like my brother. You're good for him, like my sister was. He gets his head stuck in business and numbers. You don't."

Wrinkling her upper lip, Faith confessed, "I can't stand math."

"That's where I live all day, but I'd love to bake more like you do."

"Caleb's birthday is in two weeks, let's use your recipe and bake together."

"Deal." Lauren pointed to her bump. "And throw in the cinnamon cookie recipe. The baby and I love it."

"I'll be happy to."

"Tanner and I are having a fourth of July party. Would you come along with Caleb and Jack?"

"Okay. I'd like that."

'Me too." Rising, Lauren walked over to Faith. "This was fun."

"It was."

"This pregnancy thing makes me sleepy, though, so time for my afternoon nap. Hug Caleb and Jack for me."

"Done."

With a single wave, Lauren departed.

Gathering all the mugs and plates, Faith dispatched them to the kitchen.

Willow was rinsing off dishes in the sink. "Good time?"

"Hard to believe, but yeah."

"I'll finish those." Willow put them in the sink basin. "Go see Caleb."

She raised an eyebrow and waved. "If you insist. See ya."

Birdsong accompanied Faith on the walk over to Hawk's Creek. The sun heated her arms and legs, and she eyed the flowing river at the property's edge. *Wish I could jump in and cool off.* Settling into a hammock near the outfitters, she pulled her device from her bag and began to read.

Familiar laughter proclaimed the fact that Caleb was nearby. Shifting her view from the screen to the river, she spied him paddling into the shore. He helped the family from their kayaks, and Faith admired the play of strong, corded muscles in his arms as he carried the kayaks to their holding place. Turning off the device, she alighted from the hammock and waited until he was finished speaking to his clients.

"You don't have any claw marks. So, you survived."

"Funny. Lauren and I ended as friends. I'm coming with you and Jack to the 4th of July cookout."

"Wow. Didn't see that coming. Glad, though. You two are in my life for a long time."

"Hmm, are you saying something?"

"I'm declaring it."

His wet, clammy shirt met her dry, warm one in an embrace. Her heart flew higher than the trees enclosing them in their own idyllic world for one brilliant moment.

Realizing they were drawing attention to themselves, they separated.

"The river's smooth today. Want your first lesson? We'll go slow."

"Oh-kay." Faith grimaced at the hitch in her voice. "Let's do this."

"I'm proud of you for giving this a try. You okay?" He gave her a quick hug before they put on their lifejackets.

Faith faced the river and fastened her jacket with shaking hands. She pressed a fist to her lips and stood still. Her insides were jelly and her breathing shallow and rapid. She sent a prayer for courage.

"We don't have to do this, you know. I don't ever want to put you through something that has you so uncomfortable." He stood behind Faith, his hands warm on her arms.

Drawing in a deep breath, Faith turned to him. "I want to do this."

He wrapped his arms around her, his lips drawn into a thin uneasy line. He rolled his shoulders and twisted his neck around.

He looks as uncomfortable with me as I am with this river.

Caleb surprised her as he pulled her into his arms and prayed out loud for her to be comforted. They stayed in each other's arms as her breathing slowed.

He murmured loving words to her.

Leaning back, he looked deep into her eyes. He must have liked what he saw from the deep smile he wrapped around her. She drew strength from that smile, and the prayer Caleb said on her behalf as well.

Faith experienced a warmth running through her body, and the fear binding her lessened. Her trust in God had guided her through many amazing and terrifying things. She'd moved to a new city and opened a business, fallen in love, and gone paddle boating, just to name a few. Her heavenly Father was guarding them both. She lifted her head and smiled. "I'm ready."

His smile radiated pleasure. "Let's go." Caleb held her hand and kissed her cheek as she climbed into the two-person kayak. The boat shook with her nerves. Once Caleb clambered aboard, it settled with his weight. He took up the paddles and cast off the line then twisted toward her. "Keep your eyes on my paddle, and stroke with the same rhythm as me. It will take a bit to get used to it, but you can do it."

"Okay."

The yellow boat lurched backward and then plunged forward, like a tug-of-war game. She was distracted by Caleb's well-muscled arms as he paddled with the current. The tenseness left her body with each stroke of the paddle as it dipped into the clear liquid. It was almost like flying. Faith couldn't believe it.

Taking a break from paddling, Caleb swiveled to face her. "Ready for little rapids?"

Her heart quickened. "Bring it on!" He rewarded her with a warm smile and thumbs up.

Caleb steered them to the side of the river where the water bubbled and rippled as it coursed along.

Faith squealed as the water crested over the side and splashed her legs. She paddled harder to get out of the small rapids. Caleb followed suit. He pointed to the far shoreline and steered the kayak in that direction. Caleb jumped out, holding the boat steady so Faith could climb out.

The Hawk's Creek bus they all called the "Yellow Canary" crested over the hill as they waited at the landing site. Faith chattered about their experience while they waited for the bus to arrive. It creaked and groaned then exhaled while parking. Its door swooshed open. Dylan came out and threw them some towels.

Faith ran over to give him a hug. "Hi."

He grinned, pointing his thumb at Caleb. "Beautiful summer day and this guy has me working." Dylan shook his head and squinted at his brother.

"You told me you needed to save money for your study abroad next year."

"Yeah, well . . ."

Caleb's eyes twinkled, belying the scowl he shot his brother. "Don't put it on me. Come help me drag this thing to the trailer." He threw his towel onto the bus.

Faith climbed the rubber-clad steps onto the bus and heard a phone ding. She spotted Dylan's blue and black phone on the vinyl dashboard. While Faith didn't want to be nosy, his phone kept buzzing. She glanced at the screen and saw her sister's face. Guilt crept over her. Faith decided to walk away and gather their wet towels, putting them in a basket in the front seat. Caleb squished his massive shoulders into the small green seat beside her while Dylan closed the door and started up the squawking bird. He checked his phone, and a smile lit his face. He glanced back at them and put the phone face down on the holder.

"You were brave. First the air in the balloon, now the waters. What next?"

"No more for me, you've got your airplane ride next weekend."

Dylan said over his shoulder, "Take me, bro."

"Focus on the road. The Canary is a fine piece of equipment, and it can't get damaged."

"It's missing a few feathers."

"I'm saving for something else. None to spare on this old bird."

"What?" she asked, inching closer to him. She kissed his cheek. "Is it for Jack?"

"No."

"Business?"

"Off the mark."

As they held hands, Faith felt his fingers touch her ring finger several times. Holding in her air, she prayed for a ring from Caleb to occupy that space. Doubts crawled into her happy thoughts. All their money was tied to the coffee shop. She'd have to be patient or force herself to be.

Their phones rang at the same time.

Faith saw his eyes crinkle as Caleb read the text. She quickly checked hers. It was from Jarod. Her heart skittered. She shouted, "They had the babies! Hurry, Dylan." Faith planted a kiss on Caleb and texted Jarod back.

Faith and Caleb jumped into his car and peeled out of the parking lot like joy-riding teenagers.

Faith clutched a hand onto his shoulder. "We'll get there, don't panic."

"This is the first time anyone I've known has had a baby." He eased his white-knuckle grip on the wheel and slowed.

"Me too."

They pulled into the first spot at Asheville Regional and jogged to the hospital entrance. Out of breath, she held up a finger, asking him to wait a moment. He nodded.

Once inside the hospital, they asked for directions to the maternity ward at the information desk. A kind looking, salt-and-pepper-haired man swiveled his large computer monitor and showed them the map.

"Gift shop." Faith moved with a purpose toward the large gift shop. Some minutes later they emerged with Caleb holding a balloon bouquet of pink and blue. With each step the balloons crashed into one another. "They sound like my dad's bongo drums," Faith commented.

"Your dad?"

"A holdover from a band he was in during college."

Caleb shook his head. "I'd never guess he had been in one."

"You know that old saying about a book and a cover?" Faith pressed the elevator call button.

"Got it."

The elevator pinged as the doors opened. They whispered on the elevator ride to the fourth floor, not wanting to wake one of the other passengers—a sleeping toddler who clutched a pink baby doll in her fist while her dad gently rocked the stroller back and forth. He had circles under his eyes and a two-day-old beard, yet his smile was contagious. "Thanks, my wife and I just had our second. A boy, yesterday. This is his big sister's first time to see him."

"Congratulations." Caleb held the door open for the man as he wheeled his daughter out and down the hall. Then Caleb turned to Faith and put his arm around her waist as they went down the hall searching for the room.

A nurse making his rounds escorted them to the room and knocked on the door. He peeked inside and spoke in hushed tones, then turned back to them. "It will be just a minute while she and the babies are getting settled. You can wait in the waiting room over there."

Faith half-waved. "Thanks." They went down the hall and sat in the waiting room.

Jarod came through the doorway wearing a smile that could light up Manhattan.

Faith stood to greet him. "They're here?"

"Come see."

Caleb clapped Jarod on the back as they walked toward the room.

Both sets of grandparents beamed from around Taylor's bed. Faith clipped the balloons on the corner of the curtain and gave each of them hugs and congratulatory greetings followed by Caleb. Faith looked at her tired but happy friend holding two beautiful blessings. Jarod stood next to her with his mouth hung open slightly. It was easy to see he was already in love with his babies.

She went over to Taylor and hugged her. "Congratulations, they're beautiful. How are you doing?"

Taylor kissed both the babies' downy heads and looked up at Faith. "It feels like Christmas and my birthday all mixed together. It's wonderful. I'm doing well. They arrived into the world after only twelve hours of labor."

Faith swallowed. "That's... good. I wasn't sure how long it took."

"The doctor said I'm fortunate to have had such an easy birth. All I can say is thank goodness for epidurals."

Both grandmothers nodded their heads in agreement.

Caleb walked closer to the bed and hugged Taylor. "Congrats. What are their names?"

Taylor and Jarod glanced at each other. Jarod's voice was hoarse as he spoke. "Our daughter is Olivia Anne, and our son is Joshua James."

Faith's lips tipped upward. "Those are beautiful names. I love how Olivia Anne is named after her grandmothers and Joshua James after his grandfathers." She ran a gentle finger over their doll-sized hands.

The babies began to whimper and move around.

Taylor's mom, Grandmother Olivia, grinned. "It sounds like feeding time to me." Jarod's mom, Grandmother Anne, pulled her gaze from her grandbabies and motioned for everyone to leave.

Faith took one last peek at the babies before they said their goodbyes. She hugged Caleb outside the door as busy hospital staff whisked behind them. "I can't believe it. Our best friends are parents."

Caleb kissed her, and they began to go back to the elevators. "I'm still shocked. Maybe someday we'll be married and have our own babies. I've never asked. You're great with Jack. Do you want kids, too?" He turned to press the down button.

A lump lodged in her throat and tears came to her eyes. There wasn't any room for the words to come out. She smiled and nodded as his comment sank in. Marriage and children? The idea was both terrifying and thrilling.

CHAPTER THIRTY-SIX

*C*aleb tore into his green paper with the gusto of a six-year-old at his birthday party. He hefted the box in his hands, measuring how much it weighed.

"Go ahead, I want you to see it. I couldn't wait to give it to you."

"Come on, Dad." Pulling on Caleb's arm, Jack said, "Then more cake?"

"All right."

He fumbled with the sticky tape and finally freed the edges from the adhesive. Caleb held up an envelope to the lamplight. His fingers tore along the envelope corners, and a piece of paper peeked from the edges. Pulling it out, his eyes grew large as he read the certificate.

"What? A WWII plane ride?" He let go of the certificate. As it twirled to the floor, he thanked her with a kiss.

"Yucky, Daddy. It's from me, too."

Pursing his lips together, he made a smacking sound.

Giggling, Jack ran to the kitchen. "Cake, then story."

Rising from the sofa he stared into Faith's gorgeous face, forgetting his words.

"Were you asking me about cake?"

Between Faith's caressing fingertips on his chin, and her lips hovering near his, the pounding sound of his blood pressure beat inside his head.

"I want some, too, Jack." Faith ran like a track star to the kitchen.

Begrudgingly, he went to join them, but a kiss was always nicer than cake. To him.

~

Planes whirred overhead as Caleb opened the car door in the parking lot next to the silver hanger. His gaze followed the path of a biplane in the sky. It did a series of steep climbs and tumbling loops.

Faith reached out and grabbed his arm. "Maybe I can get another present for you. This looks dangerous."

"Don't worry. I'll be safe. Have I ever said how proud I am of you for overcoming your fears? You can paddle a kayak or raft better than most, and you own a business. You've followed where your trust in Jesus led." Caleb brushed a kiss on her lips and grinned. "Riding in a biplane is something I've wanted to do since I was a kid. Trust that He'll keep me safe."

"I am. I've already prayed."

"Me too." He gave Faith a quick hug. As they watched another plane do a death roll, Caleb rubbed his hands together. The nose of the blue and white plane was pointed to the ground, then catapulted into the light blue sky. On the ground, an orange-suited crew member waved a small commuter plane out to the runway. Caleb fished three pairs of tethered earplugs and gave one to Faith and another to Jack as the plane's motor sputtered and roared to life. Before they could cross the side-walk to go into the hangar office, they stopped to let a small silver plane taxi by. The pilot gave them a military salute and moved forward. Once he'd cleared, they stepped into the cool office, listening to the dull drone of the aircraft outside. All three of them took their earplugs out, letting them dangle around their necks.

A gentleman in a green flight suit with goggles wrapped around his neck came in through a side door. "Afternoon. Caleb and Faith?" The gentleman bent down. "Who's this young man?"

"Jack."

"Hiya. I'm Rex Cranford. Nice to meet you folks." Captain Cranford handed a clipboard to Caleb. "Please sign these release papers before we go into the hangar."

"Of course." He scrawled his name with the provided silver pen.

Once they stepped inside the cavernous hanger, Caleb surveyed all the awards and photos Mr. Cranford had on his walls. It became apparent to him that Rex Cranford was a decorated Air Force hero and seasoned pilot.

Captain Rex gave them a rundown of his military and flight experience. Caleb grinned as he donned the flight suit over his jeans and shirt. He noticed Faith's smile mirrored his own as she took out her camera and snapped numerous photos of him and Rex next to the captain's 1918 Curtiss Jenny Biplane. Its shiny brass trim gleamed in the light.

Caleb grinned and patted the wing. "She's a beauty. Not as much as you are, Faith, but close."

Faith glanced heavenward and rolled her eyes.

Captain Rex launched into a ten-minute discourse on the history of the plane. He quieted and cleared his throat, returning from his memories. "Let's get into the air. Sorry I went on for so long."

Caleb would have enjoyed hearing more, but his girl, probably not. "It was interesting."

As he threw a stool next to the plane, an easy smile deepened the creases on either side of his mouth. "If you're ready, climb on board."

Caleb hugged Jack who was smiling up at him.

"If it gets too loud, tell Faith you two can sit in the car."

"Me watch you."

"You will, son." He then leaned over to Faith and planted a kiss on her lips before he climbed on the stool, then onto the wing over to the front seat. "I love you."

Faith gave him a thumbs-up. "Caleb, buckle up and hold on. Be safe. I love you, too."

Captain Rex climbed aboard and fastened his goggles after he handed a pair to Caleb. He turned toward Faith and hollered out to her, "You'll want to go find a spot out on the grassy area beyond the hanger. People sit there and watch the flights all day long. Just keep off the runway."

"Have fun." Faith and Jack trotted to the viewing area as the plane shuddered and the propeller started to spin. He tugged on his three-point harness to show Captain Rex he was secure. The pilot nodded. The motor vibrations beat in his chest, and he shoved the earplugs back into his ears as they cruised down the runway.

Caleb clutched onto the sides of the seat as the engine throttled higher. He nodded in Faith's direction as they passed by. They climbed into the sky, his stomach threatening to eject his lunch. As the wind whipped around his face, he released his death grip on the seat and adjusted his goggles. When Captain Rex tapped his shoulder, he forced his head around to look at the man seated behind him. Rex made a looping motion with his hands. Stomach in his throat, Caleb nodded. The plane barreled skyward and his sweaty hands had trouble holding onto the seat edges. Even though the safety harness held him in place, he craved the extra amount of security. He viewed the runway from the bottom of the plane or top, he wasn't sure, but whatever it was he shouted, in either abject terror or pure exhilaration. He picked up on the captain's deep laugh as they turned out of the loop and pointed behind them. Caleb squinted at the smoke trail in the shape of a heart. *I love Faith with everything in me. I've got to show her how much.* Caleb held in a breath as the plane nose-dived. *Once I can see straight.*

CHAPTER THIRTY-SEVEN

*F*aith scrubbed a hand over her face and yawned as she walked into the bakery. Ryan came through the door with a big smile splitting his face, followed by Willow, the assistant baker.

Willow held a treasure in her hands, showing Faith with a sparkle in her eye. "Happy Friday. Ryan and I have finished the baking. Here is a latte and cinnamon twist."

Faith's eyes widened as she drank from the mug with greedy pleasure then bit into the flaky sweet pastry after.

"Thanks for finishing the baking. Willow, make one for you. Grab something to eat, and sit down. Let's talk about the list for tomorrow."

"I don't know about eating more food. I already had a protein shake. It'll go to my hips."

Faith glanced at Willow and grumbled. Willow was as thin as a runway model. "Great genetics," she always said.

"I'll get my coffee. Be right back."

Willow returned and pulled out a chair. Her first sip ended in a moan of gratefulness. "I needed this today. Last night I binge-watched a new Victorian romance series. The lead actor was swoon worthy. He kind of reminded me of Ryan."

Mother hen that she was, Faith shook her head, addressing Willow. "You know what Ry and I've both told you. Save the marathon show watching for the weekend. Last time you did, I worried you'd fall asleep driving back to your apartment. I almost followed you home."

"It's too good to wait." Faith groaned at Willow's comment. Willow held out her hands, palms up in surrender. "I know, I know. Next time, only on the weekends." She bit her cinnamon twist. "Pure heaven."

"An old family recipe from my Grandma Christine. She couldn't boil water but baked like an angel." A wistful smile crossed her lips. "Great woman could tell the best stories. Okay, now tell me, please, what you two have baked."

"Hang on, the list's in the back." Flying from the seat, Willow went to the kitchen. With the fleetness only a caffeinated person could possess, she returned. "Ryan, are you coming?"

"Sure, last tray's in the oven."

Moving the chair back to touch the table, Ryan sat down and put his elbows on the table. "We've got a couple cake orders to do Monday."

"Good. What else?"

One after the other, both Willow and Ryan listed the baking they did that day and the schedule for the beginning of the week.

"Busy days ahead. We all need to rest this weekend. Anyone have any plans this weekend?"

Willow shook her head. "Faith, what are you and Caleb going to do to top last weekend's flight? I'm sure your adventurous spirits will have you doing something challenging."

Faith turned in her seat and cocked her head at an angle, thinking through their calendar. "Nothing's planned. Maybe a

A PROMISE FOR FAITH

hike or a rafting ride. I don't know. I've already taken all my kayak lessons. He's probably too busy to do much more."

Willow sighed. "Sounds like fun."

"Life's never dull with him, that's for certain. If you need me, I'm going to my desk. Need some quiet. I see we've got customers waiting already."

"We'll open in a sec," Ryan said. "Willow, let's get the cookies out of the oven."

Walking to her built-in desk in the kitchen, she opened her laptop and sighed. It was never fun trying to figure out the numbers in the computer program and how they made sense. Business necessity. She rolled her shoulders back and forth. Concentration was not coming easily today.

The back door shushed open and closed. *Delivery person.* The hair stood up on the back of her neck. *Someone was staring. Who...?* Faith turned her head to the side and flicked the pony-tail away from her face. "Can I—"

Caleb stood near the door dressed in a bright green button-down long-sleeved shirt which showed off his gorgeous eyes. Jet-black shorts completed the ensemble over his strong, muscular legs. "Hey, gorgeous, want to go somewhere with me?"

Confusion buzzed her brain. Caleb often dropped by if he had time in the evening, knowing her early mornings were chaotic. She swallowed some air and spoke. "Hi. This is totally unexpected." Faith glanced at Ryan and Willow for answers. They were smiling and giggling.

His dimples deepened, and he repeated his offer.

"Come on. I want to take you somewhere."

"I'm working."

Peering over her shoulder, he stated, "I'll do that later. Come on, Ry and Willow have it covered." Both looked like mischie-vous little elves.

She looked down at her rather casual outfit of jeans and a Briar Creek Bakery t-shirt. "Am I dressed okay?"

"Perfect."

"I could run home and change."

Caleb kissed her cheek. "You look beautiful. Let's leave before Willow puts us both to work."

Willow shooed both toward the door laughing. "Have fun."

"Thanks, I think. Call me if you need me." Shrugging, Faith left arm-in-arm with Caleb as he led her across to Hawk's Creek.

"What are we doing?"

"Don't worry."

"What's the rush? You seem in a hurry."

"No rush. I want to get in the water before…"

"Before what?" Faith noticed the color fade from his face, and sputtered. "You're ashen. We'd better go back. I don't want you getting sick. I'll go back to work, and you go home and rest."

He turned his head toward her. Sweat beaded on his face. He wiped it with his shirtsleeve. "I'm okay, don't worry. I went for a run earlier today. I'm probably still warm from it… I took a hot shower, too."

She dug a water bottle out of her bag and handed it to him. He gulped its contents down.

"Better." He whisked the door to the outfitters open.

"Kayaking or rafting?"

No answer. She repeated her question.

A sheepish grin split his face. "Sorry. My mind was on something else."

"Understandable. You're busy."

His answer was clipped. "Yes."

"Sure you're fine? You never answered my question. Kayaking or rafting?"

Pulling on his shirt collar, he replied, "Both."

Faith shrugged at his highly unusual behavior. He seemed jumpy, which was not like him at all. She hoped he wasn't coming down with the flu. He handed her a life jacket, his mind somewhere else as he looked beyond them down the river.

She soon had her answer as they neared the kayaks. He dragged one closer to the river. Faith climbed into the rear seat, and he hopped into the front after pushing off from the shoreline. Caleb took the paddle from the clamp and started cutting into the water with deep strokes. He remained silent.

Other sounds seemed to take the place of her quiet boatmate. A raucous red cardinal call pierced the morning air, calling out for a mate. Faith occupied herself by paddling and taking in the surroundings. She admired the cool water glistening like diamonds in the sun.

She repositioned her sunglasses and let the sunshine fully on her face. "Great idea. How'd you talk Ryan and Willow into working the bakery all day without me?"

He darted a glance back. "I told them my plan for our day, and they were excited."

That raised questions in her mind, but she decided to just enjoy the time with him and see what the day might bring. Faith noticed another kayak coming toward them and raised a hand to wave. They seemed familiar but were too far away for her to see their faces. She found it odd that Caleb began to paddle harder and faster when the water was calm and smooth. Faith dug in and matched her strokes with his.

Caleb became breathless and shifted in his seat, causing the kayak to tip to the left side. Faith counterbalanced and tilted her body to the right. She glanced at him and noted he was becoming more agitated. Faith averted her eyes to the other kayakers. They held a sign in their hands that had the word *Will* written on it. Faith took off her sunglasses and leaned forward. *Caleb's parents and Jack.* Her hands shook as she tried to keep a steady grip on the paddle. *What's going on? Why are they here?*

Caleb waved at his family and turned to smile at her. She returned a wobbly smile. Once again he cut through the water, building their speed to cut around the bend in the river. Ahead was another pair of kayakers.

She stopped paddling. Her parents crookedly held up the sign that said *You* as her mom dabbed at her eyes with a tissue and her dad wore a tremulous smile *Will. You. Is the next word what I think it is?* Faith's hopes soared higher than the gliding hawks above.

With a shaky hand, she blew them a kiss and bit her lip to stop the flow of moisture from her eyes. Ahead, in a kayak, were their siblings. As they came closer, Hope jumped up while Grace tried to steady their bobbing watercraft as Dylan paddled. Hope and Grace pulled out something from Dylan's backpack and held it up. She spied a white banner with *Marry* painted on it. They whooped at the couple when they cruised by, and she giggled as she wiped the happiness leaking from her eyes.

Caleb pulled them to the shoreline and hopped out. Her tingling, wobbly legs didn't want to cooperate, so he picked Faith up and put her on dry ground.

Caleb started to remove his long-sleeved shirt. Feeling a little dizzy, Faith closed her eyes.

"Look at me, please, love."

She peeked through her lashes. Where was he? Then she looked down. There knelt Caleb, on one knee, with a t-shirt that read *Me*. In his hand he held an open box, revealing a stunning diamond ring. She stared at the beautiful piece of jewelry with its sizable center stone surrounded by a halo of smaller diamonds before returning her gaze to his face.

"Faith Elizabeth Fuller, there is no one I'd love to go on this adventure with than you. Will you marry me?"

She fell in a mushy puddle of love in front of him and took his hands as she made her promise. "Yes, Caleb Dalton Gaines. I will marry you."

He leaned over, gathered her in his arms, and they sealed that promise with a kiss. With clammy, shaking hands, Caleb gently placed the ring on her finger. Their families applauded and cheered, startling Faith.

"For you, Fay."

She got down to Jack's level and hugged him. Taking the package that was offered, she unwrapped the medium-sized square. Her eyes danced with happiness. A superhero shirt in her size.

"Oh, Jack, we'll match."

"Yup. Dad got one, too."

"I love it, but love you more."

Placing a wet kiss on her cheek, Jack stood next to his dad. "Love you, Fay."

With Jack's words, the last piece missing from her heart moved into place. Family. Standing still, she surveyed all the loved ones around to seal this wonderful moment in her heart forever.

Cresting over the hill, the Canary' brakes squealed and her doors opened for them to alight.

Minutes later the old "yellow bird" noisily deposited them at Hawk Creek's parking lot. She walked with Caleb and Jack to their cars.

"Let's take mine—the car seat."

After fastening Jack into his seat, Caleb held her door open and Faith got in. He ran to the other side, climbed in, and held her hand in the sunlight coming through the windshield. A kaleidoscope of silver-white specks danced in his dark-grey interior. Faith took a deep breath and exhaled. "I can't believe it."

"I've wanted to for months, but I waited until we could do this on the water."

She took her gaze off the glittering ring and stared deep into his eyes. "It was perfect. More than I could have imagined. Months ago, I was too scared of the water." Faith swallowed a little twinge in her throat. "Now I've learned to fully trust our Father, and you, to keep me safe."

He touched his lips to the ring and then transferred them to her own lips.

"I promise to keep you as safe as I can. I'm fortunate to have found you again. A year ago, I thought I was destined to remain single. Funny how the Lord works."

Faith smoothed her finger across the platinum band. "It is. I haven't ever been this happy or felt this at peace."

Caleb ran a finger down her arm. "Me neither." He put his car in drive, and they made their way to the restaurant.

Ducking inside, they were taken to a side room where their families waited, along with Taylor and Jarod.

Jarod grinned and dipped his chin. Taylor swiped at her eyes and hugged them both. She cocked a hand on one hip and smiled. "Your niece and nephew didn't cooperate and woke up too late to be at the landing point. I hope someone filmed it."

Dylan raised his phone aloft.

Her exhale in relief was audible. "Good."

The jovial group sat at a long table for their family-style dinner, and both fathers gave toasts to the happy couple with their teas.

Faith's mother, Cat, gave a toast to the joyous couple. "I wish you two every blessing and happiness, and Alexander and I finally get a son."

Grinning, Caleb's mom, Georgia, stood up once Cat had sat back down. She raised her glass to Faith and Caleb and gave them a wink. "I'm relieved to see my oldest boy so happy. He's made a wonderful choice. Welcome to our family, Faith! Look, Steve, we've got a daughter."

Faith and Caleb clinked their glasses together and raised them to their family afterward.

Cat darted a glance at her husband. "You know what this

means, hon. Dress shopping!" She grinned wider than the Mississippi River.

Alexander groaned. "I think I've got this handled, honey." He took out a dollar bill from his wallet and gave it to Faith, a smile tweaking his mouth's corners. "Does this cover it, sweetie?" Alexander waggled his eyebrows.

"Um, not quite."

"I'll add more to this later. It's your special day."

Cat sat up straighter in her chair and grinned at Faith.

Alexander's smile widened. It was evident he was enjoying the lighthearted banter. "Now, Cat, don't spend a fortune. We've still got to pay a few dollars for the rest of the wedding."

The ladies chortled.

Two months later, Faith flew to Florida with Taylor who'd left Jarod and Uncle Caleb in charge of Olivia and Joshua Jen's plane from New York landed moments later.

Faith introduced Tay and Jen when they found her in baggage claim.

"Let's go, the appointment is at two. I already called Uber." Faith led the way out into the muggy Florida air.

At Belle Marriage, they were accompanied by Faith's mom and sisters. A middle-aged woman with the grace of a princess flowed over and held her hand out to Cat. "Hello, I'm Madame Anna Le Clerc." Her eyes scanned each girl before settling on Faith. "And you must be the fiancée." Years of serving excited brides-to-be must have honed her skills in choosing which lady had the special honor.

A bridal consultant pulled several dresses that Faith thought were pretty. With her mother in tow, Faith and the consultant were heading for a dressing room when Madame Anna herself stopped the little entourage. The stylist and boutique owner spoke a few complimentary words as she looked the bride-to-be up and down, took some measurements, nodded and waved her hand toward the dressing room.

Once there the consultant closed the door and turned to face the mother and daughter, beaming. She clasped her hands in front of her and rocked up and down from heel to toe. "You were just madamed." Her wedding charges looked at each other, puzzled. "Madame does not often take a personal interest in a bride any longer; she is so busy. We can try these other dresses on if you'd like, but I will almost guarantee you, the dress she brings will be the one you choose. It's happened every time I've witnessed it, though it's only been a few times." Moments later Madame Anna came back into the room with a dress still in its protective cover. Her light accent held a slight lilt. "This came in yesterday. I'd like to show it to you, but I had it set aside to be steamed. Do you mind if it is a bit wrinkled?"

Faith's hair swished across her shoulders. "It won't bother me. I'd like to see it."

Madame Anna hung it on a silver peg near an antique mirror and unzipped the opaque dress protector. Before the dress was even free of its bag, excitement wove its tendrils throughout Faith. Chill bumps prickled her arms. As Madame Anna slipped the dress out, fluffing it as she went, the gown was liberated from its cocoon. Faith and her mom held hands as the garment came into view. She gasped. It was stunning. The ivory silk bodice was over-laid with delicate French lace and adorned with seed pearls and crystals which glinted in the sunlight from the clerestory windows. Faith was captivated.

Her mom squeezed her hand. "Try it on." Her voice caught in her throat, so Faith agreed without a sound. She followed Madame Anna into the curtained dressing room and awaited her instructions, as her heartbeat ramped up in excitement.

Madame Anna's deft fingers adjusted the back of the train, and she stepped aside and touched a hand to her chest. "It's made for you, cheri. C'est magnifique! Let's go dazzle your family in the showroom. Then you can see for yourself. This little mirror doesn't give you the bigger picture."

Heart skipping Faith stepped into the high heeled sandals she'd brought with her and left the dressing room.

A gasp sounded as she stopped in front of her family and friends. Her mom sniffled. "Look at yourself, sweetie. That dress is gorgeous on you."

Faith dared to peer into the Cheval mirror. Her breath rushed out. The sweetheart neckline emphasized her femininity with a delicate grace. She ran her hand down the side of the gown and admired the cut of the dress. It accentuated her slim hips and didn't cling to the areas that she didn't want to be showcased. She turned around to view the train. The stunning lace fanned from her waist like Rapunzel's hair from the tower. It flowed two feet beyond the heel of her sandal. The dream dress was a perfect blend of contemporary and romantic.

"It's more than I'd hoped to find."

Taylor took Faith's picture as she wiped her eyes and handed Hope, Grace, and Jen the tissue box. "This is it; you'll bowl him over."

Jen added, "It's a home run."

Faith glanced at her sisters and their matching wide-eyes and tears helped her make the easy decision. "This is it, Madame Anna." Her loved ones clamored to give her a hug. She couldn't wait to become Mrs. Caleb Gaines.

EPILOGUE

*F*aith threw open the curtains and caught site of two dolphins leaping in Tampa Bay past their boat dock. It was hard to believe it was the day of her wedding. She whirled past her tissue-wrapped gown, now fully steamed and pressed in pristine condition, and put on her robe and went downstairs, where most of her favorite people were seated in the dining room enjoying her mom's French toast.

"Morning, sunshine. How are you?" Faith's dad enfolded her in a hug.

"Let's see after a cup of caramel mocha. Excuse me while I go get one." She scooted around the crowded table and through the door to the kitchen. Her eyes lit upon a lone loaf of oatmeal bread and homemade jelly. She grinned and sliced a small piece, put it on a plate, and poured herself a cup of coffee. Back in the dining room, everyone moved their chairs to fit one in for her. Faith ate bits of her bread between answering questions. The beverage warmed her chilled body, but her insides rebelled with unexpected nerves. She pushed away from the food and excused herself to go shower. After she finished, she dressed and lay on her bed.

Sometime later her stomach growled, so she went downstairs and made herself a sandwich. Everyone else was scattered throughout the house. Eventually she heard chatter from the hallway, and a baby's cry sounded. *I hope when Caleb and I have a baby, ours will be as precious as Tay and Jarod's.* She glanced at the clock on the stove. Twenty minutes before her first appointment. Faith finished her lunch and walked back to her room as someone answered the door. Voices from below echoed in the large hall. She put her book in her suitcase and exited the room to greet her first appointment with her family's hair stylist. Brenda did her hair and makeup, as well as that of all the ladies in the wedding party. Faith eyed her subtle makeup in the bathroom mirror. Her artfully upswept hair, held up by a whole package of bobby pins, framed her face. She was pleased with the results.

A knock on the door stole her attention away from the mirror.

"Sweetie, Caleb came by with something." Her dad cracked open the door, jiggling an envelope and gift bag in his hand.

"Thank you, Dad."

"Welcome. See you later." She heard his footsteps on the stairs.

She tore into the light blue envelope and pulled the card out. The "diamond" heart on the front made her smile. Dots of joy appeared in the corners of her eyes, and she whisked them away with a tissue. His scrawled handwriting inside made her heart lurch.

"My beautiful Faith, in a few hours we'll be making our own family history. I thank the Lord for you. You are the most gorgeous, kind, and wonderful lady I've ever known. We've ridden the seas, laughed, and flown to the heavens together. I can't wait until our married adventure begins. I love you, wife-to-be. You hold the key to my heart, forever and always. Caleb."

Faith peeked inside the red rose petal filled gift bag. She

sniffed the heady fragrance and sighed. Faith pulled out a small red box as several petals floated to the floor. Diamonds glittered in the light as she opened the lid. His gift, a diamond key on a dainty white-gold chain, made her laugh. A literal key to his heart. Faith held it up to her neck and grinned. *I hope he likes his present.*

~

A stringed quartet played as Taylor walked down the aisle with Jarod, followed by Hope and Dylan, Grace and Ryan, and Jen and Will. A white wagon festooned with yards of ribbon wheeled behind the last of the adult wedding party. Six-month-old Olivia, the flower girl, dozed upon a pillow embroidered with flower wreaths in the colors of taupe, ivory, blue and apricot around the border. Joshua, the ring bearer, slumbered on his pillow embroidered with intertwined silver rings. As Grandpa Joshua pulled them down the aisle, guests' faces erupted in smiles.

Minutes later, the church doors swung wide open as the quartet played the "Wedding March." Faith glanced around the large church, noticing most of the seats were filled. She swept her gaze to the front of the church and her husband-to-be in his black tux. *He's so handsome. I can't believe I'm going to be his wife.* Her heart thumped wildly in her chest. She wanted to treasure this moment forever. She'd never felt so loved and cherished. Caleb gazed at her and smiled. He made her feel beautiful.

"Ready, sweetie? You look gorgeous."

Faith swallowed a lump in her throat and nodded. Her dad led her down the aisle. *It seems surreal, like it's happening to someone else.* Stopping next to Jack, who was seated with his grandparents, Faith pulled a miniature airplane from her dad's tux pocket and gave it to him.

Her parents' pastor, Reverend Herb, performed a portion of the sermon, including a story of a young, freckle-faced Faith running around the church with her sisters. Pastor Tim, who flew in for the ceremony, snuck in a story about Caleb's well-known love of airplanes. Caleb grinned and pulled up his tux sleeve to reveal his present from Faith, a pair of Tiffany's silver airplane cufflinks. Faith laughed along with many of the guests. Once Pastor Tim composed himself, he performed the final, touching vows. Caleb wrapped his arms around his wife and leaned in. Faith captured his lips in a kiss, sighing when it ended. Caleb grinned and gave her another quick kiss before they walked down the aisle.

Faith giggled at Caleb's exasperated sigh when the photographer wanted even more poses. He leaned in and whispered, "Will this ever be over? I want my bride to myself."

Faith's heart pounded when they finally dashed to the waiting limousine as Mr. and Mrs. Gaines. He gripped her hand tightly as they pulled into the driveway of the Don Cesar on St. Petersburg Beach. "Ready?" She nodded. The camera person arrived moments later to snap some photos of the bride and groom on the beautiful white-sand beach. Caleb picked her up in his arms and took her back to the grassy area near the sidewalk. He carefully lowered her to the ground. Caleb put a steadying arm around her waist as she slipped her sandals back on her feet. Together they walked toward the expansive shell-pink historic hotel.

The hors-d'oeuvres and refreshments were served on the terrace where the wedding party and other guests could enjoy the live music while affording Caleb and Faith a chance to linger a moment in the reception area, taking it all in.

Faith's breath caught in her throat, her eyes growing large and misty as she noticed the

bride and groom's table. Her late paternal grandmother Emma's lace tablecloth was placed upon it, and his late maternal grandmother Christine's peach hand-painted vase sat in the middle, filled with beautiful sunset-hued flowers.

Caleb drew her in for a kiss. "I love you, Mrs. Gaines."

Electricity sizzled through her as she grabbed him by the lapels and deepened their kiss. "I love you, Mr. Gaines. We've waited a year to get married. Let's go start our night."

The bandleader announced the couple, and they crossed the floor to begin the festivities with the first dance.

His lips met hers on the final note as he held her in his arms and dipped her to a round of applause from those nearby.

Faith's face heated, and he led her off the wooden dance floor and into the waiting arms of her father for the beginning of the traditional parent dances.

He pecked her cheek. "We're so excited for you both, sweetie." Faith smiled as they danced to "Daddy's Girl."

"Love you, Dad." He smiled and, finished with their turn, took her to the edge of the floor so they could watch Caleb dance with his mom. Faith noticed Mrs. Gaines wipe a tear away with her lace handkerchief as her face wrapped in a smile.

"Someone else wants to dance." Faith's dad motioned to Jack.

"I'd be honored." Taking her little son's hand in hers, she danced step-toe-step with him.

In the middle of the song, Jack stopped dancing and ran toward his grandfather. "See you."

Holding in a giggle, she waved.

Caleb returned to her side and she wiped away his mom's peach lipstick from his cheek with a finger. He held her hand to his lips as he escorted her to the center of the dance floor. One of his wedding guests, a former fellow fraternity brother, brought out a chair for her to sit. Several other guests who were Caleb's fraternity brothers also came over.

Faith was at a loss for words as he and his fraternity brothers surrounded her in a semi-circle and sang their fraternity song. Never had an off-pitch college song been more exciting. She giggled and clapped at the close. Clinking glasses sounded as he wrapped her in his arms. Murmurs filled the room along with laughter. Dinner was served but interrupted often by silverware clinking against water glasses, shearing through the band music. Each time the newlyweds indulged their guests with a kiss. After dinner and the cake cutting, many people streamed out onto the dance floor once again. Caleb and Faith wound around the room, stopping to chat with their departing guests before making their way to the front entrance.

Bubbles bobbed and danced around them as they headed toward the rental car. Faith laughed as Caleb popped some of them that were trapped in her hair, the smell of clean soap floating down from them.

Caleb eyed the car, groaned, and turned to give the whole wedding party the evil eye. No one took him too seriously but all wore guilty expressions. Brightly colored balloons and streamers trailed from their car.

Dylan came forward with a pair of scissors and clapped his brother on the back with his free hand. "Had to do it. The ladies asked us to." High pitched voices protested behind them.

Caleb shook his head as he cut the traditional wedding clutter away and gave it all to his brother. "I expected nothing less from you and the guys." He searched the crowd and witnessed all the groomsmen, including Jarod, high fiving each other. Caleb chuckled and shook his head, more interested in turning back to his bride than their good-natured antics. After hugging their family and friends, and hugging Jack who was staying behind with his family, Caleb and Faith drove off amidst the cheers and well-wishes of the guests.

She nervously changed into a gorgeous satiny nightgown and bathrobe. The butterflies from earlier in the day nested in her stomach once again. The card she held in her hands tap-tap-tapped against her knee. Caleb came out of the bathroom, crossed the room to her, and gave her an appraising stare. "Have I told you, Mrs. Gaines, how beautiful you are?" He leaned over and kissed her, the smell of mint lingering on his breath.

Faith fanned herself with the card. "Not in the last few hours, my handsome husband." She handed him the card.

Caleb opened the envelope and pulled out a photo of a gorgeous wooden kayak. The one he'd dreamed of owning.

"Look closer."

"A check, too?"

"For your MBA program. I've paid for the rest of it."

"No."

"You gave me my dream. I'm giving you yours."

He picked her up, kissed her, and whirled her around. She giggled into his neck. "I've got something for you, too." Caleb placed her on the edge of the bed and turned to rummage in his suitcase. He pulled out a medium-sized box. It was wrapped in glossy paper that featured one of her favorite photos of them taken during their engagement photo session. Caleb and Faith held a large wooden heart between them and were kissing.

"This is beautiful."

"I'm happy you like it. We've got more back home."

Her heart thrilled at the word home. "I love you, my mushy husband."

"I love you, too, my gorgeous wife. Are you going to open it?"

Faith grinned, ripped open the paper and took out a cute white apron with "je t'aime" printed in red all over it. "I like it, thank you."

He sat down next to her and grinned. "Look in the pocket."

Faith pulled out the handwritten note. She read the words

aloud. "My beautiful wife. Since we've been together, you've given me so much happiness. We've flown together in a hot air balloon, and now I want to fly with you over the sea. Let's discover England, Ireland, and France together. We'll heat things up in our cooking class in Paris, too. My love, my life-time, I can't wait for our journey to begin. Yours, Caleb."

"Oh, Caleb, is this our honeymoon? It's only three weeks away. I can't believe it. I love you." She leaned over and gave him a loving kiss and then turned and put the presents on the dresser.

Smiling, Caleb turned off the main light, leaving only the soft light spilling from the bathroom nightlight, and ran a hand over the covers.

~

The next several days were a whirlwind. July 4th came and went before they knew it.

Finally, Hope arrived to watch Jack the day before they left on their honeymoon. Dylan was bunking with Ryan to run Caleb's portion of the tours for Hawk's Creek. The couple double-checked their instructions with Mrs. Settles for the fourth time and agreed everything looked to be in order. Caleb and Faith hugged and kissed Jack twenty times before they left.

"Ready?"

"I am, husband."

Faith leaned over to brush a kiss on Jack's cheek, a tear slip-ping from her eyes. "Bye, sweetie. I love you."

Jack looked up at her and wrapped his arms around her neck. "I love you too, Mom."

As the water fell from her eyes, she laughed. "That's the most wonderful words I could hear."

Caleb hugged her and whispered. "I love it too. We need to

tell him about how you'll be adopting him when we get back. The papers should be in by then."

She squeezed his hand. "I can't wait." Faith swiped away the tears and grabbed her carry-on. "We'll leave after one more kiss for our son."

"Agreed."

Both gave a final kiss for Jack and they headed to the car as Dylan and Hope slid into the backseat. The group parked and Faith gave Hope a sideways look as Caleb took her bag and they headed to the entrance.

"Thanks for coming out, Hopeful. Let me know if anything happens or you need anything."

"You're welcome. It ought to be fun. Jack's awesome. It's going to be good."

They stopped behind the check-in line.

Caleb clapped Dylan's back and hugged his sister-in-law. "Appreciate the both of you helping take care of your nephew."

Dylan grinned. "Always. See you in two weeks."

Caleb grabbed a suitcase.

Hope grinned at her sister. "Go have fun, you two. Don't forget to text your family… but no need to call!"

"Remember the alarm system at our house."

Hope smirked and waved. "I've got the code memorized, don't worry."

Dylan added, "I promise, we've got it. Be safe and have a good time. I'll keep her company while you're gone."

"Call us if you have questions." Caleb shook his head at his wife. "Never mind, see you." He put all the bags next to the airline check-in stand. The woman whisked them through the process. "Thank you for the help."

"Come on, sweetheart, we'll miss our flight." They began to walk down to the security line.

Faith pulled on her husband's arm. "Forgot to tell her something."

Caleb stopped mid-step and checked the time on his phone. "We've really got to go." They both turned to see if Hope and Dylan were still near check-in. Instantly, they looked at each other and then glanced back to their siblings. Dylan and Hope were locked in an embrace. As they watched, Dylan moved a piece of hair away from Hope's cheek and kissed her, neither noticing they had an audience.

Caleb looked at his wife. "We knew, didn't we?"

She giggled. "Yes. Stop gawking or we'll miss our flight."

Caleb settled a kiss on Faith's lips and grinned. "Lead on, gorgeous. Our honeymoon awaits."

The End

ABOUT THE AUTHOR

Stacy T. Simmons writes uplifting fiction that delights the reader's romantic sensibilities. Thirty-four years of marital bliss is a great contributor. She is a mom of two grown children, and she and her family have a menagerie of pets she likes to call "Noah's Ark." You can find her working on her next manuscript with a piece of dark chocolate and a cup of coffee nearby. She loves to connect with her readers via her website at www.stacytsimmonsauthor.com

Celebrate Lit Publishing
Is proud to endorse

Finding the pictures to capture your words

http://www.roseannawhitedesigns.com/

MATCHMAKER IN 3B

A PROMISE FOR FAITH BONUS SHORT STORY

STACY T. SIMMONS

CHAPTER ONE

$\mathcal{F}$aith quickly stepped into her apartment building. The door swung back and threatened to swat her into the lobby. She shifted a plastic encased dress from hand to hand, careful to not drop the three-thousand-dollar Gio Fabriotti on the dingy tile floor by the mailboxes. She fumbled with the tumbler on her mailbox. Inside were the usual suspects of junk mail, and something addressed to the former tenant. In the stillness of the lobby, her mailbox door slammed shut on its own. Heart in her throat, she held the bookstore sale postcard like a knife, ready to give someone a vicious papercut, if nothing else.

"So, you're going to pommel me with a piece of junk mail?" A raspy voice questioned.

Her neighbor's bright pink velour tracksuit and Sunday ready lacquered blonde hair belied her 60-ish years of age. "Hi, Mrs. Carlucci." Faith shoved a smile in place. "No, I get jumpy when my mailbox closes by itself."

"Didn't mean to startle you, hon. What is that gorgeous dress you've got?"

"A friend surprised me with it, she works in the garment district. She couldn't bear to put it in the castoff pile."

"That color is splashing. It'll look pretty on you." Mrs. Carlucci's pencil drawn eyebrows bunched. "Anyhow, you've been busy recently I noticed. I see a lot from my apartment down the hall."

I'm sure you do. "Working on getting a promotion. The test kitchen head chef's retiring."

"Well, I hope you get it." Mrs. Carlucci punctuated her words with swift hand gestures like a younger version of Mr. Miyagi. "You need a break though. Do you have plans for Saturday?"

"I don't. Did you need me to pet sit?"

"No, Harold and I aren't going to the shore this weekend. Mr. Tibbles won't need his favorite pet-sitter." Mrs. Carlucci pursed her posy-pink mouth, eyes narrowing. "Did you ditch the guy you were dating? What was his name? Dirk?"

"Yes. We dated three weeks, and he wanted me to make a commitment. And he had an extra set of hands, it seemed." Faith pressed the elevator call button. It glowed, and as usual, the temperamental elevator apparently was having another hissy fit. The ladies made their way to the stairs. "Isn't that awful?"

Gruff laughter caused Mrs. Carlucci's words to come in bursts. "He sounds desperate. I've got a Cousin. Ramona. She's thirty-five and getting baby fever. He might make marriage material for her. Got his number?"

"I deleted it."

"Good thinking. He might be. . . What do you call it?" Her fingers formed air quotes. "A shifty customer. Squirrely, you know?"

"Mmhmm."

"Speaking of animals." Mrs. Carlucci motioned to her eyebrows. "He had worms for eyebrows, thick and fuzzy. Didn't look right."

Faith decided not to correct her. Dirk had been a worm.

"Anyway, we're almost to our floor," Mrs. Carlucci paused and took Faith's arm. "The reason I asked about Dirk is. . .I know this great guy, single, good job, my stockbroker." They paused at Faith's door.

"I've got an insurance agent who handles my 401K plan at work. I'll keep him in mind."

Mrs. Carlucci stuck out one aqua fingernail toward her. "Not for business, but a date. I thought you were single. I took the first step for you and set you up with him."

Faith gulped. Her mouth grew dry.

"You two are going to my uncle's restaurant, not the Italian place. The other one, who owns the nice steakhouse. Remember? We went there for Harold's 60th."

"It was wonderful, I remember." Faith was simultaneously touched and irked. "I don't know this man. What if he's got squirmy eyebrows?"

Mrs. Carlucci waved a hand in the air. "No, he's one of those metrospecial guys, little bit of a beard, very handsome man. I love my Harold, but I got eyes." She winked. "Bella, let my uncle Dominick cook for you. It's mine and Harold's treat. We'd be disappointed if you didn't go." She shook her mushroom cap of Barbie blonde hair back and forth. "You work in that kitchen all day long. Wear something pretty. Show off your nice figure. Guys go for that."

"I'll think about it." Looking at the ceiling, Faith smirked. "Night, Mrs. Carlucci."

"Night, sweetie. Don't forget about Saturday. Seven pm. Do you need me to come over to remind you on Friday?"

She laughed. "I won't forget."

No one denied Rose Carlucci anything. She made the best lasagna in New York City.

~

Faith entered the glass walled corporate building the next morning, grabbed a coffee at one of the kiosks on the main floor and rode the elevator to the thirty-second floor of Erika's Eatery corporate office. Alighting, she made a quick dash to her friend's cubicle. "Morning, Jen."

Her friend rose from the chair and yawned. "Morning. Did you see the Yankees game last night?"

"No, didn't catch it."

"What did you do last night?"

"Read. Binge watched the next season of Misty Road."

"Fun."

"Before that, Mrs. Carlucci commanded me to do something."

"She's not a high school teacher for nothing." Jen giggled. "Let me guess. You're pet-sitting that little dog of theirs."

"No. Worse than Mr. Tibbles."

"What's worse than that six-pound dog? He's got a raging case of dog halitosis. His kisses are sweet, but his breath is disgusting." Jen motioned to the kitchen beyond the row of cubicles. "Tell me on the way to the kitchen before The Ring of Fire-Erika sees us."

"The boss has eyes all over the place." Faith matched steps with her friend. "About Rose's decree, she's asked me to meet her stockbroker for dinner Saturday night."

"A set up. Or is he giving you advice on your 401K?"

"She promises he's handsome, so a date." She held the door open and Jen whisked through the entrance. "I didn't know what to say. She's practically like a mom. Aagh, who knows? Maybe he's a winner."

"Did she use a 'Rose-ism?' I love Mrs. Carlucci's way with words."

"She said he was 'metrospecial.'"

"That's a new phrase for her, she's a sweet lady."

"She is. It's part of her charm."

"Agreed. Back to the command, this man with a good job, and supposedly good looking. That kind doesn't last long in this city." Jen handed Faith an Erika's Eatery imprinted apron and hairnet. "There's something wrong with him."

"More than Dirk?" Faith slipped on the green apron and glanced at her friend as she tucked her hair into the dark net.

"Did ya see his eyebrows?" Jen raised her ebony sculpted brows. "Something funky going on there."

"I didn't really notice. He had nice teeth though."

They quieted as they began chopping vegetables.

A sound of squishing footsteps neared the prep area.

"Are you finished?" The head chef, Ingrid, stood in front of them, frowning, points of red hair spiked from the chef's hat. "We need to pick up the speed ladies. There are five more things to create today. And Erika's visiting the kitchen."

Faith and Jen's knives flew with practiced precision through the small dicing.

"Good morning, Chef. And assistants." Erika's, the owner of the company's, voice boomed as she came closer to the prep area. "What's being tested today, soups, sides, or desserts?"

Ingrid adjusted her chef's hat. "Soups and a new sandwich to make a combo for fall."

"Good idea, Chef Ingrid, October will be here soon." Erika's smile widened, her cover-shoot eye-shadowed eyes rounded. "When you retire in the new year, I wonder who will be trying to fill your shoes?"

Me. Once the application window opened. Faith planned to put her name forward as a candidate for the position. Three years as sous chef earned Faith many great reviews and credit assists on creating delicious foods for the restaurant company.

"Maybe you?" She pointed to Faith. "You've been here longer than Jen."

"I'm going to apply."

"Good, good. Carry on." Erika departed with a tidy wave, stilettos clacking on the tile floor.

Mid-day, Faith entered the finished and approved recipes onto a computer file. A folded piece of paper landed on her desk. She glanced around to see who'd dropped it. Jen laughed as she race-walked away from her desk. As she unfolded the copy paper, she read the words written in red.

For you and "the mystery date" to do.

Below the script, Jen had printed the list of "The 10 Most Romantic Things to Do in NYC." A knot formed in her middle as she texted Jen.

Ha-ha, Jen. Not happening. Faith's hand hovered over the recycling bin near her left leg.

Don't throw it out, you might need it.

Too late, it's already there. The crumbled paper landed in the crowded bin.

Wear a dress.

Nope. I'm wearing my pj's.

Sure. Tell me all about it after, or I'll get Mrs. Carlucci to pay you a visit.

Did I tell you that you're annoying?

Every week, you put up with me, that's why you're my true friend.

She left her phone keyboard and returned to the one waiting on her desk, in a hurry to finish before leaving work that night.

Saturday, she shifted through the sea of clothing in her dark closet and rejected all but a few possibilities. An ocean foam colored dress stood out from the sea of dark colors in the back of her closet, shining like a lighthouse on a stormy night.

She lifted the plastic covering and sucked in a breath. The Gio Fabriotti. Faith wiggled into the dress and checked in the mirror. It was shorter than she usually wore, but the cut of the dress accentuated her curves in the most flattering way. She felt gorgeous. Her wavy brown-red hair curled over her shoulders, and the thirty-minute makeup session made her hazel eyes greener. Faith glanced down at the dress. *I just hope nothing happens to this dress.* She opened the door and stepped into the shared hallway.

Both Rose and Harold Carlucci loitered in the no-gawking zone, outside their apartment, no doubt waiting to see Faith.

"You look marvelous." Mrs. Carlucci elbowed her husband's rounded middle. "What do you say, Harry?"

"Yes, you do."

"Now look for a guy that has brown-blonde hair, tall, good looking. He'll be by the host stand."

"I'll watch for him."

"Tell us all about it tomorrow."

Mr. Carlucci held out his hands in front of him. "Rose, the game—"

"Harry, TVR it. This is urgent."

Mr. Carlucci mumbled to himself and ducked back into the apartment.

"Have fun, sweetie. You look beautiful." Mrs. Carlucci waved and closed her door.

Faith hailed a taxi and swept the short skirt underneath her as she lowered to the pleather bench seat.

"Where to?"

Faith gave the address. The cabbie lurched from the curb and swept into the speeding traffic. The cab shimmied back and forth in the five inches of spare room between the taxi and vehicle in the other lane. In her five years of living in the city, a cab driver's adventurous antics didn't surprise her anymore. She was a NYC road warrior.

"We're here," the cabbie yanked on the wheel and pushed the gear shift to park.

She gathered her handbag, and alighted from the car, careful to miss the gap from car to sidewalk. Faith scanned the exterior to Dominick's Steakhouse. The red doors marked the entrance. As she drew closer, the door was whisked open by a restaurant employee.

"Welcome to Dominick's, miss."

"Thank you." She tugged on the hem of the dress and stepped into the dimly lit restaurant. The soft evening light didn't aid her trek to the host desk. Faith squinted to see more clearly, and noticed people sitting in dark leather chairs against the wall. Low tones of conversation filtered around her. Ahead, a tall gentleman was standing apart from couples and families with his back to her. *Must be the stockbroker.* Ten more steps to go. Her left eyelid twitched like a glitchy computer game. She ran a finger over the pulsing peeper. *Calm down, Faith.* Eight more steps. She slowed.

When the man turned, Faith held in a sigh. With lines crossing his lower face, and radiating from alongside his eyes, it was clear he'd experienced many years of smiling and laughing. The gentleman motioned to someone seated nearby, and a lady rose to her feet and stood by his side. He gave his loved one a little smile as the two trailed slowly behind the host.

A deep male voice spoke, "Sorry, I'm late. Rose texted me what you were wearing so I'd know you."

"It's okay." Faith turned to face the speaker. "I got here a few moments ago." *Mrs. Carlucci deserves one of my chocolate cakes.* Dim lighting did not conceal his green eyes, blonde mixed into chocolate hair, and a physique that merited triple glances. She held out a hand, he took it in his. "Faith Fuller."

"Caleb Gaines. Nice to meet you." He shifted his feet on the wooden floor. "Did you put our names in with host?"

"Nice to meet you too. Not, yet."

He moved around her and spoke to the host. An attention-commanding, masculine, spice scent marked his path. Several sneak peeks on Faith's part, and he returned. "Do you do this often?"

"No." She played with the long gold link necklace around her neck. "My first blind date."

"I meant go out to eat. I heard you're a chef. So I thought you'd cook yourself."

Goof. "I do. I'm thankful Rose and Harold are treating us, then I don't have to cook." She stole a glance at Caleb. The angles on his beard shadowed face were very appealing. "Do you cook?"

"Not much. I eat takeout. Fish and quinoa are my favorites."

"Vegetarian?"

"No, but I eat pretty healthy."

"We can go somewhere else."

"I won't turn down a dinner at Dominick's. It's legendary. And with a pretty woman as well."

Flutters moved in her midsection. She smiled.

The black-jacketed host led them to the cobblestone patio where lush foliage surrounded the perimeter, softening the noise of the city beyond the emerald walls. Fairy lights wound round the arching limbs of the oak trees scattered along the edge of the cobblestones. They twinkled brightly as the sky darkened to a purple hue. Soft conversation from other diners wafted through the air, intermingling with the strains of classical music piped in from the restaurant. The host exited after he instructed a nearby server to bring them water and menus. Faith ran a finger around the rim of her glass and slid a peek at Caleb while he perused the menu. She liked how his eyes seemed warm and quick to dance, like the smile on his lips when he'd noticed her in this dress.

Their server, a tall gentleman with dull copper-colored hair glided to a stop next to their table. His bass voice rang true in the surrounding elegance. "May I take your order?"

"Yes, I'll have the petite filet with sautéed mushrooms, wedge salad, and a diet cola please." The wait person tipped his head and looked at Caleb.

He eyed the menu again before ordering. "I'd like the Ribeye, rare please, with a side of potato frites and an unsweet tea." The waiter efficiently put their order in the system and moved away. "I've never had mushrooms with steak."

Faith quickly put the napkin on her lap to make sure the dress was covered. She sipped her glass of water and a smile stretched across her lips. "You're welcome to try mine when it comes. Are you from here? Your accent is telling me you're not."

"Originally from Asheville, North Carolina. You sound like you're from someplace else too."

"I am. Tampa, Florida."

"Nice place to live, right near the water."

She grew warm at the mention of being on the water. Not a selling point to her. "Yes, it's great."

"Have you lived here long, Faith?"

"Between culinary arts school and my job, five years. How long for you?"

"A year. It's a big switch from a quieter town, to here."

"You get used to it. I really love it now."

"Maybe you could show me around." Caleb's eyes connected with hers. "My job keeps me busy most weekends, though."

"Find an open date, and I'll take you sightseeing."

The server politely interrupted with an "excuse me," and both leaned back from the small table to give him ample room to set down the exquisitely prepared and presented plates.

Faith sliced off a piece of the meat and moved it to the edge of the plate. "I cut a piece for you."

"Thanks. It looks great." Caleb's fingers brushed the side of her cola glass, knocking it over. It splashed onto the beautiful white dress, spreading across the thin fabric, and dripped down her legs. Frowning, Faith grabbed her napkin as the brown liquid spread across her lap. Caleb offered his napkin, but she waved it away. Blood rushed to her head as she eyed the dark blob. The sticky-sweet, cold cola made Faith shiver, but it did nothing to cool down her frazzled nerves. She jumped out of the chair and covered the stain as best as she could with her handbag. "I've got to clean this. I hope it's not ruined." She turned on her heel and rushed to the restroom. Blotting, patting. . . nothing. The thin fabric was translucent. Fire singed her scalp and she disguised the area with her handbag.

Caleb waited in the restroom hallway. "I'm sorry, I can pay for the dry-cleaning."

How about for my embarrassment? "I've got to go." With each step, her wet shoes squeaked, and the dress clung to her legs. Faith waved a hand back and forth. "No need." She walked outside, while Caleb attempted to fill the silence with small talk as the restaurant valet hailed a cab.

"I'll pay for your taxi."

"Great, thanks."

The yellow cab pulled next to Faith.

Caleb motioned for her to roll her window down. He handed the driver a fifty. "Keep the change."

"Thanks man."

"Make sure she gets home fast, but safe."

"Will do."

Once the taxi pulled away, Caleb returned to the restaurant, his steps slower than before. *Way to botch it, man.* Sitting at the now clean table, he stared across at the empty seat.

The server inquired. "Will the missus be returning?"

"No. She left."

"I'll put it in a to-go box."

"No. I don't really know her—where she lives." The server raised his eyebrows. *Great, he thinks I'm some stalker.* He ran a hand over his jaw and continued. "First date. A blind date."

"We all have a rough night now and then." The server pointed to his barely touched dinner plate. "Do you need this put in a box?"

"Sure. Thanks."

Returning, the server handed him the container. "Hope your night gets better."

"Me too." Caleb exited by the side gate and hailed a taxi.

On the ride home, he dialed Rose Carlucci's number.

"The date sounds dramatic. I'll see her tomorrow after church and let you know how she's doing.

Sunday afternoon, Caleb's phone rang as he came in his door from the afternoon service.

"Hi, Mrs. Carlucci. Did you see Faith?"

"She showed me the dress, a beautiful number, designer too. I told her to soak it in club soda."

"Any mention of me?"

"She said you were nice."

"I'd like to see her again."

Rose clucked her tongue. "Get her something memorable, and there could be a re-do date."

"You think so?"

"She might. I'm known in the neighborhood as a match-maker. Try it. Let me know how it goes." She ended the call.

He turned on his laptop and streamed an action movie. When the good guy climbed onto the base of Lady Liberty, it gave him an idea. He clicked off the movie and researched where to buy the "sorry for the bad date" gift. Smiling, he placed the order for the surprise for Faith. This lady intrigued him. Not many did.

~

Ready to get the busy Monday behind her, Faith rode the elevator up to her floor. As the door opened, Mrs. Carlucci popped her head from her apartment down the hallway.

"Looks like you've got a delivery, I kept an eye on it for you."

"No school today?"

"Day off." Mrs. Carlucci's house shoes shuffled along the wooden floor as she followed Faith to her door. "Who's it from?"

She eyed the label. "Must be a mistake. It's from a tourist shop on 7th Avenue. But it's addressed to me."

"Go on. Open it." Mrs. Carlucci stepped toward her door. "I think Harry's calling me. Have a good night."

"Thanks. You too. Night." Faith triple bolted the door after she'd entered. Curiosity bubbled inside. She slit the rectangular package with her scissors on the desk in the family room. Crumpled newspaper tumbled from the box. She dug deeper into the mystery gift. Her fingers contacted something unidentifiable, Faith extricated it from the wrapping. It was an elephantine pink eraser with the Statue of Liberty imprinted on it, and a People of Times Square calendar. Who did this? After dumping the paper onto the floor, an order form fell on top of the pile. The customer was listed as Canwe Tryagain. The stranger's address was 100 I'm really sorry Avenue. Faith grinned. Caleb. Her phone buzzed on the small hall table. She answered.

"Did you get the delivery?"

Faith's laughter echoed in her tiny foyer. "I did. It was clever, erase the date?"

"You got it, I thought it might be a little confusing." Caleb stated. "So, can we try it again?"

"All right. How about the zoo?"

"Sounds fun. Sunday?"

"It works. Two?"

"See you then."

They talked for a few minutes then ended the call.

One more check in her hall mirror, and Faith left from her place. Once outside, the warm Sunday sun beat against her shorts clad legs. She adjusted the collar of her turquoise top to let a breeze cool her skin. Walking the three blocks to the Central Park Zoo, she stopped several times to admire some "designer" handbags on a corner and buy two bottles of water the next block over. She spied Caleb at the zoo entrance and snapped a quick selfie to see what she looked like. After viewing, Faith decided all was well. She picked up the pace to cover the distance between her and him. "Hey, how are you?"

"Hi, doing great, for a September our weather's pretty warm. I'll get some waters for us inside."

She pulled the waters from her large backpack and gave one to him.

"A person that's prepared for anything. I like it. Were you a Girl Scout?"

"Nope, a veteran of many Florida summers in church camp. With all the humidity, you needed to hydrate a lot." *Oh, gosh, score one for the water doof.*

"True, it gets pretty warm in North Carolina too. Ready to go in?"

She nodded and went to an available ticket booth and began to take out her wallet.

"I'll pay."

"Great, thanks."

They followed behind a large family, the children were laughing at the birds flying overhead from tree to tree and chittering squirrels searching for dropped popcorn or peanuts. In the middle of the park, sea lions were being fed by trainers. One flew into the air and made Faith giggle.

"Isn't that great? It reminds me of the aquarium in my hometown." She brushed a strand of hair away, but it returned with the next gust of wind. Faith attempted again to get it out of her face, but it tangled in her sunglass arm. Taking them off she held in a sigh.

"I have that problem too." He pointed to his short hair. "Such an absolute nuisance."

"I'm sure it is."

Caleb was surveying the map and suddenly pointed to an area and showed her a specific point. "I'd like to see the tigers. Would you?"

"I'm up for anything."

Deeper into the zoo, they traversed, past the howling monkeys, and slow-moving elephants and found the tiger enclosure soon after.

Both stood silently as the majestic striped tiger stared in their direction.

"Amazing." Faith snapped a photo with her phone.

A stranger was walking by and grinned. "I'll take a photo of the two of you."

She handed her phone to the person.

Faith wasn't sure where to put her hands, so she clasped them in front of her. A warm hand encircled her waist, very lightly. Tickles of happiness ran through her. She placed an arm around his waist, with a butterfly touch.

"Here you go." The lady handed back her phone and joined her awaiting family.

"Thank you," Caleb offered.

Neither of their arms moved from the position. Faith's gaze went to Caleb's more than pleasant face. A roar echoed in the late afternoon sky. "Um, we'd better go see the lions next." She dropped her hand back to her side.

Caleb's followed as he said with a grin, "Lions it is."

~

One November evening, Faith and Caleb alighted from the theater. Orchestral music sounded in the speakers in the lobby, her heart still dancing in the ballroom with the book-loving character and the handsome prince.

"You know what you are to me, Faith?"

"A tour guide?" She giggled and shot a glance up at him. "I've had so much fun these past four months."

"Me too." He brushed a kiss on her cheek. "Belle."

She clutched the Playbill tighter in her hand, her heart free and light as summer warmth caressed her. "I like that."

"How about a turn in the bookstore next door?"

"Lead on."

Rows and rows of books stood at attention in the well-lit bookstore. Faith oriented herself to the different sections of the store. Dramatic, dark colors on a book's cover, begged for attention. "I'm looking for Aurelia Baine's next mystery. Want to come with me?"

"Belle is the perfect nickname for you." He laughed. "We've been to almost every bookseller in the city. You go. Meet me in the reference section upstairs."

She squeezed his hand quickly and walked away.

With the book purchased, she took the steep escalator upstairs and searched for her "Beast." She giggled to herself as she snuck up on him, curious to see what he was reading. "Find anything good?"

Caleb held the book close to Faith. She glanced at it. "How to start a business?" Her heartbeat in staccato fashion. "Here?" She attempted to swallow past the heaviness in her throat. *He'll stay here. Don't be silly.*

"I've been thinking about my own business for a long time now." He sighed, then spoke. "My boss is saying to work longer hours, more than twelve to fourteen I'm already putting in every day. Unrealistic."

"We all hit those slumps in our jobs."

"True. It's getting old tied to a cubicle, no windows, nor fresh air. I like being outdoors. New York City doesn't have the mountains or rivers like back home. No place to raft or kayak. Pray for me?"

"Of course, like you've been doing for the possible promotion for me."

"When do you find out?"

"After Christmas." She glanced at the clock on the store's wall. "It's after ten. Tomorrow's Monday. Why don't you and I head out?"

"I'll meet you by the door." He held the business book in his hand. "I need to buy this."

Faith walked in the opposite direction, stopping to browse books on various tables.

"Found you." Caleb had one arm behind his back. "For you, Belle." It was a paper flower bouquet made from book pages.

She twirled it in her hand and kissed his cheek. "Thanks, Beast."

His bass laughter filled the bookstore lobby. They held hands as the symphony of honks and motor noise wrapped around them.

In a taxi headed home, she recalled the bookstore conversation. *He never said he'd start a business here. And he mentioned back home.* She pulled the flowers from her bag, playing with the delicate petals. Worry tugged at her heart and mind. Her feelings for him were growing, and it had her absolutely petrified.

~

Christmas time in the city was full of cold nights, bright lights and people bustling in and out of stores. Faith smiled at all the happy faces as she trod along Fifth Avenue after work. Robots wrapping gifts were showcased in one large store chain's window the next store over held a dancing ballerina while her automaton male counterpart looked on and clapped. She took a photo and mailed it to her best friend, Taylor Starke as she thought she'd like to see it. Her stomach began to rumble as the pizzeria ahead wafted heavy scents of garlic and cheese from its open doors. Faith stopped in and ordered a few slices to go, then added on what Caleb would enjoy as well.

Warm pizza boxes on her hands and determination in her steps, she wove through groups of pedestrians covering the narrow sidewalks. Faith soon pressed the buzzer to his apartment.

"Hello?" Caleb said. "Can I help you?"

"Pizza delivery."

"I didn't order any."

"It's says here that it's for you." A buzzer sounded and Faith pulled the door and soon was at his place. The door swung open, and Caleb looked impossibly cute in his navy joggers and orange workout shirt.

"I got back from the gym a bit ago." He smiled and took the boxes from her hands. "Smells great, I'll go shower. Make yourself at home." Caleb disappeared into an adjacent room and closed the door.

Faith surveyed the photos on the wall. Smoke shrouded mountains, in one frame. In another, a white-capped, tumultuous river. *No thanks to the water. The mountains are pretty.* She pulled out her phone and sat on the brown leather sofa. It buzzed in her hands. It was Taylor.

Thanks for the photo. I'm jealous. I've never been to New York City at Christmastime.

Taylor, I wish you were here.

Me too. Guess where I'm going?

Where?

I'm going home with Jarod to meet his parents.

Faith's lips rounded and her fingers flew over the keyboard. *This is the man you told me you'd met in July?*

The same. We're going to be engaged soon, I know it. There might be a wedding in 2016.

I'm so excited for you.

You'll have to meet him soon. How about you and the Beast?

I'm at his place now for dinner. Things are going well. It's just. Shoot, I think he's coming back. Text you later.

Have fun!

You too, see you when you get back.

Dinner time conversation covered both of their days, which they agreed were super long, and plans for the weekend.

"So, you leave at the end of this week for Christmas vacation in Florida?"

"I do, my little sisters, Hope and Grace, are so excited and my parents as well." She sipped from her glass of water and questioned. "You leave on Sunday for North Carolina?"

"I do. I can't wait. I've not been back in almost a year."

"You had to have missed your family."

"I have. My family's happy I'm coming home soon, even my little brother Dylan. He'll have someone to game with. Our parents aren't exactly willing to play."

"I'll miss you, Caleb."

"Me too."

As his fingers played on a spiral curl near Faith's arm, she warmed at his touch.

Maybe he was feeling more than friendship too?

"I've been wanting to tell you for a while now." His face

moved closer to hers. She noticed the gold flecks in his irises as a breath was captured in her lungs. "I like you."

"You do? I like you too." She flicked her glance away, playfully. "Is there more?"

"You could say that I love you."

"You." Fireworks exploded in her body. "Love me?"

"Uh huh." His lips hovered near hers. "You're beautiful, funny, you make me happy."

"I love you too. You're handsome, smart, and I'm wowed by you."

Once their lips collided, Faith lost all bearing on time. With shallow breaths, she pushed herself from the sofa, shaking with unspent adrenaline. "That was amazing."

"I knew it would be good, but oh man. I'm glad you had the sense to stop."

His kissable lips begged for more, like the very last chapter in one of her favorite books. She took a step forward toward the kitchen. "We'd better clean up from dinner."

Caleb's eyes shifted from her to his phone. "It's past eleven. I'll clean up."

"I didn't know it was that late. How long were we on the sofa?" Her face torched at the question.

"Not long enough."

She gathered her things and both left the apartment, disappointment firing inside.

One taxi passed by as they embraced and shared a kiss, then another.

Faith pointed as she separated from him. "Here's a taxi."

Caleb groaned, and held the taxi door open.

She brushed a finger on his jaw and slid into the back seat. The door barely closed, and the car catapulted into the night.

As she put a finger to her lips, she noticed the warmth—a bit of his heart on her lips. For the remainder of the ride, she grinned. A life-is-wonderful kind of smile.

During Christmas, Faith and Caleb texted back and forth. Both decreed their families were way too nosey for their liking. In early January, she flew back to her place in New York City, anxious to see Caleb.

Her luggage clacked behind her as she maneuvered around the snow piled on the sidewalk and entered the apartment lobby.

Mrs. Carlucci held her arms open. "Happy New Year. We missed you."

Faith dropped her grip on the bags and gave her a hug. "I missed you too, Happy New Year." She stepped through the elevator door Mrs. Carlucci held open.

"Have you seen Caleb?"

"He's not coming back for another week."

Mrs. Carlucci put a hand to her head. "Oh, I must have forgotten. We have an appointment with him soon."

"I can't wait for him to get home."

Rose's lips moved upward, then decreed. "It's a regular heavenly match."

"I hope so, I really like him."

"The feeling's mutual. He looks at you like my Harry does with me."

"Thanks again, Mrs. Carlucci."

"You're welcome, sweetheart. See you."

Faith waved and closed her door.

Caffeine pumping through her system, Faith made her way to the cubicle and put away her lunch and purse.

"Today's the day." Jen's black pixie cut peeked from above the gray cubicle wall.

"Someone said?"

"No, not exactly. Erika's been on her computer since I got here, not marching around talking to everyone like she normally would do."

"Hmm, that's not very telling, friend."

"Maybe not, but Ingrid leaves at the end of the month. The clock's ticking, so to say."

She clicked onto her corporate email and noticed one from Erika at the top of the long after-vacation list of notifications.

Come see me.

Her palms became damp. "She wants to see me."

"Someone's getting a pro-mo-tion." Jen sang in a blend of jazz and cat yowls.

Faith looked away and winced, and eyed Erika's closed door. "Who knows? How do I look?"

"Twirl."

"Why?"

"Let's see how the back of your hair looks."

Like a ballerina in a child's jewelry box, Faith did a spin inside her tiny office space. "Good?"

"All is great." Jen cracked a large smile. "Go, we'll celebrate after work."

She forced her body to move toward the office. The usual chatter around the large office hushed as her hand clasped the door.

Inside the inner sanctum, Erika's secretary pointed to a seat and kept her focus on her computer screen. "She's on a conference call. It'll be a while."

She eyed the walls and noted all the awards that her bosses chain restaurants, Erika's Eatery, had won. In the center of the notable achievements, was a photo of Erika herself, signature red stilettos in full view.

A rush of air fanned Faith's hair from her face. She smoothed it down with a palm and went into the corner suite.

"Have a seat. Good Christmas?"

"Yes, thank you." She sat on the hard chair's edge. "And you?"

"Fantastic. Charles and I went to Southampton with the rest of our family. We had a charming time." Erika's smile didn't reach her eyes. Faith settled back and attempted not to wince as the chair pinched her back. "I've got some papers for you to fill out. I discussed your merits with our board, and the job is yours."

As tears veiled her eyes, she willed them no to not spill. "Thank you, I am very exc—"

Erika charged ahead. "There'll be a week for you to look over the agreement, then bring the papers back signed to my assistant. Before Ingrid leaves, she'll make sure you know what to do." She shifted a stack of papers on her desk. "You can go now."

Faith's legs carried her through the office and back to her desk chair before she collapsed.

"Good news."

"She gave me these papers." Faith held up her hands. "I forgot them in the office, I'm going to look ridiculous."

"No, go get them." Jen began the discordant tune again.

Erika's office door closed on the last syllable of the song.

"Forgot these." Erika's assistant waved the thick folder in Faith's direction. "I've put you down to meet with me in a week, 9 am sharp."

"Yes, Ma'am." She faltered at the woman's granite gray eyes. "Thank you." Once again, she exited the office as people came to congratulate her.

"How did you know?"

One co-worker decreed. "What Jennifer De Lotte knows, everyone will know."

"Hey, hey, give room to the new test kitchen chef." Jen swooshed her arms to part the thin stream of well-wishers. "We've got to get in there, Ingrid's in a MOOD."

"Not even her temper's going to bother me today, I am so happy."

"Me too. Maybe I'll move up to sous chef."

Faith gave her friend a quick embrace. "I hope so too. There's not another Yankees fan I'd like to work with."

Jen snorted and went through the test kitchen door.

Today was a fantastic day, she was sure of it.

Gathering with her cluster of co-workers at a local restaurant, Faith's good mood continued. *The only thing that'd make it better was if Caleb were here.* Her phone buzzed on the table beside her and she turned it over to see who had called. Caleb's name showed on the screen.

"I'll be back in a few." Faith pointed to the phone and dashed outside. "Hey, how's everything?"

"Good. Congratulations on the promotion. I'm so glad for you."

"Thanks, I was shocked when she told me. Guess I'm here to stay in the city."

Caleb cleared his throat. "Yeah, it seems that way."

Faith saw Jen motion to her through the window. "Jen's wanting me to come back in. See you soon?"

"I'll be there by the end of the week."

"Okay." A dial tone blared in her ear. She walked back into the noisy restaurant.

"Caleb okay?" Jen yelled to Faith.

"Fine, we got disconnected." She tucked the phone in her bag, her mood dimmed by the short conversation.

"Ugh, cell phones are so unreliable." Jen frowned.

"Yeah."

"Time to celebrate." Jen pulled Faith on the small dance floor to join their friends.

Letting the pulsing beat wash through her, the doldrums disappeared. She danced until her feet argued for her to stop.

A busy week kept Faith's attention training to be head test kitchen chef took all her focus and endurance. Ingrid was a tough instructor, more exacting than even her culinary art professors in school. Friday night, she grabbed a Knish from a street vendor, and bit into the soft dough as the potato and cheese filling awakened her taste buds. Once finished, she visited her favorite bookstore four stores down from her apartment building. The smell of old paper, and worn leather relaxed her after the week's hubbub. She spied a book about mountains on the shelf below and bent down to look at it closer.

"I'd look at the 100 Ways of Dressing A Chicken if I were you," a familiar voice suggested.

Faith stood and turned around. Delight creased her lips. "That sounds like some fun reading." She reached her arms around Caleb's shoulders as her heart thudded. "When did you get back?"

"Two hours ago." He brushed a chaste kiss on her cheek. "I've been gone two weeks and completely forgot how crowded this place is."

"I absolutely love it for the blend of people here, tourists and residents alike."

Caleb's head shook. "The quiet of the mountains was good."

"Is your family well?"

"Yes, thanks."

"Are you looking around here more?"

"No."

She pulled on his hand. "Come home with me, I'll make dinner."

"I ate, thanks."

"We can talk."

"Raincheck?"

"Oh. Sure." Faith attempted to brush the disappointment that stuck on her heart. One more kiss near her mouth and the two separated and walked away from each other. Like a piece of a puzzle that didn't fit, something was off. Faith prayed it was her imagination, and not the actual truth.

Busy schedules led to putting their date off for an excruciating twelve days. They sat in Faith's living room next to one another on a snowy January Saturday.

"How's work going?" Faith readjusted her position on the gray sofa and pushed a teal-colored pillow away that dug into her back. "You're busy like me."

Caleb's hands folded. "I'm leaving the company."

"Did you get a new job?"

"Not yet. I'm looking."

"Would it be here?"

"I'm open to it."

Faith reached over and patted his knee. "I know you'll get one soon."

"I've only applied with a few companies. I had one interview recently."

"That's wonderful. Whomever meets you, they'll hire you. Let's start the celebration."

"Always positive." Caleb pointed to his lips. "We can celebrate here."

Her insides glowed and she moved closer to him, lips within touching distance. Both came together and Faith sighed.

A short while later, they were chatting again.

Caleb's fingers were twined in her hair. "You are what I've

needed, a person who has her own mind, and understands what I do."

She bit her lip, as her eyes lingered on his. "No one's ever said that to me. Our relationship has grown faster than any other I've been in. Deeper, too. I definitely need you in my life."

The couple stayed in one another's arms as the snow swirled and danced outside the windows, and the small fireplace provided extra warmth and ambiance. Faith's heart was content.

Daffodils and tulips sprang from the Central Park beds as Faith and Caleb walked hand in hand on an early May day.

"Beautiful day, isn't it?"

"Not like you though. You're stunning."

Heat warmed her face. "Thank you, you're pretty cute too."

"Pretty cute." He laughed.

"Yes."

"I can't believe we've been going out for nearly a year."

"Me neither. It's incredible to think we were set up by a matchmaker."

"Thank the Lord for Rose Carlucci."

"Amen to that."

He swept her in his arms and placed a kiss bullseye center on her lips, quick as the flying birds above in the trees.

"I hear a phone buzz. My phone's off."

Caleb frowned and dug in his chocolate brown coat pocket. "I need to take this, I'll be back in a bit." He strode some distance away by the lake.

Several chittering squirrels running around held Faith's attention as well as the clip clop of the sturdy horses pulling white carriages on the street beyond the hedges. She wrapped her arms around herself to ward off the fingers of chill cutting through her light peach tinted coat. Faith purchased a couple of coffees from the vendor close to where she waited. Several sips of coffee later, and he returned.

"I didn't mean for it to take so long."

Faith gave him the coffee.

"Let's go sit over there."

She eyeballed the empty park bench. "Okay."

"The call was from a company that I'd interviewed with." Caleb's lips turned down, he put his coffee on the ground and pulled on his sweater collar. "They need an in-house financial person for their sporting goods company, and they've given me an offer."

"Caleb, that's amazing." She grabbed onto his arm. It tensed below her fingers. Dings of alarms rang in her mind. "You're frowning. What's wrong? It's here, isn't it?"

"No. It's not here. North Carolina."

Faith pivoted her face away from him. Every nerve in her body fired, pain plucked an unbidden tune in every strand. She forced a glance back toward him, not quite meeting his eyes. "North Carolina."

"I applied for it thinking it was a long shot. We did the phone interview a week ago."

"Why didn't you tell me? I thought we confided in each other."

"We do. It happened fast. The second interview was yesterday. I had no clue they'd want to hire me." His shoulders sagged. "Would you move there?"

"It makes me ill to say it, but no." She gripped her midsection. "All the schooling and long hours were to get this job as a head chef somewhere. I love my co-workers and job. Are you going to take it?"

"Do you want me to stay?" He stood and paced back and forth. "I absolutely can't stand this job anymore. Four hours of sleep a night. They want everything from me but my blood.

Sitting in a Wall Street chicken coop cubicle, no windows, no sunshine. It isn't me."

"I'd be a real jerk if I said yes." As water pooled in her eyes, his face became fuzzy, like an out of focus camera lens. "Go."

"Move to North Carolina." Caleb grabbed her hands.

She squeezed his hands and dropped them. "I can't leave."

"We'll be together still. You can come visit me some weekends, and I'll visit you."

In the sidewalk bend nearby, a violinist began to play for their paycheck. The subtle cries of the strings were a twin to her bereft heart. "When do you leave?"

"In a month."

"This is a great opportunity for you." As her cold lips mimicked a smile, there was not a spark of warmth in her entire body. The walk to her apartment was filled by Caleb's chatter about his new job. She could sense his excitement with the rise and pitch of his tone. With each word he spoke, the reality of their fractured future stung. No more seeing each other almost every day. No more spontaneous visits. No more knowing he lived in the same city.

At the building's entrance, Caleb kissed the baby hairs by Faith's ear.

"You're sure."

No. I want you to stay. I want to be selfish. Turn it down. "I am."

With a hug, he turned and melded into the thronging crowd, phone in hand. She dropped the keys at her door. As she stooped to get them, she noticed a pair of blue flats beside the dulled keys. Rising, she looked beyond Mrs. Carlucci's face.

"You've got sad eyes. Bad news?"

Faith nodded.

"Work?"

"No."

"Ah, man troubles."

"He's moving to North Carolina." Faith's chin dipped to her chest, as a thin stream dripped down her cheeks.

Mrs. Carlucci put a gentle finger to Faith's chin. "Look at me," Faith raised her head. "Whatever this is between you two. Jesus is bigger than this." Rose swiped at Faith's eyes with a tissue. "He'll help you. You'll see Caleb again."

"He is. As for the other, I hope so. We're going to visit each other when he moves."

Rose stated softly. "If things don't go to plan I'll find another guy for you."

Faith went into her apartment, slept the weekend away, and went to work that Monday.

For five months, Faith and Caleb texted and called one another. Yet, no plans to visit were ever carried out. Life was simply too busy. All the while, Rose Carlucci stuck to her statement and tried to find another match for Faith. All were rejected. At the core of all of us, is our heart. Who we love is what causes it to beat. Faith's heartbeat was a green eyed, sweet, and handsome man. Caleb.

Made in United States
Orlando, FL
18 May 2023

33246397R00167